The Money Hole

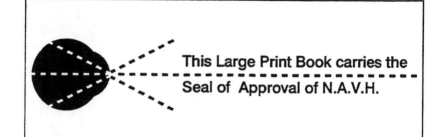

This Large Print Book carries the
Seal of Approval of N.A.V.H.

Bonanza™ 5

THE MONEY HOLE

STEPHEN CALDER

G.K. Hall & Co.
Thorndike, Maine

Published in 1996 by arrangement with Bantam Books, a division of Bantam Doubleday Dell Publishing Group, Inc.

G.K. Hall Large Print Western Collection.

The text of this Large Print edition is unabridged. Other aspects of the book may vary from the original edition.

Set in 16 pt. News Plantin by Al Chase.

Printed in the United States on permanent paper.

Library of Congress Cataloging in Publication Data

Calder, Stephen.
    The money hole / Stephen Calder.
       p.   cm. — (Bonanza ; 5)
    ISBN 0-7838-1725-8 (lg. print : hc)
    1. Ranch life — West (U.S.) — Fiction. 2. Large type
books. I. Title. II. Series: Calder, Stephen. Bonanza ; 5.
  [PS3553.A39493M66 1996]
  813'.54—dc20
                                             96-5475

For Joe and Ella Mae,
Who shared with me their summers,
their *Ranch Romances*,
and their *True West* magazines

Ben Cartwright — The rugged, respected patriarch of the Cartwright clan. His Virginia City mine has been a bust, and his dream of a silver empire has turned into a nightmare. Thurston Smalley, a notoriously corrupt financier, plans to take over the mine — and the Cartwright fortune. Sinking deeper into debt, Ben must choose between humiliating surrender to Smalley . . . and the loss of his beloved Ponderosa.

Adam Cartwright — Ben's eldest son, a mining engineer, and a shrewd businessman. He urged his father to invest in the Bristlecone Mine, and he knows it will pay off . . . in time. But with losses mounting — and Smalley poised for the kill — time may only be bought at the cost of his father's dynasty.

Little Joe Cartwright — Ben's youngest son, handsome and reckless, a ladies' man and a prankster. Quick with his fists and with a quip, he knows little about mining or financial manipulation. But he knows when his family is threatened — and he knows how to fight.

Lucia Sinclair — Pretty, bright, resourceful, the woman who has won Adam Cartwright's heart. She knows more law than any man in Virginia City but is prohibited from practicing law because of her sex. Then Smalley makes her an offer — turn on Adam and his family and she'll realize her wildest dreams.

Thurston Smalley — The Vulture of Virginia City, feared and despised. A vicious and remorseless speculator, he has ruined more mines — and mine owners — than any man in the West. Now he has decided to crown his hateful career; he won't just ruin the Cartwrights — he'll grind their faces in the Virginia City dust.

Hoss Cartwright — Ben's second son, a big man with a heart as big as the great Sierra Nevadas. Only the vast open spaces of the Ponderosa can hold his outdoorsman's spirit — but the Cartwrights face financial ruin, which could destroy the Ponderosa legacy and Hoss's cherished freedom.

CHAPTER 1

"Would you look at that?" Hoss Cartwright said, stepping inside the Odd Fellows Hall to attend the annual dress ball of Zephyr Engine Company No. 7.

Little Joe grinned, removed his flat-brim hat and tossed it toward a table stacked with head gear. "She's something," he answered, eyeing a demure blonde who fluttered her eyelashes, then turned coyly away.

"No, dad-blame-it," Hoss sputtered. He pointed at a long table that stretched the length of the hall. "Food! Have you ever seen such a spread?"

"Never have," Little Joe answered absentmindedly, standing as tall as his five-foot-nine frame would allow and confidently straightening his string tie. When the blonde peeked at him again, Little Joe strolled her way, cocky as a lone rooster in a henhouse.

Hoss turned to suggest they grab a bite, but Little Joe had already abandoned him to chase a skirt. Just as the sixteen-piece orchestra struck up "Camptown Races," Hoss spotted Little Joe squiring a pretty blonde toward the dance floor. Hoss lifted his hat and ran his hand through his receding brown hair, envious of Little Joe's charm with the women. Hoss always found himself as awkward as a three-legged mule when it came to talking, much less dancing, with women.

Instinctively he fingered the string tie strangling him. He had promised Pa he would wear a tie to the dance, but he hadn't agreed to keep it on. Pa and Adam were probably so engrossed in assay reports at the Bristlecone Mine that it would be at least an hour before they came to the dance. Hoss jerked his tie from under his stiff collar and dropped it into his coat pocket. Undoing his collar, he skirted the dancers and ambled for the food.

Scattered among the women in fancy dresses and the men in black suits were Zephyr Engine Company volunteers, ablaze with color, their red shirts like cloth flames swirling in the crowd, their leather helmets protruding like brown islands above the sea of dancers. No event on the Comstock Lode was so anticipated as the Zephyr Engine Company's annual fund-raising ball.

Hoss gaped at the decorations. In the hall's center, an elevated fountain spurted four-foot-high jets of water which landed in a lower pool filled with goldfish and tiny frogs. Trellised arbors bordered by pots of colorful flowers angled away from the fountain to the corners of the room. In each corner stood an evergreen taken from the high country. A dozen songbirds, bewildered by the music and the noise of the dancers below, flitted from tree to tree.

Though Hoss found the decorations impressive, they failed to match the table of food, heaped like ore in bowls and on platters. Studying his dining options, he drew himself a mug of cold beer from the keg planted beside the table. The beer would knock the clabber from his throat and maybe give him the courage to ask a woman to dance. As he quaffed down the golden liquid, he heard a familiar voice.

"I should've known I'd find you here!" Sheriff Roy Coffee laughed and slapped Hoss's back.

Grabbing a plate, Hoss turned around to greet Coffee, noting the sheriff's newly clipped gray hair and his freshly trimmed salt-and-pepper mustache. "Had your ears lowered, Roy?"

Coffee tilted his head. "As much as I need hair," the sheriff said, flicking his finger at his dwindling supply, "it does seem foolish to pay someone to mow it, now doesn't it?" Coffee picked up a plate himself, then trailed after Hoss, watching his generous helpings. "You need sideboards on your plate, Hoss."

"They'd help," Hoss answered, then cleared his throat. "You bring Sara Ann with you?" Hoss was nervous about Coffee's granddaughter, Sara Ann. He had known her since she was a toddler. Now she was a striking young woman of seventeen, a woman he would like to court. But being eleven years her senior, Hoss felt as inept as a blind gunman around her.

Coffee glanced at Hoss. "You think I could come to the biggest dance of the year without

Sara Ann? She's dancing, I'm sure."

Hoss swallowed his disappointment. She was dancing with someone already. Now it would take another beer or two to get the courage to ask her to dance. Hoss changed the topic. "Zephyr Engine Company's really outdone itself tonight."

Coffee nodded and looked about the hall. "I hear they've even got a monkey walking about."

"A monkey?" Hoss crowned his plate with three slices of bread.

"Yep, the volunteer fire departments are running scared after the big fire. Been talk about the city taking over the fire-fighting duties. The volunteers don't like that, and Zephyr's fire captain, Big Jim Fowler, is trying to impress folks."

"A monkey?" Hoss repeated, pointing to an empty table by the far wall. He almost tripped when he saw Sara Ann Coffee waltz by with a red-shirted volunteer fireman. Hoss's spirits fell like debris in Virginia City's deepest mine shaft.

Hoss ambled to the table and dropped his plate atop the lace tablecloth. Lowering his beer mug, he caught a flash of brown from the chair beside his. A long furry arm appeared and grabbed his sliced bread. "What?" he shouted, recoiling as a monkey jumped on the table, then watching it stuff the bread in its mouth and vault away. "Dad-blame that durn rodent," Hoss shouted as people around him laughed. Red-faced, he sat down.

His embarrassment burned even deeper when

he saw Sara Ann grinning, then flared to anger when Little Joe sauntered by, the blond-haired woman on his arm.

"Maybe the monkey'll dance with you, Hoss," his brother taunted.

Hoss remembered the string tie in his pocket and considered knotting it around Little Joe's throat, where it could do some good.

The sheriff slid into the chair beside Hoss. "Who's the woman with Little Joe?"

Hoss shrugged, studying her long blond hair, ruby lips, and green eyes. "Little Joe probably doesn't even know."

"She's a looker," Coffee said.

"Roy," Hoss said, "you're too old for that."

"You're never too old to look, Hoss."

As they began to eat, a man of Hoss's dimensions approached the table. He wore a red shirt and a leather helmet with a numeral 7 embossed on its gold frontpiece. The gold helmet shield represented his position as captain of Zephyr Engine Company No. 7.

Hoss took in the fireman's broad shoulders, his dark eyes and the neatly trimmed beard. Around the fringe of the beard and on the top of the man's hands, Hoss spotted splotches of pink skin; badges, Hoss suspected, of burns from fire fighting. The fireman acknowledged Hoss with a smile as sincere as a snake-oil salesman's grin.

Coffee introduced the two big men. "Hoss, this is Jim Fowler, captain of Zephyr Engine Company Seven; and Jim, this is Hoss Cartwright."

"The Ponderosa Cartwrights?" Fowler asked, extending his hand.

Nodding, Hoss took Fowler's hand and stared into dark eyes scorched of all emotion. Fowler tried to intimidate Hoss with his powerful grip. "Just call me Big Jim."

The handshake a standoff, Hoss withdrew his hand.

"Sorry our monkey upset you," Fowler said. "Since the big fire, some folks've said us volunteers were a bunch of monkeys. We thought we'd have a little fun with that, and brought him from San Francisco."

"If you boys fought fires as good as you throw a dance, Virginia City would be safe forever," Hoss replied.

Fowler's eyes narrowed and his hands balled into fists. "Been a lot of lies since the big fire," he responded coldly. "These socials raise money, money we'll use to buy a new steam pumper, money that'll protect Virginia City. Enjoy yourself, Hoss, and pray you never need a volunteer fireman to come to your aid."

Fowler strode away, anger in his step.

"You know, Hoss," Coffee said, pointing his fork at Fowler's back, "Big Jim's playing politician. He's more interested in himself than anything else, including the Zephyr Engine Company."

"I'm not much for politics or politicians," Hoss replied, then sipped at what was left of his now warm beer.

"You learn to deal with both as sheriff," Coffee answered.

The orchestra's next tune was "Lorena," and Hoss spotted Little Joe dancing with the same blond-haired woman. Usually Little Joe was not so selective, preferring to share himself with all the girls. Hoss shook his head in envy.

As he looked around the room, he saw his father approaching. Behind Ben Cartwright strode Hoss's older brother, Adam, whose arm was linked with that of Lucia Sinclair, assistant county clerk of Storey County. Lucia was slender, with a full bosom and long black hair that she usually wore in a bun. Her gray eyes were as penetrating and studious as her mind. Rumor had it that she had read enough law to outsmart every honest lawyer in Nevada, even though women were not permitted to practice law. Hoss considered her a fine-looking woman, though too bookish for him.

"Evening, Roy," Ben said.

"Good to see you, Ben, and you too, Adam. Lucia."

Adam nodded his greeting, and Hoss could see the strain in his older brother's eyes. The Bristlecone Mine was not producing ore of sufficient quality to keep it from draining Cartwright Enterprises.

Hoss felt his father's penetrating stare. "Evening, Hoss, I see you forgot something."

Sheepishly, Hoss slipped his hand in his coat pocket and retrieved the black string tie, waving it like a limp worm. "I wore it in," Hoss grinned. "I didn't promise I'd keep it on."

Ben slid into a seat beside Roy, motioning for Adam and Lucia to join them. "Where's Little Joe?" he asked.

"You know Little Joe. He's dancing and charming the girls, Pa."

"He can be too charming for his own good," Ben said.

Lucia pointed to the dance floor. "There he is, dancing with Holly Lucas."

"Who's Holly Lucas?" Adam asked.

"Big Jim Fowler's girl," Lucia answered softly.

Hoss pegged Fowler for the distrustful, jealous type who would resent his girlfriend dancing with another man. Little Joe usually got the girl of his choice, but seldom without trouble. Hoss shrugged. "Need another beer, anyone?" When no one accepted his offer, he scooted from the table and plowed toward the keg.

As Hoss moved into line with a dozen other men, he caught a glimpse of Sara Ann Coffee sliding delicately across the dance floor with another fireman. Then he saw Adam and Lucia, moving as one to the music. Adam was an accomplished dancer whose skills Hoss envied all the more every time he saw Sara Ann pass. Hoss got his refill and drank deeply into the mug. When this song was over, he would ask Sara Ann to dance. He would put it off no longer. He would ignore his own shortcomings as a dancer, and hope Sara Ann would too. If only he didn't step

16

on her toes. And she was so petite, five feet, four inches at most, and him more than a head taller. What would people think? Would they laugh? He didn't care. Then the music stopped and Hoss slammed the mug down. He gulped and stepped toward her, his courage building with each step.

"Ladies and gentlemen," came a strong voice from the vicinity of the orchestra, and Hoss glanced toward the back of the hall. He saw Big Jim Fowler standing on a chair, a silver megaphone to his lips, as if he was issuing orders at a fire. As the guests quieted, Fowler continued. "Ladies and gentlemen, it's time to give these fine musicians a break." He lowered the megaphone, tucked it under his arm and began to clap. The crowd joined in as the musicians took bows, then ambled away.

Hoss lifted his hands to clap, then dropped them in defeat, his courage slipping away like the musicians from their instruments. When he looked for Sara Ann Coffee, she had disappeared. With brow furrowed and shoulders slumped, he retreated to the beer keg and more disappointment. The musicians had taken all the clean mugs.

As he trudged to his table, Hoss passed Little Joe, whose arm was around the waist of a giggling Holly Lucas, while Big Jim Fowler's megaphone-enhanced voice reverberated through the hall. "The great fire last year devastated this community," he shouted. "We all know that." He nodded, as did most in the audience. "There's been talk of disbanding the volunteer fire companies and letting Virginia City create its own department, a paid department, paid with tax monies that'll come out of all our pockets." Fowler paused.

The room was hushed, except for the fluttering of songbirds among the trees and an occasional muted call from one to another. Here it comes, Hoss thought, Fowler's plea to keep the volunteer departments active. Reaching his chair, Hoss sat down.

"The fire was a tragedy, all of us agree," Fowler said as every fire helmet in the room bobbed up and down in consent. "Zephyr Engine Company Number Seven was there, fighting the flame at great personal risk. Of all the volunteer companies, only Zephyr Engine Company Seven escaped without loss of a single foot of hose or a single piece of equipment." Fowler hesitated, then shook his head. "I take that back about losing no equipment. We did lose a bucket."

The crowd laughed, and the firemen applauded and stomped their feet on the wooden floor.

Roy Coffee turned to Ben. "They didn't lose any equipment because Fowler stationed them upwind from the fire. They put out embers while the other departments were battling flames."

Up front, Fowler continued. "Some say it was the volunteers' fault so much of the town burned, but who else was there to fight the fires? Some have asked me here tonight about the monkey. If you haven't seen him, he's around. Just ask

Hoss Cartwright. Now, why are we letting a monkey wander around?"

Hoss felt his cheeks flush at the mention of his name.

"I'll tell you why," Fowler said, "because it's time us firemen quit letting folks monkey around with our good reputations."

Spontaneous cheers erupted from the floor. Several red-shirted firemen lifted their leather helmets in the air.

Fowler doffed his helmet in reciprocal salute. "The money we raise tonight," Fowler shouted as he lifted his head gear toward the ceiling, "will help Zephyr Company purchase a new steam pumper to better protect the homes and lives of all of you."

Cheers arose again.

"Now, if you good folks should decide your city needs a paid fire department," Fowler shouted, "you can be assured that I and the members of Zephyr Engine Company Seven will work with you to make that possible."

Again cheers arose, but not nearly so enthusiastic as before, the firemen more muted in their response.

"Zephyr Company is behind what's best for this community."

"And what's best for Big Jim Fowler," Coffee said to Ben.

"And now what's best for this community and for you fine folks," yelled Fowler, "is for the music and the dancing to continue."

This drew the loudest cheer and longest applause as Fowler jumped down from the chair. The musicians scurried from the refreshments back to their instruments, and shortly the music of the orchestra drowned out the din of the crowd.

Hoss stretched his arms and excused himself, searching the crowd for Sara Ann. By the orchestra, he saw a few firemen around Big Jim Fowler, shaking his hand, slapping him on the back, nodding their support. Most everybody else seemed more interested in food or dancing. On the dance floor, Hoss saw Little Joe and Holly Lucas stepping to the music and laughing.

Standing with his balled fists on his hips, Hoss scanned the room fruitlessly. He turned to head for the beer keg when he felt a tapping on his arm.

"Hoss, who are you looking for?"

It was Sara Ann Coffee. Hoss's fists melted from his hips and he stammered. "Ah, uh, someone to dance with."

Sara Ann smiled. "How about me, then, at the next song? A couple men I'd promised dances have had too much to drink by now."

"Sure thing, Sara Ann," Hoss answered as she stepped to his side and slid her arm in his. Hoss felt his chest swell with pride. He didn't care what others thought anymore. Just having Sara Ann at his side was enough. If only the orchestra would finish this song.

Finally the music stopped, to polite applause, and Hoss stepped awkwardly onto the dance floor with Sara Ann. He took her hand in his and slid his arm around her waist, realizing that he had made a mistake in stopping where he had. Little Joe and Holly Lucas were beside him. His younger brother winked at him, then planted a kiss on Holly Lucas's cheek. At Holly's giggle, Hoss turned away.

Just as the music started, Hoss stepped to the tune, then was staggered by someone plowing full body into his back. He stumbled over Sara Ann, who gasped, but he maintained his balance and released her. He lifted his massive fist and saw Little Joe on the floor behind him. "Dad-blame-it, Little Joe," Hoss cried.

Then Hoss saw Big Jim Fowler, standing over Little Joe, waving the silver megaphone like a weapon. "You stay away from my woman."

Little Joe rubbed his chin, then clambered to get up, but Hoss caught his shoulder and kept him from attacking the fire captain. Holly Lucas spun around and pointed her finger like a dagger at Fowler. "You wouldn't dance with me, and nobody else would either, but him."

"Nobody else was that dumb. They know you're my woman."

Hoss pushed Little Joe aside. "You want to fight a Cartwright, try me for size."

Both men took a step toward each other, but before they loosed punches, Sheriff Coffee jumped between them. "Hoss, you and Little Joe come with me. Sara Ann, you too. We're leaving so there's no trouble."

CHAPTER 2

Thurston Smalley tugged the cuff of his yellowed shirt as he strolled down the plank sidewalk skirting the Bristlecone Mine offices. His beady eyes scrutinized the two-story building and his tongue flicked snakelike across his lips. Smalley tugged the brim of his beaver hat, long out of style, then thumped a mote of dust from the wide lapel of his swallowtail coat, frayed around the edges from years of use. When he bought the coat years ago, it had been stylish and barely affordable on his pauper's wages. Even though money was no longer an impediment, Smalley still wore the threadbare coat. It reminded him of what it was like to be hungry, what it was like to want everything. Now that he had money enough to buy anything, he wanted little but more money, more power.

Though his five-foot frame cast but a slight shadow on the plank walk, his mere name cast a sinister pall over the Comstock Lode. It was said he had ruined more mines and made more money by stock manipulations than anybody in Virginia City. Smalley crossed the dirt street and angled for the morning shade cast by the facade of a local brewery, preferring shade like vermin prefer darkness. He leaned against the brewery's weathered wall, watching the Bristlecone office as a predator studies its prey. Occasionally Smalley glanced beyond the Bristlecone and the city itself to the slopes of Mount Davidson. Halfway up the slopes stood the remains of the Montgomery Mine, the property that made him his first million without ever producing an ounce of silver. The abandoned mine works stood as a monument to Smalley's stock manipulations.

Smalley pulled a gold watch from the pocket of his green-checked vest and noted the time. Nine-twenty. When Ben Cartwright left, as he usually did by ten o'clock, Smalley would approach Adam with his offer. In the days before the Big Bonanza was discovered, the silver-bearing veins of the Comstock Lode seemed to be headed in a westerly direction. When prices plummeted, Ben Cartwright had bought a claim east of what became the Consolidated Virginia Mine. But instead of west, the true course of the Comstock Lode had been east, aimed straight for the Bristlecone claim. Two years of litigation had certified Ben Cartwright as sole holder of the claim. No other mining claim in all of Nevada held more promise than the Bristlecone, not just for silver, but also for manipulating stock, if only Ben Cartwright would sell.

But despite the mine's promise, the mother lode had proven elusive in the Bristlecone. The longer Ben Cartwright held the mine, the greater the drain on the vast Ponderosa empire. Smalley had bided his time, but now with the mine at thirteen hundred feet and still not producing a profitable ore, Smalley figured the Ponderosa fortune had been stretched enough to worry the Cartwrights.

At a quarter of ten Ben Cartwright emerged from the Bristlecone office and headed down the street; likely for the Washoe Club, Smalley thought, to meet with Monville Pyburn, his stockbroker, and Clarence Eppler, his attorney. Cartwright had been meeting them daily for two weeks, further indication that Cartwright resources had been stretched thin.

Smalley watched Ben Cartwright disappear around the corner, then extended himself to his full five feet and tugged on the lapels of his frayed coat. He strode from the brewery, stepping out into the street, his beady eyes squinting at the mild morning sun. As he marched across the street, Smalley poked at his bared teeth with a gold toothpick, then laughed in a low growl.

With this visit would begin the destruction of Ben Cartwright and the Ponderosa fortune.

The Washoe Club fronted on C Street just down from the International Hotel, where Adam maintained a suite while overseeing the Bristlecone. The club permitted only men of wealth, clout, and esteem as members. Ben Cartwright was a member. Thurston Smalley was not.

Entering The Crystal, a drinking establishment known as the "millionaires' saloon," Ben nodded to several acquaintances. He marched up the carpeted stairs to the second-floor Washoe Club and opened the thick, mahogany door. Thaddeus Bradford bowed slightly as Ben entered this retreat of thick carpets, plush chairs, cut crystal chandeliers, oil paintings, and bronze sculptures. As overseer of the Washoe Club, Bradford chose the cooks, the waiters, the wines, and the menus for the members. Without violating a trust, he had overheard conversations upon which millions of dollars had been invested. As always, he wore a black tie, a cutaway coat, and a somber expression.

"Morning, Mr. Cartwright," Bradford said. His lips squeezed out a thin smile as he took Ben's hat. "Mr. Eppler and Mr. Pyburn are awaiting you. I shall bring you your coffee momentarily."

"Thank you, Thaddeus," Ben said, striding into a well-appointed parlor just off the large dining room.

Clarence Eppler paused in lighting a Cuban cigar and nodded at Ben. Monville Pyburn quickly finished cleaning the thick lenses of his wire-rimmed glasses, then hooked them over his ears. Eppler, tall and slender, with stooped shoulders that made him seem to hover over the cigar and match, finished lighting his Cuban. He exhaled a cloud of smoke that momentarily obscured his face and the magnificent head of chocolate-brown hair. Pyburn scratched his gray muttonchop whiskers as he adjusted his glasses on his nose, then blinked. The thick glasses magnified his eyes, giving him an owlish look that mirrored

26

his stockbroker wisdom.

Pyburn studied Ben. "No good news, I gather."

Ben shrugged, then slumped into his accustomed chair, one of three fronting a redwood table. Bradford entered with a silver coffee service and a bone-china cup and saucer. The aromas of coffee and cigar mingled well. Bradford filled Ben's cup. Depositing the cup on the table, he pointed to Eppler's brandy snifter and Pyburn's glass of warm milk. Both men shook their heads, so Bradford turned and exited, closing the door behind him.

Ben picked up the coffee cup and sipped its hot liquid. As he put the cup back in the saucer, he shook his head. "Assaying reports still have too much quartz and too little silver. Not enough to make it profitable."

Pyburn stroked his chin and wriggled his nose. "Ben, it's no longer a question of whether it's profitable."

Nodding sadly, Ben reached for his coffee cup. He knew what was coming next. Pyburn always skinned money issues to the bone. That was what made him an exceptional stockbroker, that and his impeccable honesty.

"The question," Pyburn continued as Ben swallowed a mouthful of coffee, "is no longer whether it's breaking even. You've got to start turning a profit fast, and not just a small profit. Your mining debts now exceed a third of a million dollars. The Bristlecone has drained your accessible resources, Ben. You know that, and you've got

27

suppliers to pay and a payroll coming up."

Studying the cup of coffee, Ben nodded. "Monville, the silver's got to be down there somewhere."

Eppler exhaled a cloud of smoke, then pulled the cigar from his lips. "Who's to say the vein didn't make another abrupt turn, missing the Bristlecone? Mining's like playing with a crooked gambler. You never see all the cards until it's too late to throw in your hand."

"I'm not quitting, gentlemen."

Pyburn shrugged. His owlish eyes narrowed. "Were you a greedy man, Ben Cartwright, I could understand, but you're plenty wealthy, with enough for you and the boys to live out the rest of your lives."

Ben tipped his head back and drained the last swallow of coffee from the fine china cup. As he lowered his head, he looked from Pyburn to Eppler. "Adam's got faith the mine'll come in."

"Don't let Adam's belief ruin all you've built since the rush of 'forty-nine," Pyburn implored him.

For an instant Ben's gaze hardened. His brown eyes, the color of fine mahogany, softened as he realized Pyburn's comment had been issued without malice. Monville Pyburn had been a trusted advisor for fifteen years, and Ben valued his judgment. But he valued Adam's as well. Adam had a sensible business head and had studied engineering back East. And Adam was his son. Ben spoke softly: "We'll go awhile longer, no more

28

than a month, then make a decision."

Pyburn shook his head. "You can't go any longer, Ben, without an infusion of cash."

Ben nodded. "I'll take out a loan."

Eppler pointed his cigar at Ben. "I can't let you do that, Ben. Too risky if the mine doesn't come through."

Leaning forward in his chair, Pyburn shook his head vigorously in agreement. "Unwise, Ben, unwise. I'd recommend you sell stock in the Bristlecone, assess your stockholders for working capital. Everyone else does it, and there's no point in you Cartwrights going it alone."

"Once you sell stock," Ben shot back, "the speculators get their teeth in you quicker than a wolf can get his in a lamb. The Cartwright name is too important to me and the boys to let the speculators toy with it."

Shaking his cigar at Ben, Eppler offered precautions of his own: "Word on the street is you're stretched, Ben. Take out a loan, and the unsavory types will smell blood for sure. You've got to keep your luck, good or bad, quiet, so people don't use the information against you. Should you have to sell stock, bad rumors can cost you thousands of dollars, whether they're true or not."

Ben placed his coffee cup on the silver tray and stood up. "Clarence, I want you to arrange a loan with the Bank of California. A half-million dollars for one month. That'll be enough to pay off our creditors and keep the mine operating."

"Ben, Ben, Ben," Pyburn moaned, running his

fingers through his gray hair.

Eppler's head drooped like his sagging spirits. "The bank will want collateral."

"My word is as good as the Cartwright name," Ben shot back.

Nodding reluctantly, Eppler looked up at Ben. "Yes, sir, it is, and the bank'll give you a loan on your word because they know what stands behind your name — the Ponderosa. If you can't repay the loan, it means the mine hasn't produced, and the bank won't come for the mine, they'll want the ranch. A lot of speculators have coveted your place because it's the closest timber that hasn't been cut down for the mines. You've got good water to boot, but most of all, they want the land to see if they can find more silver. It's a grave risk you're taking, Ben Cartwright, because even a personal loan is the equivalent of putting a mortgage on the Ponderosa."

"If the Bristlecone doesn't make it," Pyburn cautioned, "you'll lose the Ponderosa, at best. At worst, you'll witness its destruction."

Thurston Smalley entered the Bristlecone office and slammed the door behind him. A pair of startled clerks looked up from their desks and the paperwork piled there. By their calm expressions, neither clerk recognized him, and that was fine. Both would know who he was by the time he left. He would make sure of that. Ignorant clerks such as these helped fuel the rumors he started.

Smalley poked at his yellowed teeth with his gold toothpick. Both clerks hesitated, and Smalley took advantage of their delay by opening the swinging gate that separated the foyer from the business area. He headed for the stairs leading to Adam Cartwright's office.

"Pardon, sir," said a freckle-faced clerk with wide eyes, "this is for employees only."

His smile deflating as he jerked the toothpick from between his teeth, Smalley pointed the gold splinter at the clerk. "You're the first one I'm firing when I own the Bristlecone," he said.

The clerk gulped, but his friend at the adjacent desk shot up from his seat. "Just who the hell do you think you are?"

Smalley smiled as he answered. "Thurston Smalley is my name."

Both clerks paled visibly.

Smalley enjoyed the fear in their eyes. A bad reputation humbled the bit players in life. These two wouldn't challenge him, and in fact they would unknowingly help him by spreading word of his visit to the Bristlecone, just like past visits to other ailing mines before he had devoured them financially. He secretly relished his nickname as the "Vulture of Virginia City."

Sliding the gold toothpick into his vest pocket, Smalley sneered at the two clerks. "I'm here to see Adam Cartwright."

The clerks looked at one another, confusion clouding their faces. "Mr. Cartwright left word not to be disturbed," the freckle-faced clerk said.

"Did you have an appointment?"

"I don't need an appointment and I don't need your impertinence. Would you care to tell Adam Cartwright that you sent me away angry?"

"N-No, sir," the clerk stammered, then ran up the stairs.

Before he reached the top step, an office door upstairs swung open and Adam Cartwright appeared. He stood six feet, one inch tall, a muscled 190 pounds. His black eyes stared over a patrician nose. The approaching clerk seemed intimidated by Adam's commanding gaze and hard-set jaw.

The clerk spit out his message in short puffs. "Thurston Smalley. Downstairs, here. To see you."

Adam looked from the clerk down to Smalley, then back at the clerk. Smalley was certain he saw a tremor of fear in Adam Cartwright's eyes.

Adam slammed his door. Things had not been going well in the mine, and now this. The "Vulture of Virginia City" on his doorstep meant things had deteriorated even worse. Adam walked around the room, picking up every assaying report from his desk and the worktable. He carried them to a black safe which squatted in the corner. The tumbler clicked between his fingers as he twirled the dial and finished the combination. He grabbed the handle and twisted. The lock clanked and the iron door swung open. He shoved the reports inside, then shut the door, spinning the dial.

As he straightened up, he tugged his shirt sleeves and turned around, surprised to find Thurston Smalley standing in the open doorway, watching him like a wolf watches a lame rabbit. Adam felt his muscles tighten.

"I took the liberty of letting myself in, Mr. Cartwright," Smalley said, "my time being pressed, and you, I'm sure, having more important things to do. Mind if I sit down?" His arm pointed toward a worn chair at the worktable.

Adam shrugged. "As you like."

"Thank you," Smalley replied, seating himself without taking off his unfashionable beaver hat. His hand worked its way into his vest pocket and pulled a gold toothpick from inside. He poked at his teeth, his beady eyes watching Adam cross the room and close the door. "I regret your father is not present to hear my offer," he began, "but I know you can be depended upon to pass it along."

Adam clenched one hand into a fist, then forced his fingers to relax. He told himself to control his anger. "We're not interested in any offers."

Smalley pulled the toothpick from between his lips, which sprouted an antagonistic smile. "You will be before I'm through with the Bristlecone. The longer you wait, the more it'll cost you. I'm prepared to offer you a fair price for controlling interest in the Bristlecone."

"We're not selling."

"Think about it," Smalley said. "The Bristlecone is slowly bleeding the Ponderosa. And ev-

33

eryone knows the Ponderosa means more to the Cartwrights than all their other enterprises put together. Think about it, Adam, you are tearing the Ponderosa up and throwing it piece by piece into the Bristlecone. You Cartwrights can't keep both going. You can save the Ponderosa if you get rid of the mine, but none of you — yourself included, Adam — have the smarts for mining operations and mine investments."

Adam took a quick step toward Smalley and stopped. Smalley was trying to manipulate him like he exploited stocks. Cartwright resources were stretched now, Adam knew, but to give in to someone like Smalley would betray the Cartwrights' good name. "We don't have your smarts for larceny," Adam challenged.

"I merely pluck the fruits of capitalism, sir. Your mine's financial position is precarious. The mine's worthless, except for potential, potential you'll not realize without an infusion of cash."

Adam shook his head. "No deal."

"I'll offer you a hundred thousand dollars for controlling interest in the mine, or $175,000 for everything."

"That's a twentieth its value at best," Adam shot back. "It's ludicrous and you know it."

Smalley answered with his predatory smile. "I also know you're at thirteen hundred feet, with monthly expenses running at least a third of a million dollars, likely more."

Adam's throat went dry and he tried to hide his shock. Over the past twelve months, Bristlecone expenses had averaged $356,000 a month.

Smalley continued. "You are extracting less than five hundred tons of ore a day. With your ore assaying at less than twenty dollars a ton, you are grossing at most ten thousand dollars a day, less milling and reduction charges."

Adam stared straight ahead, hoping his eyes could hide the surprise at Smalley's uncanny analysis. It was dangerously close to the truth.

"By my estimate," Smalley nodded, "you are losing thirty- to seventy-five thousand a month, maybe even a hundred thousand. That's quite a sum to make up, even for the Cartwrights. You can't last forever."

Adam felt his lips tighten and his stomach turn. Smalley had an accurate feel for the mine's trouble, that or good spies. "We'll go as long as it takes."

"It won't take long," Smalley snarled.

"No deal. If or when we need money, we can raise it from friends, sell them shares if that's what it takes."

Smalley stood up and pointed his toothpick at Adam. "Discuss it with your father. See if he'd rather lose the mine or the Ponderosa." He inserted his toothpick back in his vest pocket and thumped the brim of his hat. "I'll expect an answer from you in a week, if you can hold out that long."

"The answer's now and the answer's no," Adam shot back.

Tugging the lapel of his frayed coat, Smalley

CHAPTER 3

Little Joe opened the door to Adam's office and held it for Hoss.

"Thank you, little brother," Hoss said, taking off his Carlsbad-cut hat and rolling the brim in his hand.

As Hoss passed, Little Joe slid the tip of his boot in front of Hoss's foot. Hoss stumbled forward, his hat falling to the floor, his foot just clearing the seven-inch crown before landing on the edge of the four-inch brim.

"Dad-blame-it," Hoss mumbled.

Little Joe's snicker died at the sound of his father's voice.

"Joseph," Ben called from the office's worktable, "I didn't call you here for foolishness." Ben's voice was as somber as his expression. Adam sat as solemn as his father. On the table before them were stacks of reports and papers.

"Close the door," Ben commanded. "We've family business."

Little Joe shoved the door and it banged shut, drawing the disapproving stares of Ben and Adam. Little Joe swallowed hard and jerked off his hat. He hated these business meetings.

As Little Joe moved toward the table, Hoss

retrieved his hat. Little Joe avoided his father's angry stare. And the day had started off so well too, Little Joe recalled, with him running into Holly Lucas on the street. She had coyly told him how delighted she would be to see him this evening when she finished work at the eatery. Little Joe seated himself meekly at the table, enjoying Hoss's scowl as he dusted his hat. Hoss tossed his hat on the table and plopped his 240 pounds into a chair, which he scooted as far as possible from Little Joe. Hoss was a big, strong man, but one of the gentlest creatures on earth, except when it came to Little Joe, the family prankster.

Ben ran his fingers through his silver hair and looked at his two youngest sons, but the gaze from his dark brown eyes seemed to extend somewhere beyond them. The crow's-feet etched into the tanned corners of his eyes seemed deeper than before. "We have problems with the Bristlecone," he said.

"Serious is it, Pa?" Hoss asked. "Are we going broke?"

The words hit Little Joe like a slap in the face. "What?"

Ben shrugged. "It's costing us more than it's bringing in. Right now we have more than a third of a million dollars in debt related to the mine, and no available funds to pay those debts. Short of a loan or disposing of the mine, we don't have acceptable options."

"Let's sell," Little Joe shot back.

"It's not that easy, Little Joe," Adam answered.

Hoss held up his hand, then scratched his head. "How can we be going broke? We got the Ponderosa and our livestock interests."

"And," interjected Little Joe, "Pa has timber leases and stock in the Virginia and Truckee Railroad."

Ben nodded. "But those aren't readily accessible assets."

"Huh," answered Hoss, scratching his head again.

"By readily accessible, I mean an asset like cash which is easily spent. The Ponderosa is worth a lot, but you can't spend it without selling it."

"But mining can't cost us that much," objected Little Joe.

Adam shook a stack of papers at his younger brothers. "It's all here," he said, scanning the top page. "Over the last twelve months, the Bristlecone has cost us $4.2 million."

Little Joe whistled and Hoss coughed, scratching his head even more vigorously.

"That comes to more than $350,000 a month, and $11,700 a day," Adam continued.

Hoss shook his head and leaned toward Adam. "How did we spend that much on a hole in the ground?"

"I'll give you an example," Adam replied. "Candles! We spent $15,950 on candles last year."

Hoss sighed and slumped into his seat. Little Joe's eyes widened like saucers.

Adam continued. "We spent almost as much

on candles as we did on blasting powder, $17,340. Ice to cool the miners, almost two million pounds of it, cost us $21,899. It's more expensive to run a mine than a cattle ranch, Hoss, and you couldn't raise enough cattle on the Ponderosa to keep the Bristlecone going."

Ben grimaced. "That's the truth of the matter, boys. We are bringing up 475 tons of ore a day, which is producing less than twenty dollars a ton of silver. That means we're only making some nine thousand dollars a day, which is some $2700 less than our daily expenses. We've carried the loss until now, but we've suppliers to pay and a payroll coming up. We need a loan."

"Fine," Little Joe said, "take out a loan."

"A half-million-dollar loan," Adam pronounced.

"A what?" Little Joe gasped.

Hoss slumped deeper into his chair.

"A half million dollars," Ben said, "to pay off our debts and keep us running for another month."

"Pa," Hoss asked, "I still don't understand why we don't sell."

Adam shook his head. "A mine that hasn't produced a solid profit has a value only as great as public confidence. A speculator named Thurston Smalley visited me today. His stock manipulations have made him a fortune and ruined hundreds of investors. He ran the Montgomery Mine into the ground and several since. Now he's targeted the Bristlecone. He'll start rumors to drive down public confidence in the Bristlecone. If we sell out, we may not even make what we paid for it and what we owe on it."

"But won't it cut our losses?" Little Joe asked, his head cocked, his expression as murky as his understanding of the situation.

"The short-term answer is no," Ben responded. "We've certain contracts for timber and for equipment which we must pay off, even if we close the mine. And even if we shut down the Bristlecone, we could still jeopardize the Ponderosa because of those contracted commitments and our debt. And our position is complicated by Thurston Smalley. Smalley's a vicious speculator, as greedy as they come. The next two weeks will tell, that's why I'm gonna ask you two to stay in town for a while instead of returning to the Ponderosa."

Things weren't looking so bad after all, Little Joe thought, if the Bristlecone's dilemma meant he could stay awhile in Virginia City.

"We need you nearby," Ben continued. "Decisions may have to be made quickly, and they'll be made as they've always been made for Cartwright Enterprises. I'll have two votes and each of you one vote. For now, we're mining the Bristlecone. Any questions?"

"Yeah, Pa," Hoss said, "anything Little Joe and I can do to help, us not being business-minded as much as you and Adam?"

Ben spoke softly. "Trust no one outside of this room, don't talk to anyone about assaying reports, don't speculate on the mine's potential, and don't let rumors go unchallenged."

"Pa," Hoss said, his furrowed brow pinching the bridge of his nose, "is there any chance we could lose the Ponderosa?"

Ben pursed his lips and nodded slowly. "The loan will be issued to me without contractual collateral. But, Hoss, if the Bristlecone doesn't come through, the bank will try to claim the Ponderosa."

"Damn," Hoss said, standing up slowly. "I need some lunch. Any of the rest of you?"

Adam and Ben shook their heads in unison, but Little Joe smiled. "I sure do," he said.

"Little Joe," Pa said as his youngest son pushed himself up from the table, "stay out of mischief."

"Sure, Pa, no trouble," Little Joe replied, tugging his hat on his head and turning for the door. "No trouble."

Hoss followed his younger brother outside Adam's office, then down the stairs and through the office where he heard two clerks talking about Thurston Smalley. As he stepped outdoors into the warm sunshine, Hoss felt like a boy who had lost his dog. The thought of life without the Ponderosa was too much to comprehend. How a man he had never heard of before, Thurston Smalley, could threaten the Ponderosa with lies about the Bristlecone perplexed him even more.

The door slammed shut in Hoss's hand, rattling the glass panes. The two clerks inside glanced from their desks to Hoss. Hoss didn't realize his strength when he shut doors. It was nothing intentional, but when his mind was fixed on something else, he didn't always keep his strength in check, particularly when it came to shutting doors.

He stepped down the plank walk and in a couple of moments was beside Little Joe. He was surprised at his younger brother.

Little Joe gave Hoss one of his charming smiles, then began to whistle a snappy tune.

"What are you so all-fired tickled about, little brother? Because I feel lower than a snake's belly."

Little Joe just laughed. "Now I've got plenty of time to call on Holly Lucas."

"If you don't beat all, Little Joe. We may lose the Ponderosa, and all you can think about is chasing women. But I'll tell you this, you better stay away from Holly Lucas."

"You don't know anything about women."

"Nope, but I know trouble when I see it, and she's trouble."

It was past six when Adam locked up the office and walked toward the center of Virginia City. Behind him the hoist works of the Bristlecone mine purred as it pulled ton after ton of ore from the bowels of the earth. Mining never shut down on the Comstock Lode. The best-paid miners in the world worked in shifts around the clock, prying riches from the earth. At four dollars a day, their muscle and sweat made fortunes for many, but seldom for themselves. They were, though, honest workers for the most part, proud to be working in the world's deepest and richest mines.

A thousand Thurston Smalleys would not have the integrity of one miner, Adam thought. The worry of the Bristlecone had been a heavy burden these last few weeks, when Cartwright money had been stretched. Adam felt he alone was responsible for the ruin facing the family. Though all of them had originally voted to invest in the mining operation rather than sell stock, they had done so at his urging. Even his father had gone along with him, but Adam was never certain if Ben's heart had been in such a speculative endeavor, particularly with all the capital that mining required. And now, with Thurston Smalley eyeing the venture like a scavenger, Adam felt even more pressure.

Ben had been smart enough to diversify Cartwright Enterprises, and today the family had livestock, timber, and railroad interests to draw monies from. Adam had convinced his father and brothers to go into mining as well, because of the Bristlecone's prime location. With himself as superintendent, Adam was confident he could bring the mine in. With common yields amounting to $34 a ton on the Comstock Lode, Adam would never have suggested the Cartwrights get into mining. However, the Consolidated Virginia, which abutted the Bristlecone, had come across a huge vein yielding $100 to $700 a ton. Even with a yield on the lower end of that range, the Bristlecone had potential to be one of the richest mines in Virginia City.

That potential, though, was contingent upon finding silver in the Bristlecone. To the west, the Consolidated Virginia had struck the mother lode at 1150 feet and had made millionaires of John W. Mackay and James G. Fair. And yet the Bristlecone, abutting that very mine claim, had scratched 1300 feet into the earth and was making paupers of the Cartwrights. Mining was a fickle mistress. Adam had only to look up Mount Davidson at the skeleton of the Montgomery Mine, which had never produced anything, or to look behind him down F Street to the works of the Ophir Mine, one of the first on the Comstock Lode. Almost two decades ago the Ophir had been the major producer on the Comstock Lode. But it had been years since the mine had given a significant find or produced a profit. The Ophir was now a monument to bankruptcy. What if the Bristlecone had more of the Ophir than the Consolidated Virginia in its veins? Adam was worried. He berated himself that he should never have persuaded his family to let him risk the Ponderosa empire in such a speculative and costly venture.

Passing the long wooden buildings of the Consolidated Virginia mine works, he turned up Union Street, walked three blocks to C Street and turned south, heading for Bill Davis's gymnasium. He pulled the silver stem-wind watch from the vest pocket of his tailored three-piece suit. He had promised to dine with Lucia Sinclair at eight o'clock. He still had time to get in a few rounds on the punching bag before dinner, so he shoved the watch back in his pocket and picked up his gait.

Reaching the gymnasium, Adam bounded up the steps and pushed open the double door. The well-lit room smelled of exertion and sweat. The steady noise of men jumping rope and pounding punching bags was punctuated by grunts of pain and moans of exhaustion. The gymnasium was a melting pot of Virginia City's sporting crowd, ne'er-do-wells and well-to-do. In the gym and especially in the canvas ring dominating the center of the room, men's social standing was irrelevant. In the back corner at the punching bags, Adam saw a clump of men watching someone go through a workout.

Adam entered the dressing room and greeted Jacob, the black attendant who was seated in a barber's chair reading a discarded copy of the day's *Territorial Enterprise.* Jacob drew water for baths, provided towels, maintained propriety in the dressing room, and even offered free shaves to the clientele.

"Evening, Mr. Cartwright," Jacob said with a rich, mellifluous voice.

"Still think you ought to sing for a living, Jacob," Adam said.

"No, sir," Jacob replied, folding the newspaper precisely in half, then arising elegantly. "I don't sing good in front of crowds, particularly when they're throwing things as they sometimes do at a black man. Will you be needing a bath or shave when you're done, Mr. Cartwright?"

"Both," Adam said. "I'm meeting a lady friend for dinner."

Jacob smiled. "No better kind of friend than a lady friend."

Adam slipped back into a dressing booth and pulled the curtain. Before he could get his coat and vest off, Jacob slipped him a pair of boxing tights, a pair of socks, and his boxing shoes. He dressed quickly, then threw back the curtain and strode past Jacob, who gathered Adam's clothes and carried them into the locked room where he kept the attire of the gymnasium's clientele.

Out in the gym, Adam jogged to the punching bags, skirting the clump of spectators watching one boxer, and squared off against a hanging bag. Adam had a lean build, made athletic by his regular work in the gym. His muscled chest was thick with black hair and perfectly proportioned, its single flaw an eight-inch scar that snaked up his right ribcage, his medal for being tossed by a bull as a youth.

Adam attacked the hanging bag, throwing punches slowly at first, then pummeling the bag until it reverberated above all else in the gym. In his mind, he pounded the face of Thurston Smalley, the Vulture of Virginia City, and was so focused on the punching bag that it took him a moment to realize a crowd had gathered near him. He struck the bag with his left, right, left hands, then drew back and blasted it a final time with his right. He twisted around to see whom the crowd was watching, then nodded at the sight of John W. Mackay, one of the richest men in the world.

"Rough day, Adam?" Mackay said, extending his hand.

Adam shrugged. He wiped his hand on his boxing tights before grabbing Mackay's and shaking it warmly. For a man of forty-five, Mackay was in excellent physical shape, testament to his regular use of the gymnasium. An Irishman by birth, Mackay had a thick mustache and dark, penetrating eyes that seemed deep-set because of his long nose. He spoke like he boxed, slow and steady, with a tendency to anger. He had taken up boxing, he had told Adam, to help him manage his anger, though not nearly as well as he managed his mining interests. He had come to the Comstock Lode broke, but through hard work and good instincts, had invested in a series of mines before they boomed and had sold out just as they began to decline. Now he was one of the four principal owners of the Consolidated Virginia. He always attracted a crowd, not only in the gymnasium, but everywhere he went, because he was generous to a fault. According to local legend, Mackay could leave his office with a thousand dollars in his pocket and be broke by the time he crossed the street.

Mackay released Adam's hand, then turned to

the men clumped around him. "You boys mind your own affairs awhile so Adam and I can talk some business."

The men scattered about the gym, each keeping watch on Mackay in case he left in a generous mood. Mackay waited until all were out of hearing range before he spoke again.

Adam knew what was coming, and he knew Mackay could be trusted with the truth.

"Luck picking up for you?" the millionaire asked.

"Afraid not," Adam said. "Fact is, my luck's taken a turn for the worse. Thurston Smalley came by to see me today, wanting to buy me out at a ridiculous price."

"The Vulture of Virginia City, is it? Things have taken a bad turn indeed. What'd your father say?"

"We're going to hold on for awhile," Adam replied.

"I would've thought you'd struck silver by now."

Adam only nodded.

"A lot of luck in this business," Mackay offered.

"More bad luck, especially with Thurston Smalley getting involved."

"By the end of the week, rumors will be flying about the Bristlecone. I admire you Cartwrights for going it alone, trying to bring the Bristlecone in. Not many men can do it."

"We haven't yet."

"My money says you will."

49

"That's a lot of money, John."

The millionaire nodded. "I have a wife and family in Europe to support. Funny thing, Adam, I left Ireland to come to America for the opportunity this country offered. I've succeeded beyond any sane man's wildest expectations. And now my wife spends every year in Europe using my money to impress the very aristocrats who wouldn't even give me and thousands of other poor Irishmen a chance at a decent job. It doesn't make sense, Adam, now does it? I guess that's why I like these workouts, they get the bile out of me."

"At least we Cartwrights have stayed family," Adam replied.

"It's easier when you don't have a wife." Mackay laughed and slapped Adam on the back. "If I hear anything about Thurston Smalley's scheme, I'll let you know. Only good thing about him going after you Cartwrights is it'll keep him off of me."

Adam shook his head. "You're too big for him to go after."

"Nope," said Mackay, "when a snake's ready to strike, he doesn't consider the size of his prey." The millionaire turned and walked toward the dressing room, and several of the others in the gym suddenly decided it was time for them to change too.

For all Mackay's money, Adam did not envy him. With his family taking residence in Europe, Mackay had no home except a hotel room. Even

50

if it was the best money could buy, it was still not a home.

Adam attacked the punching bag with a vengeance for another five minutes, then picked up a jump rope and worked out on it until Mackay exited the gym. Adam retreated to the dressing room, where Jacob greeted him at the door. "I just drew your water, sir. The back room if you please."

Adam bathed quickly, then dried and wrapped himself in towels. He marched barefoot to the front of the dressing room and slid into the barber's chair. Jacob draped hot towels on Adam's face, then brushed lather over his cheeks, chin, and neck. After honing the straight razor on a strop, Jacob gave Adam a shave and splashed some tonic on his smooth cheeks.

When Jacob had finished, he pointed to a dressing cubicle where the attendant had already placed Adam's clothes. Adam nodded his thanks and dressed quickly. As he left the dressing room, he gave Jacob a five-dollar silver piece. "Best shave I ever had," Adam said.

Leaving the gymnasium, he turned down C Street and headed for his suite at the International Hotel. The sky had darkened, but C Street was bright with gas lamps. At precisely eight o'clock he walked into the lobby of the International Hotel.

Lucia Sinclair stood up from a sofa and walked toward him. It pleased Adam to note that several male heads turned to watch her cross the lobby.

She smiled, but her gray eyes seemed troubled.

Adam took her hand, lifting it to his lips and kissing it. "What's wrong?"

She hesitated. "Is something wrong with the Bristlecone?"

"Why do you ask?"

"Thurston Smalley came to the county clerk's office today. I overheard him telling one of the other clerks he wanted to inspect the records on the Bristlecone claim."

Adam caught his breath. "The Bristlecone is his next target."

"Well," Lucia said proudly, "he didn't find out anything about your claim today."

"How do you know?"

"When I overheard his request, I ran to the back and misplaced the record book. That will stall him for a while."

Adam leaned over and kissed Lucia on the cheek.

CHAPTER 4

The crowd filtered past the ticket takers. Men and women moved to the front of the Miners Union Hall and squeezed together on the hard bench seats facing an elevated stage, anticipation growing.

Thurston Smalley clung to the wall, away from the amber light of the gas lamps. His lips parted in a grin that bared his yellowed teeth. These fools, he thought, paying fifty cents to see Professor Harlan Beck perform sleight of hand and mind-reading feats. Smalley had seen Professor Beck's type before, men who read the vapid minds of their paid shills and then made a few coins disappear, to the audience's amazement. If the audience really wanted to see money disappear, they should watch him work, Smalley thought. Over his career, he had made hundreds of thousands of dollars vanish from mining properties ruined by his manipulations. Then, like magic, he had made those dollars reappear — in his own pocket.

Like the magician, Smalley relied on spies, men who could be trusted to do wrong. Tonight he had arranged a meeting with one of those men, Vorley Deaton, a hard-rock miner who had connections in the Miners Union, connections that could get him assigned to any mine on the Comstock Lode. Deaton had worked two other mines for Smalley and had turned a handsome profit for himself.

Smalley watched the crowd intently, knowing Deaton would be late, as instructed, so they could claim seats at the back. One couple passed Smalley arm in arm, and he instantly moved deeper into the shadows. The blond woman he did not recognize, but her escort he knew on sight — Little Joe Cartwright. Little Joe nodded at several men, then took off his hat and sat down. The blonde snuggled against Little Joe, who slipped his arm around her waist. Before Smalley could see more, other spectators took their seats behind Little Joe, blocking Smalley's view.

The back rows had almost filled when Vorley Deaton entered the hall. Dressed in typical miner's garb of woolen overalls, gray woolen shirt, and narrow-billed cap, Deaton was well-muscled, his face and hands pale from years of hard work in the darkness of a dozen mines. Deaton scanned the room, spotting Smalley but giving no sign of recognition. When Smalley emerged from the shadows, both men angled for seats on the last row. Sitting first, Deaton ignored Smalley as the manipulator slid onto the bench beside him.

Neither man spoke. Deaton leaned forward, propping his elbows on his knees and resting his chin on his interlocked fingers. Smalley studied the throng, seeking glimpses of Little Joe Cartwright whenever possible. As the room filled, the noise grew.

Without looking at Deaton, Smalley whispered his instructions. "Get into the Bristlecone. I need the regular information."

Deaton turned his head a hair, watching Smalley out of the corner of his eyes. "Not the Bristlecone."

Smalley's head jerked with controlled anger. "What?"

"Not the Bristlecone, Mr. Smalley." Deaton spoke softly.

Smalley eyed Deaton carefully. Never before had Deaton defied him. Then Smalley smiled. Now he understood. Deaton wanted more money. "No games, Deaton, how much more money do you want?"

"It ain't money," Deaton whispered. "Just I don't want to work the Bristlecone. The Cartwrights've always treated the miners fair."

Smalley's fingers knotted into powerless fists. "They pay you four dollars a day, same as everyone else."

Deaton nodded. "They do, but they give us plenty of ice and water in the hole. They pay men when they're out sick and care for their families when they're injured. They run the safest mine on the Comstock."

Smalley scowled. "No matter. Once you work for me, you do what I say. If you don't, I'll destroy you."

His jaw clenched, but Deaton nodded reluctantly. "I won't like it, but I'll do it," he said slowly.

"That's better. As a bonus, when you're done with this mine, I'll give you a thousand dollars. Until then you'll still get the two hundred fifty a month I'm paying now. After we're done with the Bristlecone, I'll never ask you to do another job for me."

Deaton shrugged. "If you'll go after the Cartwrights, you've no decency in you. There's no better mine operators on the Comstock."

Smalley snickered. "When I'm done, there'll be no poorer mine operators on the Comstock than the Cartwrights."

Deaton pounded his muscled legs with his balled fists, stood up slowly and scowled at Smalley. "What more do you want? You've got all the money you could ever need."

"Power," Smalley snarled, "power over people like you, people like the Cartwrights. People know who I am. How many know who you are, Vorley Deaton?"

The miner pushed his way toward the aisle, Smalley laughing at his departure. Smalley would have followed, except for Little Joe's presence. He stayed to watch Little Joe, thinking he might pick up some information he could use against the Cartwrights. Take the woman, for instance. Wasn't she the friend of Big Jim Fowler? Smalley had heard that Little Joe and Fowler had almost come to blows over a woman. If this were the woman, Smalley knew how to fan the flames of jealousy, flames that might just burn the Cartwrights for good.

Little Joe never felt luckier. As Holly snuggled against him on the hard bench, he smiled, wondering what Big Jim Fowler would say if he could see her clinging to him like moss to a tree. He laughed.

"What's so funny?" Holly giggled, infected by his merriment.

"Just thinking about the dance, my luck in running into you, and wondering what Fowler would think about this."

Holly leaned closer into him. "I don't care. He could've brought me here, but he cares more about the Zephyr Engine Company than he does me. I don't want to spend my evening talking about him. Tell me about the Ponderosa. It must be grand."

Little Joe nodded and began to explain about the ranch and his job overseeing the ranch's horse herd, breeding good racing stock.

Holly seemed little interested in horses and attempted to change the subject. "Can I ask you something, something personal?"

"Sure," Little Joe replied, intrigued. He leaned toward her.

Holly's lips touched his ear, sending a wave of excitement down his spine. "Are you rich?" she whispered.

He was disappointed at her question but excited

by her nearness and the chill of her breath in his ear. "You're a nosy one, aren't you?"

Pulling away from him, Holly frowned and her lower lip quivered for a moment. Her hold on his arm loosened and her shoulders sagged. "I've just heard so many things, good things, about the Cartwrights, I never thought they could all be true of folks that had money," she said, her words tinged with emotion.

For a moment Little Joe thought she might cry. "We've money," he said. "Not as much as some of the major mine owners, but more than most folks."

Holly's hand tightened around Little Joe's arm and she leaned closer into him. "I just can't believe someone with money can be as handsome and decent as you, Little Joe." She seemed contented next to him, and Little Joe was pleased.

On the elevated stage a bespectacled man appeared from behind a black curtain and lifted his arms toward the ceiling, gesturing for quiet from the audience. Gradually the hall grew hushed and the man introduced the amazing Professor Harlan Beck as the world's greatest sleight-of-hand artist and the most phenomenal mentalist in all the universe. The crowd applauded wildly as a man darted through the back curtain, a black cape flying behind him as he pranced about the stage. Holly Lucas straightened in her seat and gazed with the multitude at the man who stopped at center stage, then bowed to his audience. As he straightened up, he tossed his cape back over his shoulder. In his black suit, black vest, and black tie, he looked more gambler than professor. His black eyes and pencil-thin mustache dominated his face.

With a wave of his hand, a deck of cards appeared from nowhere. Then a red handkerchief seemed to come from thin air to cover the cards. He lifted that hand to the sky and suddenly jerked it toward the floor. When his hand stopped at his waist, both the kerchief and the cards had disappeared. The audience roared, and Beck smiled for the first time.

He clapped his hands together and a deck of cards appeared again. He fanned them, then collapsed them into a stack and spread them out on a table at his side, going through a series of fancy shuffles and manipulations, making the cards dance as if they had lives of their own, each trick drawing disbelieving gasps, then applause.

Finally he uttered his first words. "Good evening, ladies and gentlemen. Thank you for your warm Virginia City welcome. Those were the easy tricks. Now for the hard ones."

The audience roared, getting into the spirit of the act. Beck asked for volunteers, had them select cards then bury them in the deck or otherwise hide them while he made the card reappear or divined its suit and denomination.

"Isn't he good?" Holly whispered excitedly to Little Joe.

"He's okay," Little Joe answered, "but it's all

a trick. These people may be his shills."

Holly swatted playfully at his arm. "Killjoy!"

For the next half hour, Beck amazed people with his card tricks, his variations on the shell game, and his ability to pick the pockets of the volunteers who came up on stage. For his final trick Beck was even able to pull the belt off a volunteer without the man knowing it. The man returned to his seat thinking he had stumped Beck.

"Explain that," Holly said as Beck tossed the belt to the man.

"He probably had too many to drink," Little Joe replied.

Beck pranced about the stage, taking the accolades, then held his index finger to his lips for silence. When the exuberance faded away into quiet, he looked about the audience, milking the silence for dramatic effect.

"Sleight of hand is simple compared to what I am about to do. I claim to be the world's greatest sleight-of-hand artist because anyone can learn to do that, given a little practice and a lot of talent. But what I am about to do as a mentalist will astound you beyond belief, for I am truly the greatest mind reader not just in the world, but in the whole universe."

The disbelieving crowd murmured, some men scoffing loudly.

"Doubt me if you want," Beck retorted, "but I shall prove my claims after I return from intermission." He disappeared behind the dark curtain before the crowd could respond.

Holly cocked her head at Little Joe. "How's he gonna do this, if he's a fraud?" she challenged.

Little Joe just laughed, surprised at her naïveté. "He's probably backstage right now, reading notes on the shills he plans to call on stage."

Holly grinned suspiciously. "We'll see now, won't we?"

Little Joe stood up, stretching his arms. "You're too gullible, Holly Lucas."

Holly blushed, then giggled as she arose. "Oh, Little Joe," she said, waving toward the front, "there's one of my girlfriends. Oh, she sat down, I must see her."

"I'll go with you," Little Joe offered.

"I'd love for you to, Little Joe, but shouldn't you save our seats?"

Little Joe had to admit her suggestion was a good one in such a crowded hall. "I'll stay."

Holly squeezed his hand, then pardoned herself, moving quickly to the aisle.

Little Joe watched her move to the front, then lost her in the crowd. As Joe's gaze swept the room, he had the uncomfortable feeling of being watched. Turning around, he glimpsed a small man in the back row who averted his eyes. The man wore an unstylish beaver hat. Joe thought he had seen him somewhere before, but he could not place him. The man looked harmless enough, however. Little Joe had feared Big Jim Fowler slipping up on him, but that worry was unjustified. His gaze circled the room, then stopped on the stage. Had he seen Holly disappear behind the curtains? Surely not, but even so, he had an eerie feeling.

He could not shake that feeling, even when Holly made it back up the aisle, then squeezed down the row of spectators. She smiled and pointed to the stage. "They're about to start."

Little Joe helped Holly settle into her place, and slid beside her on the bench just as Professor Beck's bespectacled assistant appeared on stage again, holding his hands up for silence. Little Joe enjoyed the aroma of Holly's perfume as she leaned against him.

"You still don't believe Professor Beck can read minds, now do you?" she challenged.

"I'll believe it when I see it."

"Then volunteer when he calls for folks from the audience."

"And let him make a fool of me before everyone? No, ma'am."

"It would make me happy," she whispered, lowering her head to his shoulder.

"Nope," Little Joe said.

As the crowd quieted, the professor's assistant shouted out his introduction. "Now, the greatest mentalist in the universe, Professor Harlan Beck." The assistant disappeared and Professor Beck, black cape and all, reappeared on stage, swooping around the platform, bowing to the audience, which took up where it left off, cheering him wildly.

When the professor straightened up, he called

for a volunteer and quiet. "These exercises will require great concentration, which will be impossible without total silence." He pointed to a volunteer on the front row, and a portly woman with a huge hat waddled up on stage. As he offered her his hand, he encouraged the audience to applaud, and they did.

"Thank you, madam," he said as she clambered up on stage. "Ooops, I believe you lost this." He unwadded his fist and let a bracelet slide into her outstretched palm.

"How'd you get that?" she gasped.

"A touch of larceny in my soul." He smiled, disarming her with his charm. "Now then, I want you to think of a number. I would suggest your age . . ."

The woman's mouth dropped open.

". . . but since you are obviously no more than twenty years old, that would make my chances too easy at one in twenty."

The woman's smile was as broad as her ample girth, and the audience laughed.

"Consider a number between one and a thousand and write it on this chalkboard," he said, handing her the slate and chalk. "Do not let me see it." He turned his back to the audience.

After thinking for a moment, the woman scratched three numerals on the board, then held it up for the audience to see. The numerals — 769 — were visible even from Little Joe's seat. Still standing behind her, Professor Beck turned a quarter way around and instructed her to erase it with the rag he offered.

When the evidence was obliterated, the self-proclaimed best mentalist in the universe closed his eyes and held his fingers to the bridge of his nose, then wrinkled his lips in concentration. It seemed forever before he spoke. "The number," he said, opening his eyes and staring beyond the woman, beyond the audience, into a distance only he could see, "is twenty-two."

Little Joe snickered and nudged Holly with his elbow. The audience groaned but for a moment.

The collective groan was shattered by Beck's shout. "No, the individual numerals add up to twenty-two. The actual number was 769." Beck crossed his arms triumphantly across his chest. "Is that not right?"

Little Joe felt Holly's elbow poke at his ribs. "See there."

Professor Beck used a half-dozen more volunteers to perform similar tricks, while Holly sat on the edge of her seat and Little Joe tried to figure out the mentalist's gimmicks.

"Now," called Professor Beck, "for my last reading of the mind I want to challenge the biggest skeptic in the audience. Who is that person?"

Immediately, several men lifted their hands or pointed to nearby doubters. Others began to clamor their nominations.

Professor Beck bounded from the stage into the audience. "Who will it be? Who thinks he can stump me? Who believes all of this is a hoax? Who among you dares to challenge the universe's greatest mentalist?" Beck's knowing gaze scanned the audience.

Little Joe sank into his seat as Holly waved her arm then jumped to her feet. "Over here," she shouted, pointing at Little Joe. "He doesn't believe any of this."

Professor Beck turned around, stared at Holly, then glared at Little Joe. "Sir," Professor Beck intoned, "have we ever met?"

Shaking his head, Little Joe felt as foolish as a bartender at a Baptist meeting.

"Come on," commanded Professor Beck, motioning for him.

Behind him people began to pat him on the shoulder. For a moment Joe fought it, but the crowd began chanting.

"Little Joe, be a sport," Holly pleaded.

Grimacing, Little Joe stood up, then lifted his arms over his head like a prizefighter. The audience cheered. Bolstered by the support, he grinned and followed Professor Beck to the stage.

As Little Joe turned to face the crowd, Professor Beck stood nose to nose with him, making Little Joe wince at the smell of onions on his breath. "You do not believe in me, do you?"

Little Joe shrugged. "Not until I'm shown."

Professor Beck laughed. "Shortly, you shall believe, if you concentrate and do as I say. Now think of something pleasant."

Little Joe thought of Holly and smiled.

"Don't think of your girl, that's too easy," Beck instructed.

Little Joe felt the smile drain from his face. Could Professor Beck read his mind? No, of course not. This time Little Joe thought about the Ponderosa.

Professor Beck's black eyes bore into him like twin augers as he pinched the bridge of his nose with his soft fingers. Slowly Beck opened his eyelids. "I have seen a tree and a bush, a great tree and a small bush beside it, its branches touching the great tree."

Once again Little Joe felt a smile working its way along his lips. A tree and a bush were the farthest things from his mind.

"A tall pine tree," Beck said, "a ponderosa pine."

Little Joe gulped.

"But it's something else, not just a tree . . . it's land? Do you work land called . . ." Beck paused, letting the great silence hang in the air. ". . . Ponderosa?"

Those in the audience who knew Little Joe gasped.

Little Joe could not believe it. "The family ranch is the Ponderosa," he told Professor Beck.

Beck waved his hand in the air. "Silence. This bush, this bush that I see. It's a holly bush. Does the word 'holly' mean anything to you?"

"Holly's my company for the evening," Joe said in disbelief. "Damn," he whispered to himself.

"Silence," Beck called. "I see something more that I do not understand. You and the holly bush and a ring of fire. You and your friend were brought together by a fire? Is that correct?"

Little Joe shrugged. "I guess. We met at a fireman's ball."

"Beware," Beck warned, "what is bonded by fire can only be broken by fire."

CHAPTER 5

The latest assay reports were bad. Adam tossed them aside. He ran his hands through his hair and shook his head in frustration. The mine shaft had passed 1300 feet, now with laterals every hundred feet, from the three-hundred-foot level on, and still the vein that had to be there could not be found. There was silver in the diggings, but not enough to make it profitable. Only enough to tantalize, just enough to make a man think more was just beyond the rubble of each shift that chinked away at the earth's innards. It was just enough to break a man's spirit. And his wallet.

Adam cringed to think he was throwing Cartwright assets down a hole in the ground. Perhaps the odds would improve if he tossed dice or tried faro or played poker instead. He pinched the bridge of his nose, then wadded up a piece of scrap paper and tossed it toward the wastebasket beneath the window. The paper hit the windowsill and bounced to the floor. Adam shoved himself up from his chair and strode to the window. As he bent over to pick up the paper, he saw a thread of smoke arising from the brewery across the street.

Smoke! Just to the east of the Bristlecone property, the Comstock Brewery was smoldering, smoke wafting from the wooden shingles, weathered and dry from too much sun and too little moisture. For an instant Adam wondered why no one had yet raised the alarm, then realized pedestrians did not have his vantage point.

"Fire!" he yelled out the window, and the heads of passersby lifted to stare at him. He pointed at the brewery, its unpainted wooden walls seemingly fine. The passing men, mostly mine workers, stood fixed in disbelief for a moment, then one spotted a wisp of smoke and pointed. Then another saw it. All of a sudden the men burst down the street, sounding the call.

Adam bolted from the window and down the stairs into the Bristlecone's business office. He answered their startled gazes. "Fire, fire at the brewery." Darting outside into the street, he bent and scooped up a handful of dirt, and tossed it into the wind. The debris carried away from the Bristlecone and toward the fire.

At least the wind was favorable, so far, but winds were as unpredictable as fires. He had a shift of men in the Bristlecone. With the Bristlecone's precarious financial situation, he couldn't afford to bring them up. Even so, he couldn't risk leaving them down there. Should the hoist works catch fire, they would be stranded, or even worse, burned to death if the fire got into the mine and its volatile timbers.

A half-dozen men darted from inside the brewery, screaming an alarm at the tops of their voices. From all around Virginia City fire bells clanged their warnings. As Adam turned to attend to the evacuation of the mine, flames broke through the brewery roof, orange tongues licking at the sky and dancing in the wind, scattering showers of sparks.

Adam ran back inside the Bristlecone's offices. "Lock up and get out," he ordered his office staff, then raced out the back door for the hoist works and stamp mill. The rumble of the stamp mill grew as he neared the giant building. Startled foremen looked up as he burst inside, waving his arms to get their attention over the noise, then cupping his hands to his mouth. "Evacuate the mine! Evacuate everyone, now!" he yelled. The hoist operator paused a moment, then Adam was beside him, shouting over the machinery noise. "Fire across the street, evacuate the mine, now."

The hoist operator flew into action, yanking the signal cord that jangled alarm bells in the mine. The hoist wheel accelerated as the operator, smudged with dirt and grease, brought a final load to the surface. Ore carts were shoved from the hoist cage by men who understood the gravity of the situation. A couple of men jumped into the hoist cage to carry the warning to others who may not have heard the alarm. No sooner were they in the cage than it dropped back into the earth. Behind the operator the giant iron hoist wheel spun crazily as yards of flat cable unwound into the earth's depths.

Adam appointed a supervisor to keep the names and a final tally of all the men who came up. Then he ordered more men to prepare to shut up the mine when everyone was evacuated. Adam had had iron doors installed ten feet deep in the shaft for just such an emergency. Once all the men were out, those doors would be closed and covered with fresh ore and dirt to block it off. It would take a day to get the shaft open again and the mine operating, but Adam wouldn't take any chances with his men or with the shaft itself.

His face was etched with worry, though he felt better with each load of miners the hoist cage disgorged. When the shift foreman signaled that all the miners had been evacuated, Adam gave the command to seal the shaft. As he uttered the order, he felt a pit in his stomach as deep as the Bristlecone shaft.

His fingers ached from the work, rubbing the brass fittings on the Button and Blake hand pumper. Big Jim Fowler's anger was reflected in the spotless brass bell that he had polished with a clean rag for most of an hour. He was the only one in the firehouse now; the other volunteers were at their day work. Fowler relished the solitude, particularly after all the embarrassing talk he had heard since last night. While he and other volunteers were cleaning up the Odd Fellows Hall where they had hosted their charity ball the night before, Holly Lucas had attended a magician's show with Little Joe Cartwright. Even if she was a free spirit, Holly Lucas was his girl. His persuasive powers had convinced the members of Zephyr Engine Company No. 7 to elect her their belle. They had given Holly her own leather helmet and her own red shirt, the badges of pride and unity volunteers wore as members of a fire company. Despite the honor, she had not worn the shirt and hat to the ball. Indeed she had been comely in her dress, attracting admirers galore. Her appearance and the common knowledge among the firemen that she was Fowler's girl had been an asset to political ambitions — until she had started dancing with Little Joe Cartwright. And now this, going out with Little Joe behind his back!

Fowler wanted to strike back at Little Joe, to give him a public beating so everyone would know that Holly Lucas was his girl, one who owed her prestige as belle of Zephyr Engine Company No. 7 to him and him alone. However, Fowler knew such a confrontation could cost him support should the city opt for a paid fire department.

Fowler stepped back, wiped his hand over his face and nodded at the brass bell. The distorted reflection of his face in the bell was unblemished, the brass as shiny as new. Fowler moved to one of the brass brake arms that men worked up and down to build the pressure necessary to pump water. Many a blister had Fowler rubbed into his palm while working the brakes as a volunteer, but those days were behind him. By his skill as both a firefighter and as a politician, he was now captain of Zephyr Engine Company No. 7 and no longer had to man the brake arms. As captain, he gave the orders.

Jerking his polish rag from the hand brake, Fowler attacked the brass rod, wrapping his fingers around the lever arm as if it were Little Joe's neck. Except for his encounter with Little Joe and Hoss Cartwright, the dance had been good politics — so far. However, expenses for such a fancy ball had been so high that the small profit would likely disappoint the men of the engine company. That would be bad, but not insurmountable. He could overcome any backlash with Holly Lucas at his side, but she would have to tame her free spirit, or he would destroy her like the others who got in his way. He rubbed the brass brake arm with a vengeance.

Outside, the wind kicked up and whistled through the bell tower, the drooping bell rope swaying in the breeze. The outside door banged shut. Fowler slapped his rag against the brass arm. He hated the wind, fire's greatest ally.

When the door slammed again, Fowler turned around to latch it. He was surprised to find Holly Lucas standing meekly before him, her hands clasped together at her slender waist. She approached him warily, like a scolded child. Fowler drew back his hand and slapped her across the cheek.

"You know what that's for?" He spit out the

words and drew his arm back to slap her again.

Tears welling in her eyes, she jutted her chin forward, daring him to slap her once more.

Before he unleashed his hand again, he heard a commotion of heavy footsteps on the plank walk out front. Almost instantly the door swung open. A volunteer dashed inside, out of breath.

"Fire, fire!" he shouted between gasps for breath. "Fire at the brewery, near the mines."

Fowler shoved Holly out of the way and jumped for the bell rope, catching it high and dragging it down with him. The bell tolled.

Two arriving volunteers scurried to unlatch the wagon doors. Fowler commanded one to take over on the bell. As the volunteer grabbed the rope, Fowler dashed across the room, donning his leather helmet and grabbing the silver megaphone he would use to command his charges. With his powerful arms, he pulled the hand pumper a dozen feet to the now open door. Jumping from the front of the pumper, Fowler ran to the rear of the firehouse, grabbing the handles on a hose cart and pulling it as close as possible to the pumper.

Volunteers came in bunches. Soon, enough arrived for the run. Fowler positioned men around the tongue of the pumper, saving the lead spot for himself. He designated two of the stouter men to follow with the hose cart.

Fowler shouted above the clang of the bell overhead. "Drinks on me if we get first water." With that he tugged on the pumper's tongue, and the wagon slid out of the firehouse, gathering speed and noise as it rolled down the sloping street, its small bell clanging, its men shouting and cursing. In its wake rolled the much lighter and much quieter two-wheeled hose cart.

"Faster," Fowler yelled, "faster! First water for Zephyr Engine Company Seven."

Little Joe walked out the double door of the bootmaker's shop. At a gust of wind, he tugged his flat-brim hat snug over his head, then turned up the collar of his denim jacket. On his feet he wore a new pair of boots, the leather still stiff and fragrant. A man always felt better when he had flashy footwear and a girl to think about. Holly was all he had thought about since last night at the mentalist's performance. After he had walked her to her boardinghouse, she had allowed him a kiss on the porch, much to the dismay of her landlord, a corpulent spinster with a sour look in her eyes and a policy of "no men allowed" in her boardinghouse. Holly had held out hope that they might see each other again tonight. Little Joe smiled. With new boots on his feet and a few silver dollars in his pocket, he could certainly impress her.

Rocking on the heels of his new boots, Little Joe let his hands slide to the buckle of his fancy gun belt, and his thumbs hooked over the hand-tooled leatherwork. Of course, he wished Adam good luck in finding plenty of silver, but he just hoped it took a few more days to find it, days he could use courting Holly Lucas.

As Little Joe marched around the corner from the bank, a single bell to the north began to ring. It was joined by a second, a third, and then yet another, until bells all around were ringing. Fire bells! Two dozen men ran past him, all turning into a tall building on the opposite block.

"Fire!" shouted one of the men. "Fire at the Bristlecone!"

The mention of the Bristlecone sat like a hot coal in Little Joe's gut. He raced to the corner and glanced to the north, catching his breath as he did. Just beyond the Consolidated Virginia, a cloud of dark smoke was being blown east by the wind. He could not be certain if it was the Bristlecone or not, but something was sure burning. If the Bristlecone's hoist works caught fire, it might mean the end of the Cartwright fortune and the Ponderosa. All of a sudden the new boots, the few dollars in his pocket, and even Holly Lucas, seemed insignificant.

Behind him he heard the clatter of equipment and the clang of bells as a steam pumper plowed down the street, scattering pedestrians and horses in its wake. Little Joe pulled his hat a notch tighter and raced away toward the ominous cloud of smoke.

Big Jim Fowler shouted the order to halt, and the pumper drew up near a cistern across the street from the flaming brewery. Excitement raced though his veins as fast as water would

76

soon be pumping through the hoses of Zephyr Engine Company No. 7. Fires exhilarated him, especially when his volunteers were the first on the scene. This one was serious, especially with the brisk breeze. Holding his silver megaphone to his lips, Fowler issued orders to his men as the hose cart drew up beside the pumper. The men were a flurry of activity, securing the hose to the pumper, unreeling the hose, taking positions along the brake arms, awaiting the command to begin pumping.

Fowler studied the situation. They must get water on the fire, but they must also soak the buildings downwind to keep them from taking to flame. Where were the hook and ladder companies to knock down the brewery walls and help contain the fire?

"Now," Fowler shouted, and the men began to move up and down like human pistons. "Keep it steady, boys," he yelled, moving from the pumper along the hose. As the men worked the brake arms, the pressure built up and the hose twisted and contorted like a wounded python. Spotting a novice as one of two men handling the nozzle, Fowler dashed to the end of the hose, the searing heat knocking the breath from him. He dropped his megaphone and gasped, then grabbed the hose, shouldering the novice out of the way. As his powerful arms steadied the hose, Fowler felt the gaze of a sizable crowd gathered in front of the Bristlecone. Up the street he saw several more spectators running toward the fire, and one caught his attention. It was Little Joe Cartwright.

Fowler eased up on the hose and it jerked in his hands, swinging away from the building and down the street, the pressure making it harder and harder to handle the nozzle. When Little Joe was about seventy-five feet away, Fowler opened the valve and a powerful stream of water exploded from the hose right at Little Joe. Fowler could see nothing beyond the spray of the water. Then, as he swung the hose back toward the burning building, he saw Little Joe flat on his back in the middle of the street. Fowler shouted with glee as he turned the great stream of water on the burning building. "First water for Zephyr Company!" he yelled triumphantly as other volunteer fire companies arrived.

Winded, Little Joe sprinted down F Street to the Bristlecone. For a moment he could not be sure, then he was certain that it wasn't the mine works ablaze but the brewery across the street.

Drawing within a hundred feet, he recognized Big Jim Fowler in the middle of the street trying to control the convulsing fire hose. And the next thing Little Joe knew, he was flat on his back and sopping wet in the middle of the street. When he realized that Fowler had doused him, he shoved himself up from the street, swatting at his soaked clothes and smearing mud all over his pants and denim jacket. He jerked his hat out of a puddle and brushed the mud off. He plopped the soggy hat on his head, sending water trickling down his face, then looked down at his new boots, their shine sullied with mud. Little Joe stomped across the street. His boots splattered more mud as he moved to the front of the Bristlecone office, joining the throng of spectators who had gathered to watch, a few snickering at his misfortune.

Across the street the flames crept steadily along the roof, then began to rise up the wooden walls, crackling and sizzling as they devoured the dry wood with teeth of flames. Sparks and embers flew skyward in the draft above the flames and floated on the wind eastward, endangering every structure in its path.

With a clatter of equipment, a hook and ladder company arrived, the volunteers grabbing axes and pike poles, or hooks as they were called, and rushed buildings neighboring the brewery. Little Joe watched them attack a small office and a house beside the brewery. Men without tools rushed inside and scurried out with furniture and belongings. At the end of the street a horse-drawn wagon waited, its frightened horse balking at drawing closer to the flames. Volunteers carried their loads to the wagon and hurriedly dumped them inside. A dozen men made a couple of trips apiece, stripping the office and house of belongings like a plague of locusts culls a field of green. Then the hook and ladder captain lifted his megaphone to lips and commanded his charges to tear down the two wooden buildings.

Like a squad of vandals, the volunteers advanced with axes and pike poles, slashing and ripping at the buildings, knocking out windows, prying planks free, jerking support timbers free, pushing in walls, punching holes in the roof, working as fast as they could to level the buildings before they too caught on fire and contributed to an even greater catastrophe.

Other volunteer companies arrived, all with steam pumpers. Their boilers puffed smoke as they built up steam to throw even more water on the inferno. Even after their arrival, the hand pumper of Zephyr Engine Company No. 7 continued to pour the steadiest stream of water on the fire. Like his engine company, Big Jim Fowler was the most prominent among the fire fighters. Having turned over the hose nozzle to other volunteers, he scurried among the firemen, giving orders to his men and others, directing the fire-fighting effort with great daring, advancing upon the blaze and waving for the men on the hose to follow.

Still soaking and cold from the dousing, Little Joe watched Fowler and despised him both for the accident and for his high visibility in fighting the blaze. The anger blazed in Little Joe as hot as the fire across the street. He watched and waited for an hour while the flames gradually diminished, then disappeared behind charred walls and debris. But the fire within him only grew, particularly as volunteers and citizens approached Fowler to offer their congratulations on containing the fire.

Little Joe strode across the street, anger in his step, and pushed his way through the men around Fowler. The fire captain shook a circle of hands and acknowledged several slaps on the back, as contented as a politician at a rigged election.

When Little Joe stepped in front of him, the smile widened on Fowler's fire-reddened face. "Came to congratulate me, did you, Joe? Or do you need another shower?"

Little Joe drew back his left fist, which exploded toward Fowler's nose. On instinct, Fowler lifted his arm, blocking the blow, and Little Joe's fist slid by Fowler's powerful shoulder.

"You turned the water on me, didn't you?" Little Joe screamed, lifting his fists and squaring off against Fowler.

Fowler feigned ignorance. "You little runt, I didn't see you out here helping us fight this fire. You don't know what it's like to control a hose under pressure."

Little Joe attacked Fowler, but his flailing fists were ineffective. Though a bigger man than Little Joe, Fowler was agile on his feet, dodging Little Joe's wild punches, countering with fewer swings but more hits. When Little Joe advanced, Fowler retreated, encouraging his adversary. Then Fowler stopped and loosed a powerful punch, striking Little Joe on the cheekbone. Little Joe staggered backward, shaking his head to rid his eyes of the sudden blurriness. He studied Fowler a moment, then charged the bigger man.

Surprised, Fowler stumbled under Little Joe's

full force. Both men collapsed on the ground in a flailing heap, rolling around in a street splotched with puddles. Before either could harm the other more, a third man plowed into the fray.

"Break it up, you two," yelled Sheriff Roy Coffee. "Can't you firemen ever put out a fire without fighting among yourselves?" he said as he pulled Little Joe off Fowler.

Little Joe struggled momentarily as Fowler tried to trip him, but was pushed by Coffee out of Fowler's way. Coffee stood between the two men, then realized this was not a fight among volunteers. He looked at Little Joe, shaking his head, then at Fowler. Both men knocked the patches of mud off their clothes.

"I told you boys at the dance not to be fighting," Coffee said. "Who started this?"

Little Joe pointed at Fowler. "He did."

Fowler shrugged. "I was standing here when Joe came up and slugged me."

"That's right," called volunteers and spectators in the encircling throng.

"I was just doing my job to protect the citizens of Virginia City," Fowler said, "when Joe attacked me for no reason."

"He's lying," Little Joe challenged, gingerly rubbing the cheek that Fowler had bruised. "He turned a water hose on me and muddied me up."

Coffee looked at the crowd again.

"Big Jim Fowler ain't at fault," said the captain of a rival volunteer fire company. "He was just accepting the well-deserved thanks of several of us when this other one attacked him." The rival captain pointed his finger at Little Joe.

Coffee nodded. "Come on, Little Joe, we're going to jail."

CHAPTER 6

The county clerk's office had cleared out with the report of a fire, giving Lucia Sinclair her first break since the Storey County Courthouse had opened that morning. She finished filing a few deeds, then worked her way to the record room in the back of the clerk's office. Tomes of records were shelved one after another in the room, testament to the volume of paperwork a mining town created and to the legacy those records would leave future generations, not to mention future lawyers. The law was the thread that wove the fabric of society, she had always held. In fact, she believed it so much that she had read law, though as a woman she was not permitted to practice. It galled her like wet hemp on a sore, especially when she saw inferior or crooked men practicing law. They mocked society's noblest profession, lining their pockets with ill-gotten gains, bullying their enemies in court and ignoring their debt to the truth.

At least as assistant county clerk she could be near the law and borrow from the county's law library. Though some men resented Lucia holding a man's job, County Clerk Wendell Benton had recognized an efficient manner, a precise legal mind, and a superior intellect. Benton was as honest as the day was long, but was methodical in thought and action, his biggest asset beyond his honesty being his ability to recognize talent in other people. In his forties, Benton was a family man with three sons, three daughters, a receding hairline, a quiet disposition, and an acceptance of his station in life. He would never be rich, but with a good wife and family, neither would he ever be poor.

As she entered the records room, Lucia glanced nonchalantly over her shoulder to make sure no one was following her, then quickly checked for others among the shelves of Storey County's official documents. Certain that no one could possibly see her, she slipped to the back corner of the room and dropped to her hands and knees, pulling from among old criminal records the deed book she had hidden when Thurston Smalley had come calling. It bothered her sense of legal propriety to have removed the book, but she knew Smalley was out to take over the Bristlecone and ruin the Cartwrights. When she stood up, she noticed splotches of dust trailing down her long skirt from her knees. Quickly she moved to the shelf where the deed book belonged and shoved it back in place. As she stepped to the door, she bent to dust her skirt, but stopped when she saw Benton.

"There you are, Lucia," Benton said. "I'd begun to wonder if you had gone to the fire. It's the brewery across from the Bristlecone."

"Trying to catch up on a few things," she answered.

Wendell Benton nodded. "Efficient as ever, but would you mind joining me in my office?"

"Certainly not," she said, stooping to brush off her skirt.

"I don't recall any active records on the bottom shelves," Benton said, thus alerting Lucia that he knew what she had been doing.

Having brushed away the dust as best she could, Lucia Sinclair followed her boss into his office. She caught her breath.

Seated opposite Benton's desk, wearing his unstylish beaver hat and his frayed coat, was Thurston Smalley himself. His beady eyes followed Lucia as she seated herself at the end of Benton's desk, but he neither greeted nor acknowledged her.

Benton plopped into his chair, leaned back, propped his feet upon the desk and clasped his hands behind his neck. Lucia was surprised at Benton's informality; the county clerk always expected his staff to treat the public with proper manners, no matter how rude or difficult they might be. For a moment Lucia was shocked to think that perhaps Benton's familiarity with Thurston Smalley indicated they were allies in Storey County. Then she realized this was Benton's way of showing Smalley the same disrespect he had shown her. Lucia smiled at Benton.

"Lucia," Benton said in a serious tone, "Mr. Smalley here seems to think you've been violating the public trust placed in this office."

Sitting straight without her back touching the chair, Lucia answered Benton while staring at Smalley. "I do not recall waiting . . ." She paused for a moment. ". . . on Mr. Smalley."

"It seems Mr. Smalley was in here earlier in the week, asking to see the deedbook with records on the Bristlecone property." Benton nodded. "He thinks you overheard his request to another clerk and rushed into the records room to hide the volume."

"Sir," she said looking back at her boss, "of the many things I may indeed be blamed for in the performance of my job, I hope that I shall not be blamed every time a deedbook is misplaced."

Smalley's lips quivered with anger.

"Deedbooks are from time to time being used by others, and to insinuate I am responsible is insulting," Lucia concluded.

Smalley waved away her comments. "I know you're seeing Adam Cartwright, and I know you'll protect him every chance you get."

Benton pulled his feet from his desk and they hit the floor loudly. "I will not have you impugn the motives of a valued member of my staff," he said, standing up.

Smalley sat nonplussed. Lucia felt relieved that she had just replaced the deedbook.

Walking to his office door, Benton called for another clerk and instructed him to search for the appropriate deedbook. Shortly, the clerk reappeared at the door, deedbook in hand.

"Where was it?" Benton asked.

"On the shelf where it should be," the clerk responded, handing the book to Benton.

"Thank you." Benton took the large leather-bound volume and dismissed the clerk. He turned to Thurston Smalley. "I believe you owe Miss Sinclair an apology."

Smalley sneered. "Thurston Smalley apologizes to nobody."

"Very fine, Mr. Smalley," Benton said, "you are welcome to look at the deedbook here in my office, but both Miss Sinclair and myself intend to watch and see that you do nothing amiss."

"Are you accusing me of an impropriety?" Smalley shot back.

Benton smiled. "I'm accusing you of nothing more than you accused Miss Sinclair." Benton dropped the book on the desk before him.

As Smalley opened the book to the index, Benton winked at Lucia.

God bless him, thought Lucia, he knew all along that she had hidden the book from Smalley. Her respect for Wendell Benton grew.

Ben Cartwright strode into the jail, anger in his eyes.

"Howdy, Ben," said Roy Coffee, looking up from a stack of papers. "I was going to come for you in a bit, let you know about Little Joe."

"I got word, Roy, I got word." Ben's voice brimmed with anger.

Little Joe arose sheepishly from the cot in the cell, but his eyes avoided his father's. He slapped at his mud-caked clothes.

The sheriff stood up and shook his head. "It wasn't much of a fight, Ben, neither of them hurt. Problem is, it's just the type of pettiness that can lead to worse things."

Little Joe shook the cold iron bars of his cell door against the lock. "Fowler started it," he called defiantly.

Coughing into his balled fist, Coffee shook his head at Little Joe. "Witnesses say Little Joe attacked him, plain and simple."

Ben marched around Coffee's desk to face the cell door, his feet wide apart, his fists planted on his hips. "Joseph, I don't know what's gotten into you."

"Dammit, Pa," Little Joe said defiantly, "it wasn't —"

Ben's right hand shot up from his waist, his finger pointing at Little Joe's nose. "Don't you use another profane word, Joseph, or you'll be saddling a horse you can't ride."

The anger didn't drain from Little Joe's face, but the defiance did. When he spoke again, his words and tempo were controlled. "It wasn't me, Pa. He soaked me with the fire hose, knocked me down."

Ben crossed his arms over his chest, his dark eyes skeptical.

Nodding, Sheriff Coffee marched to Ben's side. "A couple fellows mentioned seeing that happen, but you know a fire, Ben. There's a lot of excitement, a lot of things going on. Things happen that don't make sense. Fowler could've intended to knock Little Joe down or he could've just lost control of the hose when he opened the nozzle. Either way, it can't be proved."

Little Joe rattled the cell door in frustration. "It was no accident," he said. "I saw him take the hose and turn it on me."

Coffee shrugged. "You may be right, Joe, but no witness saw what went on in his head. They saw a hero fighting a dangerous fire. And they saw you attack him when it was over."

Ben lifted his hat and ran his fingers through his silver hair, shaking his head all the while. "Joseph, the truth doesn't matter in this instance because —"

Little Joe flung his hands down from the iron bars and let his mouth fall open. "What are you saying, Pa? You've always told me to tell the truth."

"I don't doubt that you are, Joseph, but the truth of this incident is less important than how the truth appears to others."

"Huh?" Little Joe frowned.

"The truth, as most folks saw it, was you attacking Fowler." Ben pulled his hat back in place.

Little Joe backed to the cot and sat on it. "A fellow's got a right to protect himself," he said.

Ben answered sternly. "You're fighting angers me not nearly as much as you failing to protect our property, Joseph. You did nothing to help."

Little Joe jumped up. "What are you talking about?"

"You know the situation in the mine. Had the Bristlecone caught on fire, it could've spelled the end for the Ponderosa, for the easy life you've got."

Little Joe cocked his head at his father, accentuating his dimpled chin. "I didn't see Adam fighting the fire."

"He was sealing the mine, Joseph, to keep the fire from going down the hole. All you did was attack a man who was risking his life to save our property."

His shoulders slumping and his head sagging, Little Joe lowered himself to the cot. "Just get me out, Pa, and I'll do better next time." His voice was tainted with defeat.

Coffee eased between father and son. "I hate to have to do this, Ben, but I've got to treat him like everyone else, take him before the judge and have bond set. I expect it'll be about twenty-five dollars."

"Roy, you just do your job."

"It'll be an hour before all the paperwork's done," the sheriff explained. "I know I could trust you and Little Joe, but I've got to be neutral in these matters."

Ben slapped Roy on the back. A smile appeared on his face for the first time since he entered the jail. "You just take your time, Roy. I'll be back in the morning to bail him out."

Little Joe shot up from the bunk again. "What?" he yelped.

"It'll give you time to think about all this, Joseph," Ben said with a wave of his hand.

Little Joe turned to the sheriff. "Roy, would you check my belongings in your desk, see if I had enough money on me to make bail?"

Coffee shook his head. "I don't have to check, Joe. You only had about half what you'll need."

Little Joe groaned and collapsed on the bunk, stretching out and pulling his hat over his eyes. Groaning again, he rolled over on the bunk and faced the stone wall.

"We were lucky," Hoss said, leaning out Adam's office window and staring at the charred remains of the brewery. "Wind out of the east could've ruined us."

Adam grunted. The fire had been contained. The offices and hoist works of the Bristlecone had escaped unscathed, except for Adam's decision to seal the mine shaft. Now his precautions had backfired. The Bristlecone would loose twelve or more hours, time the Cartwrights no longer had, before resuming operations. At least no one had died from the wrong decision.

The door swung open and Ben Cartwright walked in, nodding to Adam, then Hoss.

"Where's Little Joe?" Hoss asked.

Ben closed the door, took off his hat and hung it on a hook by the entrance. "Jail," he said.

"Dad-blame-it, Pa, I didn't know he was in that bad of trouble," Hoss offered.

"He is with me, Hoss," Ben answered. "With

as much as we've got to worry about, this may be the only way I can get his attention."

Hoss shook his head. "Only way you'll get his full attention, Pa, is to put on a skirt and perfume."

Even Adam laughed.

Ben nodded, then seated himself at the worktable littered with paper and reports. Hoss took a seat opposite his father and both stared at Adam, seated uncomfortably at his desk. "How'd the fire set us back?" Ben asked.

Adam cleared his throat. "Twelve hours, minimum, maybe more. I hired extra men to unseal the mine and I may want to keep them on so we can move faster."

"That'll cost us more, Adam," Ben replied.

"May cost us more not to move fast. And now with Thurston Smalley threatening to ruin us, I don't see any other option, unless we admit defeat." Adam offered a limp shrug.

Stroking his chin, Ben stared hard at his oldest son. "Smalley will stop at nothing. Have you been thinking what I've been thinking, Adam, about the fire?"

"Yes, sir, I sure have."

Hoss grunted. "You two don't mind me knowing what you're talking about, do you?"

"The fire," Ben said. "It could be Smalley's way of threatening us."

Hoss jerked his head back and squinted, his ice-blue eyes moving from his father to Adam and back to Ben. "Someone would do that?" he asked in disbelief.

Adam nodded. "Thurston Smalley would. Things aren't as simple here as they are on the Ponderosa."

Ben stood up from the table and walked to the window, studying the street. "We should post guards around the mine."

"I was thinking that," Adam said. "And I was also figuring on buying a water wagon we could keep around here to fight any arson."

Hoss asked incredulously, "This is that serious?"

Without looking away from the window, Ben answered. "Yes, sir. Thurston Smalley is a man with no scruples."

Hoss stared at his father. "Wish I was back on the Ponderosa."

"Wish I could let you go, Hoss," Ben said, glancing at his middle son a moment, "but we need you here awhile. Tomorrow, after I bail Joseph out of jail, the four of us need to meet with Monville Pyburn and Clarence Eppler, discuss our options and vote our shares on what we want to do with the Bristlecone."

Adam pushed himself up from his chair. "We got a few samples out before we sealed the mine. I'll have a report on them tomorrow. We should be closing in on the vein soon." His words conveyed more hope than conviction as he walked to the door. "I'm stepping to the hoist works to see how long before we can reopen the mine."

"I'll join you and then maybe we can go to

the Washoe Club for a little supper. You care to join us, Hoss?"

"Nah," Hoss replied, shrugging. "Food's just as good at the saloon and it's all you can eat for the price of a beer. People there are more my type than the stuffed shirts at the Washoe Club."

"Suit yourself," Ben said as he and Adam grabbed their hats. They walked downstairs silently, each understanding their time and money was running out, each knowing they now had a serious threat in Thurston Smalley.

The stamp mill was silent, the hoist works still. As they neared the mine shaft, they could hear the curses of the foreman imploring his men with his strong lungs. The clatter of ore being dumped into an ore cart, the screech of carts being moved from the shaft opening, and the sound of a dozen shovels striking rock and dirt occasionally drowned out the foreman, who cleaned up his language when Ben and Adam Cartwright came into view.

A burly man with an intimidating physical presence, the foreman moved away from the mine opening and greeted the Cartwrights. "We've made about two feet, so we've eight or so to go."

Adam approached the covered shaft and stood with his arms crossed, watching two dozen men attack the dirt and rock fill with their shovels, then toss it into the ore wagons which were shoved before them. They were a hardworking group, a half dozen or so not even noticing Ben's and Adam's presence.

Adam, though, noticed one man in particular. He had the look of a miner about him, pale and well-muscled, but he moved at his job faster than any of the others, dumping about two shovels of debris in the ore cart for every shovelful any other man loaded. Adam studied the man, but didn't recognize him.

He asked the foreman, "Is this a new crew?"

"Fresh crew I hired today," the foreman answered. "So many of our afternoon shift fought the fire today, they'd been worthless anyway."

"We'll be taking on two new crews when we get operational again," Adam said, pointing to the miner who had caught his eye. "I want him to head one of those crews. What's his name?"

"I don't know," the foreman said, then hollered at the man shoveling dirt faster than the others. "What's your name?"

The miner stopped, pointed to himself with his index finger, and at the foreman's nod, said, "Vorley Deaton."

Thurston Smalley sat in a back corner of the saloon, sipping leisurely at a beer and toying with the plate of free food that went with it. He could usually pick up accurate information listening to the miners when their tongues had been loosed by a few mugs of beer. The saloon was dim in the afternoon shadow of Mount Davidson to the west, but the saloon owner never lit a kerosene lamp while there was still a drop of light to be wrung from the day's allotment. The crowd was quiet today, what little talk there was being about the brewery fire and Little Joe's fight with Fowler. There were rumors of Adam Cartwright sealing up the Bristlecone, and Smalley took them for the truth, since the Cartwrights were a cautious breed. Smalley had figured Adam would react cautiously, and that's why he had paid to have the fire set.

Smalley was prepared to call it a day when Hoss Cartwright walked in, heading immediately for the food table and heaping a load of victuals on a plate. Smalley sank back into his chair and pulled his hat down over his eyes as Hoss ordered a beer from the bartender.

A couple of men at a far table waved at him, and he moved to join them. "Where's Little Joe?" one hollered.

Hoss grinned widely. "In jail!"

The two men laughed.

"And he's gonna be there awhile longer," Hoss added.

"The Bristlecone draining you Cartwrights so that you can't pay bond for your own kind?" joked the other.

"Nope," Hoss answered. "Pa just figured not to pay his bail until tomorrow. Give him a chance to think things over."

Smalley nodded to himself. That was good information, the type of information that made regular forays into these plebeian dens worthwhile, the type of information that he had used over the years to enhance his reputation as the "Vulture of Virginia City." Speculators thrived on rumors, and Smalley was not above spreading rumors like a sodbuster scatters manure. Both were good fertilizers for their respective harvests.

But what over the years had separated Smalley from the common speculators, what had made him the most feared manipulator on the Comstock Lode, was grounding his rumors in truth. He had used spies, had bribed clerks, had eavesdropped on miners, had compromised husbands, all to get information. Rumors truthlessly fathered could damage a mine, certainly, but could not alone destroy an owner emotionally. Smalley never went after a mine without wanting to break the owner, and he never wanted to destroy an owner more than Ben Cartwright. The demise of Ben Cartwright, as respected on the Comstock as Smalley himself knew he was despised, would be the fitting end to his dark career. Smalley indeed wanted to take over the Bristlecone, but he had the scent of Ben Cartwright's blood like a wolf stalking wounded prey. Smalley could take the Bristlecone, but it would be a useless trophy without Ben Cartwright. And if he couldn't get Ben Cartwright, he could get Adam Cartwright, for to destroy the son was to destroy the father as well.

Smalley listened to Hoss Cartwright and smiled. Perhaps he could worm his way into the minds of the Cartwrights through Little Joe's lady friend. Holly Lucas was her name. Then he might not have to depend so heavily on Vorley Deaton, who seemed to be losing his stomach for handling these matters.

It was odd, Smalley thought, to have such a hatred for a man or for a family that had never harmed him. Most likely it was the conflict of philosophies. Some men, like Ben Cartwright, measured success by what they had built. Others, like himself, gauged it by what they had destroyed. He could ruin the Bristlecone, but he wanted more. He wanted Ben Cartwright. He could take Ben Cartwright without the Ponderosa patriarch ever knowing his foe, just like the man who bushwhacks an enemy from behind; but Smalley was a more sinister cut of man, the type who first tortures his victims before killing them. He wanted Ben Cartwright to know his assailant was not a common speculator, but Thurston Smalley, the Vulture of Virginia City. He wanted to torture the Cartwrights by ferreting out information that should be known to no one but them. He wanted to create so many doubts among them that they turned on one another or made poor decisions. He wanted to outwit them with his speculator's instinct, and then brush them aside like so many crumbs after a cheap meal.

And Holly Lucas would help him. Whether she liked it or not!

CHAPTER 7

The boardinghouse was weathered and unpainted, but the front parlor seemed well-kept and clean, at least that portion of it Thurston Smalley could see around the barrel-shaped owner who stood in the doorway, her dishwater hair tied in a knot, arms crossed, suspicious eyes studying him intently. The woman shook her head. "No men allowed in here, even scrawny ones like you. Once you let men in your place, folks get the wrong idea when you're boarding girls," she scowled matter-of-factly. "Now who was it you wanted to see?"

"Holly Lucas," Smalley responded.

"You don't seem her type. What's your name?"

"I prefer to tell her myself."

The landlady rubbed her pudgy chin and turned from the door. "Holly Lucas," she called, "a gentleman here to see you." She waddled to a rocking chair and squeezed into it, picking up a clump of hand sewing from the table at her side and resuming her mending under the glow of the yellow lamplight.

In a moment Smalley saw Holly Lucas amble down the hall, her pleasant smile fading as she saw Smalley. Holly looked at her landlady, then at Smalley.

"That's the one," the woman said. "You stay out on the porch, and if he bothers you, just holler."

Holly's face took on a pleasant glow again as she stepped to the door. "I'm Holly Lucas."

"Might I have a word with you, Miss Lucas? Outside?" He looked beyond Holly at the landlady.

"I guess it's okay," Holly answered, moving toward the porch.

The landlady cleared her throat. "Holler if you need help."

"Yes, ma'am," Holly said as she walked out to the porch.

"Miss Lucas, my name is Thurston Smalley," he said when they were alone. Smalley studied her face in the shaft of yellow lamplight that seeped from the window. Even in the weak light he could make out a bruise along her cheek. "I came to let you know your friend Little Joe Cartwright is in jail."

Holly's hand flew to her mouth. "What for?"

Smalley reached for Holly's chin, and she stiffened with surprise at his touch. Gently he turned her cheek into the light, nodding sympathetically as he examined the bruise. Holly looked toward the plank porch, avoiding Smalley's gaze. "Fowler do this?"

Embarrassed, Holly merely nodded. "But Little Joe?"

Smalley lied, "Little Joe heard that Fowler had

hit you, so he whipped him after the brewery fire this afternoon."

"He did?"

"Little Joe Cartwright was protecting your honor. It's just like him to do that sort of thing." He released her chin.

Clasping her hands together, she smiled. "He did that? And that's why he's in jail?"

Smalley nodded. "Bond's twenty-five dollars."

"The Cartwrights can afford that, easy," Holly answered.

"Except that old man Cartwright is a hard case and figured to leave his son in jail awhile."

"That's mean," Holly said, her voice wrought with concern. "I wish I could help."

"Maybe you can, Miss Lucas."

"I don't have that kind of money."

"Perhaps I can assist, provided you will allow me, and provided my name doesn't come up, if anyone asks."

"What do you mean, Mr. Smalley?"

Smalley motioned for Holly to step farther away from the building and toward the street, where the noise of passing wagons and horses would screen their conversation. She moved with him out of the wedge of porch light and into the darkness.

"I've long admired Little Joe Cartwright, and I hate to see him hurt by a mean father. I must admit his father and I are investment rivals and I don't like him. Even so, I hate to see the boy mistreated."

Holly rubbed her cheek.

"I'd be glad to put up the money for you to pay his bond, but I can't let anyone know I'm behind it. That's why I need someone like you to do it, someone who wouldn't raise any suspicions by posting bond. Knowing him like you do, you would be perfect."

Holly lifted her face. "I'll do it, gladly."

"And I'll give you an extra twenty-five dollars, money for you to buy yourself a new dress and make yourself pretty for him."

Instantly, Holly thrust her chin forward and planted her hands on her hips. "What are you really up to, Mr. Smalley? You're not doing this out of the goodness of your heart."

"I like a perceptive woman, Miss Lucas, and you're right. Truth is, I'm looking at investing in a mine the Cartwrights are running, the Bristlecone. Little Joe and his brothers want to sell, but the old man'll have none of it. I want to help Little Joe on this, but Little Joe's scared to cross his father, and I don't blame him, mean as the old man is. If you were to find out anything from Little Joe about the situation with the mine, it would help me fight the old man and help Little Joe get his way about selling the mine. As a favor from me, there'd be more money in it for you, money to buy new clothes for yourself."

Holly bit her lip and cocked her head. "Why can't you just work this out with Little Joe?"

"Despite how badly his father mistreats him, Little Joe is too loyal to his family to stand up to him. Little Joe's a good man, the honorable son of a mean patriarch. And if you were Little Joe, would you want to risk your father finding out you were giving information to one of the old man's business rivals? Remember, the old man wouldn't even bail him out of jail tonight. If you don't believe me, ask Little Joe when you see him next. Then you can decide if I'm telling the truth or not."

Holly pondered a moment. "You sure this won't hurt Little Joe, will it?"

Smalley smiled. "No, ma'am, not in the least. May even do him some good, helping him get out from under his father's thumb, give him his share of the Cartwright fortune so he could start out on his own, maybe take on a wife. His old man's against his sons marrying, I'm told. Fact is, Ben Cartwright had three wives, each dying mysteriously, it seems. I'd be worried for any young lady that married one of the sons while the old man still ran the family and the family fortune. No telling what might happen to her."

"Maybe I could help a little," Holly said softly, "as long as you promise it won't hurt Little Joe."

"Little Joe won't be hurt as long as he doesn't know he's got secret allies against his father. I'll not tell a soul you're helping me," Smalley said, "and you can't tell anyone either, not even Little Joe."

"Little Joe did fight Big Jim Fowler over me?" Holly asked, rubbing her cheek wistfully.

Smalley nodded. "He's that type of man. He'll

look out for others before he takes care of himself. That's why you and I have got to help him sell the mine and get out from under his father's iron hand."

"I'll look out for Little Joe, like he's done for me," Holly said emphatically.

"Good," said Smalley, reaching into his pocket and pulling out several gold coins. He dropped them in her hand. "I'll check with you periodically, see if you have any information on how things are going at the mine, assay reports, things like that."

"Thank you, Mr. Smalley," she said as her fingers closed around the money.

Smalley departed without another word.

"It's the mine, isn't it?" Lucia Sinclair gently shut the slender volume of Byron's poetry and replaced it on the abundant bookshelf in Adam's suite at the International Hotel. She crossed her arms over her full bosom. "I'd never have told you about Smalley inspecting the Bristlecone records this afternoon had I known you'd become so despondent, Adam Cartwright."

Adam, reclining on the sofa, stared silently beyond her. He felt closer to defeat than ever in his life. While he'd been giving the order to seal the mine, Smalley was sitting in the county clerk's office, meticulously inspecting the Bristlecone claim for some flaw that he could exploit.

Lucia strolled toward the window and lifted the shade, staring quietly outside. "The moon's pretty," she said. She lifted her hands to her head and pulled the pins and ribbon from the bun primly crowning her black hair. As her hands slid away, she shook her head and her hair fell gently down upon her shoulders and beyond. Attractive in a proper way with her bun, she took on a mischievous look when her hair was loosed and her full lips turned to a smile.

Never had Adam seen her prettier or more inviting, but the mine problems weighted his ardor until it sank deep in a pool of worry. "Perhaps you should read some more poetry, Lucia."

Holding her hand out for him, she shook her head. "Adam Cartwright, I'll not let you dampen the evening for both of us. You get on your feet right now. We'll either go to the opera house or walk in the moonlight, just the two of us."

"Us and everybody else'll be out this time of night."

Lucia tapped her foot. "No, sir, Adam Cartwright, I'll not spend another minute in here with your tail between your legs like a whipped dog. We'll go for a stroll."

Adam held up his hand to argue, but Lucia silenced him with the stony gaze of her defiant gray eyes. He said only, "I don't want to go to the opera house or anyplace where there's many people."

"Then we'll stroll under the moon and stars."

Slowly, Adam eased himself up from the sofa and stood, brushing away the wrinkles from his clothes. "We can check the mine, see how the work is coming."

"No, sir," Lucia said, crossing her arms. "You've paid too much attention to that mine tonight and not enough to me." Lucia stepped away from the window and marched to the hat rack by the door. She held his hat out for him.

Adam moved gingerly around the sofa, his enthusiasm dragging like his feet. He killed the light, and the furnishings disappeared in the darkness, save those by the window covered with a dainty lace of moonlight. In the darkness, Adam found Lucia, took his hat from her hand, then swept her into his arms and kissed her full on her lips. "Is that any better, Lucia?"

"It'll do for starters," she answered. "That and a walk."

They emerged into the carpeted hallway of the International Hotel and walked to the hydraulic elevator. The call button buzzed at Adam's touch and the elevator appeared in a moment, the uniformed operator greeting the pair as they stepped inside. The cage eased down, then deposited them in the lobby. The International's lobby was full of the monied, the near-monied, and the clingers-on who sought handouts or vied for the inside information that might make them fortunes of their own.

As Adam steered Lucia through the crowd, he knew that the tongues of several would be wagging about the impropriety of his seeing Miss Sinclair in his room, but for once he preferred that gossip to the speculation about the Bristlecone and the state of the Cartwright fortune.

Adam had almost reached the International's impressive front door when a spindly speculator with a wad of tobacco bulging in his cheek grabbed his arm. Adam jerked free and the speculator stepped back, shifting the tobacco from one cheek to the other.

"Mr. Cartwright," the man challenged, "any truth to the rumor you don't have clear title to the Bristlecone? That why you've put armed guards around the Bristlecone? Are you hiding something?"

Pausing a moment as another couple entered the hotel, Adam studied the speculator. The man's eyes were bloodshot and turbid, as if the tobacco in his mouth had risen to his eyes like murky water in an unpumped mine. Speculators, Adam thought, were the vandals of the mining industry.

"Is it just rumor about you sealing the mine?" the speculator asked.

Adam stepped wordlessly through the door, pulling Lucia along.

"Care to sell an interest in the Bristlecone?" the speculator shouted. "You'll never get a better price than now. These rumors floating around will hurt the mine's value. You better sell now. The price is only gonna go down over the next month!"

Adam shut the hotel door with authority, leaving the glass rattling in his wake. He shrugged, then sighed. "If the rumors are so bad, why do so many still want to buy into the Bristlecone, Lucia? Can you figure it?"

"Like it or not, it's the Cartwright reputation for square dealing, Adam. Some want in because they know you're honest."

"Not all of them are trustworthy."

"But if they get in with you, it'll give a platform for conducting their mischief behind the good Cartwright name. If the Cartwrights get out of the Bristlecone, it's guaranteed to cost more fortunes than it will ever make."

Adam nodded. "You're right."

Lucia twisted her head in surprise and studied his face with pleasure. "Right about mining?"

"No," Adam replied, "right that I should forget about mining for a bit."

Both laughed as they crossed the street. Lucia slid one way, but Adam steered her another. "Where are you taking me, Adam Cartwright?"

"To jail."

"What? Oh, Little Joe, I almost forgot. Think he's learned his lesson yet?"

"Not Little Joe. Pa's been trying for nineteen years, and it seems like Little Joe gets into more mischief all the time. Maybe if we go in and laugh at him, it'll embarrass him enough to think next time before he does something stupid."

The aroma of fresh-baked bread struck the couple as they passed a bakery. "Maybe we should take him a loaf of bread, make him feel a little better, rather than laugh at him," Lucia suggested.

Adam hesitated, but Lucia tugged him toward the bakery, open well into the night to accommodate the late shift of miners getting off work. They stepped inside, the warmth of the small shop enveloping them with the fine aroma of fresh bread. A baker with dough on his apron stepped to the counter and offered his assistance.

Lucia pointed out a loaf of white bread behind the glass counter. "Fresh?"

"Out of the oven five minutes, no more," the baker said, sliding the glass door open and grabbing the fresh loaf. He wrapped it in brown paper and tied a string around it. "Two bits," the baker said, as he plopped the bread on the wooden counter.

Adam dug into his pocket and flipped the baker his payment, then grabbed the wrapped loaf of bread. The wrapper was warm to his touch. He escorted Lucia back out onto the walk and they proceeded to the jail, the evening air brisker now.

At the corner, Adam steered Lucia down the street crowded with miners from the shift change. The brisk air carried the excitement the miners brought up from the bowels of the earth, tales of good-looking ore, anticipation of that next big bonanza just a few feet deeper in the hard rock, dreams of fortunes for all. The excitement bred wild speculation, for there had never been a better year in all of Comstock history. The lies and truths these miners revealed to their friends, to eavesdroppers, and to each other would fuel wild speculation tomorrow on the San Francisco stock market. Some men were carried away by the speculation bug, spending their hard-earned money on exorbitant stocks as thoughtlessly as a drunk buys bottles of whiskey. Others, like Thurston Smalley, rode the speculative wave, spreading rumors and innuendo that helped them line their own pockets at the expense of honest and less sophisticated men, many of them the four-dollar-a-day miners naive at finance.

A few on the street recognized Adam, greeted him and tipped their hats to Lucia. Some of the men Adam knew were miners from the Bristlecone, but he could not remember their names, if he had ever known them to begin with. Adam could remember facts and figures with ease, but to his embarrassment, names often escaped him. Little Joe, though, was one who never forgot a name, especially a young woman's name. He was also more gregarious than Adam. If only Little Joe had more maturity, Adam thought, and better judgment.

As they neared the jail, Lucia leaned closer. "I should have worn a shawl."

"We won't be long at the jail. Little Joe will think I've come to gloat."

"You have, Adam, admit it."

Adam nodded imperceptibly in the darkness. "He needs to be brought down a notch or two."

"Granted," Lucia replied, "but you need to quit brooding about the Bristlecone. There's only so much one man can do, even you."

They approached the jail door, Adam pausing a moment to take a deep breath. As he reached for the doorknob, Lucia tightened her grip on his arm. "Don't aggravate him."

"I'll be on my best behavior, Mama," Adam teased.

"I'm not that old!" She laughed and pinched his arm.

Adam opened the door and followed Lucia inside.

Roy Coffee looked up from his desk and a plate of beans and fried steak. He wiped his mouth with the sleeve of his shirt and smiled beneath his salt-and-pepper mustache. "Evening, Adam, ma'am," he said, moving his chair to get up.

"Keep your seat, Roy. We just came to visit Little Joe," Adam said, looking from the sheriff to the three cells in the back of the office. Two men stood at the bars, a couple were passed out on the bunks, and one squatted in the corner, like a roach hiding from the light. "We brought Little Joe a loaf of bread."

Coffee shrugged. "I can't let you give it to him."

Adam jerked his head toward Coffee. "Roy, what do you mean? It's nothing but a loaf of bread."

The sheriff held up his arm. "Now hold on, Adam, I believe every word you say, but the fact of the matter is Little Joe is gone, bailed out an hour and a half ago."

Adam's head dropped. "I knew Pa would back down."

"Nope, not your Pa. It was Holly Lucas, the one he danced with at the fireman's ball. She came in, paid his bond, and they left together."

"But Pa said for him to stay the night." Adam deposited the loaf of bread on the corner of Coffee's desk. "He should've stayed."

Coffee stood up and walked around the desk until he stood in front of Adam. "Would you've stayed if a pretty little lady was willing to pay your bond?"

Adam hesitated.

Coffee laughed. "Maybe you might have, but not Little Joe."

"You should've kept him like Pa said," Adam countered.

Coffee laughed again. "Someone comes in here to pay bail, it's not my job to say no just because some relative says not to, even when it's someone I respect as much as Ben Cartwright."

Adam scratched his head. "Roy, this is mighty peculiar."

Coffee folded his arms across his chest. "Adam, you run into a lot of peculiar things in my line of business. Guess that's why I stay at it, to keep from getting bored."

"Then, Sheriff," Lucia interrupted, "we'll leave you this loaf of bread." She picked it up from the desk and handed it to Roy. "We've got business to attend."

"Thank you, ma'am." Coffee said, taking the

bread from her. "Why, it's still warm." He turned to face Adam.

"Now what's this I hear about title problems at the Bristlecone and you putting guards on patrol around the clock? Some are saying you're about to sell out, now that the title's unclear. And to keep prices up, you've put guards on duty to make it appear you're trying to keep a major find a secret. Any truth to that?"

Adam shook his head. "Thurston Smalley's behind it all."

Coffee whistled. "Then you do have problems."

CHAPTER 8

Ben Cartwright took in the somber faces. Adam, Hoss, lawyer Clarence Eppler, and stockbroker Monville Pyburn realized the seriousness of the situation. Little Joe sat with a smirk on his face, proud he had gotten out of jail without his father's money. Ben had said nothing about Little Joe's release, but it rankled him like saddle sores sour a horse. Little Joe spent too little time considering wealth's responsibilities and too much time enjoying its privileges. A night in jail might have given him pause for reflection, but Holly Lucas had spoiled that. He stared at Little Joe until the trace of a smile evaporated from his son's lips.

Adam passed the assay reports around the table. Eppler and Pyburn studied them closely, nodding and making notes. Hoss, his brow furrowed, examined them quickly, then offered them to Little Joe. Hoss thought he understood the report, but not necessarily its implications. Little Joe barely glanced at it before sliding the report to Ben. As a second report made it around the table, Ben stood up, his hands knotted into fists. He leaned over the table, anchoring his fists on its polished surface, and stared intently at Little Joe as he took the stack of papers. This time Little Joe gave appearances of reading it before passing it to his father.

Clarence Eppler straightened his stooped shoulders and looked at the ceiling. "Not good, not good," he said, "especially when rumors are questioning your title to the Bristlecone."

Adam slapped the table. "Thurston Smalley started that rumor, we all know that!"

Monville Pyburn stroked his gray muttonchop whiskers, then toyed with one of the sleeve garters he always wore. Behind the thick lenses of his wire-rimmed glasses, his eyes blinked owlishly. "No argument there, Adam," he said. "Smalley's a snake, but whether his rumors are true or not, they decrease the mine's value at a time when you can't afford it, neither figuratively nor literally."

"Precisely," Eppler said. "If you sign loan papers, Ben, you better pray you strike the mother lode, because the Bank of California won't be interested in a worthless mining claim. They'll come after the Ponderosa for collateral."

"What?" Hoss interrupted. "A loan, the Ponderosa?"

Holding up his hand, Ben nodded. "I'll explain in a minute."

Pyburn pulled off his glasses and held them up toward the window. He blew off a speck of dust and hooked the wire earpieces back in place. "Putting the guards around the place was a good move, Adam, making people think you might be on to something in the mine."

"It was no gimmick, Monville, we meant it to keep Smalley from burning the hoist works and mill," Adam replied impatiently.

"Rest assured," Eppler said, "that Smalley's unlikely to burn down a property he wants to acquire."

"Gentlemen," Ben interrupted as he took his seat, "we're here to decide our next course of action. Adam, bring us up to date."

Adam nodded, then stood and walked over to the window as he spoke of the Bristlecone's unfulfilled promise. He noted that the mine was unsealed that morning and fully operating. He reported that the shaft itself was down to 1350 feet with operating laterals at 1100, 1200, and 1320 feet. Adam called them the Nina, the Pinta, and the Santa Maria. The Nina, the oldest and longest of the mine's three laterals, extended 262 feet toward the mother lode's suspected location. The Pinta reached 178 feet away from the main shaft. The Santa Maria had gone but eighty-five feet from the shaft.

"To date," Adam said, "our best ore's producing under twenty dollars per ton, $18.90 to be exact, but it's costing us $24.60 a ton to mine and mill. With a daily production of 475 tons, we're losing around $2700 a day."

Hoss sputtered. "Where's the extra money coming from to pay for that loss?" He looked around the table.

"That's where the loan comes in, Hoss," Ben

replied. "Clarence has had the papers drawn up for a half-million-dollar loan from the Bank of California."

Hoss threw up his arms, then slapped his palms against the table. "Let's get out of mining."

"Yeah," Little Joe piped in.

Ben looked to Adam and saw disappointment in his black eyes. Then Adam turned away from the table and stared out the window.

"It's not that simple, boys," said stockbroker Pyburn. "Right now's the worst time to sell because all the rumors are reducing the Bristlecone's value. If you get out now, you've still got debts you can't pay. Knowing your father, he'd make good on his debts, and that would mean selling part of the Ponderosa anyway."

"Huh?" Hoss said. "We've still got money, don't we?"

Adam cleared his throat. "Hoss, I showed you and Little Joe the other day how much mining costs."

"Let me explain," Pyburn continued. "Cartwright Enterprises has expended its available reserves of cash to keep the mine going. So, you have no convenient source of funds to cover the current losses. You have contracted for certain expenses such as timber, milling, and transportation, which must be paid over the next three months. Even if you closed the mine today, it would be at least that long before you would quit losing money on existing contracts. Your father has opted not to sell mine stock publicly because

118

of the speculative fever that might tarnish the good Cartwright name, particularly now that Thurston Smalley has targeted the Bristlecone. You have but two options: to sell the mine and eat your losses now, or to take a loan of a half-million dollars and hope you strike the mother lode before the money must be repaid. If you try to sell the mine now, the price will be so devalued because of the bad rumors that you stand to magnify your losses because you can't recoup as large a percentage of your investment. If you take out a loan, you're gambling that you can bring the mine in within the month, the term of the loan. Stated simply, the Bristlecone's got you over a financial barrel."

Hoss slapped the table again. "How'd we get ourselves into this mess? I don't care about mining. This mining business is keeping me here when I'd rather be back on the ranch working, and now you tell me we might lose part or all of the ranch." Hoss glared at Adam.

The worst that Ben feared was unfolding before his eyes. The mine could turn his sons against each other. He slumped back in his chair, knowing Little Joe would voice his displeasure too, now that Hoss had broached the subject.

"This is Adam's doing?" Little Joe stated. "I'm with Hoss and ready to get out."

Adam spun around from the window and stormed to the table. "My doing? Maybe so, but I've put more into this mine, sweated more over it, than you two have over anything in the last

year. Take it out of my share of Cartwright Enterprises until I'm no longer a partner." He
pointed at Little Joe, then at Hoss. "If I go broke,
I can make it back. You two can't, not at —"

Ben pounded his fists on the table. "Adam,
enough! You three listen. We're not going to tear
this family apart over this mine. We'll put it to
a vote and let it stand at that. Once it's voted
on, we'll work together whatever the decision.
Right?"

Adam retreated to the window and Little Joe
grumbled something unintelligible.

"What, Joseph?"

Little Joe took a deep breath. "I said you'd
side with Adam and that would be it. You always
side with him on these matters."

Pointing his finger like a pistol at Little Joe's
nose, Ben gritted his teeth. "You know how Cartwright Enterprises is divided up, a fifth for each
of you boys and two-fifth for me. One vote for
each of you, two for me because I built up
Cartwright Enterprises and the Ponderosa. One
day it will belong to you boys, but until then,
Joseph, I'll vote my conscience. If you are dis-
satisfied, you can return your fifth share. You
too, Hoss."

Ben felt the hard gaze of both upon him.

"Pa, it ain't that," Hoss offered. "It's just that
I don't like risking the Ponderosa for no hole
in the ground."

Little Joe nodded vigorously. "I'm with Hoss."

Ben studied both sons. "I'll call for a vote. The

losers will abide by the vote."

Little Joe shot up from his chair. "Then, Hoss, we might just as well leave, because Pa will vote with Adam. He always does."

Hoss grabbed Little Joe's arm and jerked him back into his seat. "Hush up, little brother."

Turning his scowl toward Hoss, Little Joe jerked his arm free.

Ben shook his head and looked at Eppler and Pyburn. "I apologize that you've had to see us this quarrelsome." Then Ben looked toward his sons, his gaze lingering on the defiance in the set of Little Joe's mouth and the fire of his hazel eyes. "We're voting whether to sell the mine or take out the loan. Clarence has the paperwork with him. If we approve the loan, I'll sign the papers. If we vote to sell, we'll set that process in motion. Does everyone understand?"

Each son nodded.

"Now," Ben continued, "I'll call for the vote. Adam, you first."

Striding from the window toward the table, Adam pushed his chair aside and leaned over the table, planting his palms atop it and staring at his two brothers. "I'll reserve my vote until later," he answered.

Hoss and Little Joe quickly looked at one another. Why wasn't Adam voting?

"Hoss," Ben called, "your vote."

For a moment Hoss looked from his father to Adam and back. With resignation he shrugged and voted: "I say we sell the mine."

"One vote for selling," Ben repeated. "Joseph, your vote?"

Little Joe answered Adam's withering gaze with a confident vote. "I vote we get out of the mining business for good."

"Two votes for selling," Ben said. "Adam?"

"I'll reserve my vote until last," Adam said, his hands defiantly planted on the table, his hard stare focusing on Little Joe.

Ben nodded. "Thank you, Adam." Ben knew what Adam was doing, though he could tell by the puzzled expressions of Hoss and Little Joe that they didn't. Had Adam voted before everyone else, Ben's two votes would have been the deciding ones. By voting last, Adam would cast the deciding vote, deflecting Hoss's and Little Joe's anger from their father to him. There was a subtle difference here, but Ben caught it easily.

As much as it pained him to risk the Ponderosa, it pained him even more to risk the family harmony he had managed over the years. Money or the risk of losing it had a way of tearing families apart. But in siding with one son, was he turning against two others? The mine didn't mean as much to Hoss and Little Joe as it did to Adam. Were it to collapse under him, Ben wondered how bad a blow it would be to Adam. Still, as Eppler and Pyburn had pointed out, now was not the best time to consider selling out.

Ben cleared his throat. "I cast my two votes in favor of taking the loan. That's two votes for selling out, two votes for signing the loan agreement. Adam?"

By the surprise on their faces, only then did Hoss and Little Joe realize why Adam had withheld his vote. Little Joe groaned until Ben glared at him.

"I cast my vote to keep the mine going another month and accept the loan." He turned around and walked triumphantly back to the window.

Ben clenched his jaw. Why did Adam have to turn his back on his brothers after casting the deciding vote? Adam's self-righteousness could easily be perceived as arrogance. Why hadn't he just cast his vote graciously? "By a three-to-two vote, Cartwright Enterprises will sign papers for a half-million-dollar loan and continue mining the Bristlecone."

Little Joe shoved his chair away from the table and stood up. His lips twitched in anger as he pointed at Adam, then his father. "You two don't need me, not when you outvote me and Hoss on everything."

"Joseph," Ben commanded, "don't you talk to me that way." Ben shot up from his chair as Little Joe strode for the door.

"You two decide what's best for us since that's how it'll be anyway." Little Joe grabbed his hat from its hook and stormed outside, slamming the door behind him, his boots hitting noisily as he bounded down the steps.

Ben slumped back into his chair, leaning his head against the backrest. When he straightened, he saw Hoss stand slowly up from his seat.

"Sorry, Pa, but you know I don't take to this business so well as Adam. I ain't angry, I just don't get it all, and I don't like doing anything that could endanger the Ponderosa. Right now, a cold beer sounds better than all the silver in Nevada. I've been outvoted fair and square, so you and Adam make the decisions and I'll go along with it."

At that, Hoss walked meekly around the table as if he were trying to make himself smaller. This damnable mine! Behind him, Ben heard the door open then click shut as Hoss stepped cautiously out of the office. "Gentlemen," Ben looked at Eppler and Pyburn, "I apologize for our family differences."

Both men nodded. "Tough decisions always make for tough times," responded Eppler, "but Ben, once you sign the loan agreement, the Ponderosa may never be the same." With his admonition, Eppler pushed a half-dozen papers across the table toward Ben. "Here's the loan agreement. It's in good order, but I don't recommend you sign it."

Pyburn piped in. "You could still sell stock, Ben. You know that is my recommendation?"

Ben spoke solemnly. "Folks around here associate the Bristlecone with the Cartwright name, and I'll not have our name sullied by speculators like Thurston Smalley."

Pyburn looked to Adam at the window. "Don't take this wrong, Adam, but with your father unwilling to sell stock, I'd have voted with Hoss and Little Joe, just to cut your losses and hang on to as much of the Ponderosa as you can."

Adam turned slowly around, anger simmering in his eyes. "There's silver down there, we all know it."

Pyburn scratched his gray whiskers and nodded. "We know that, but we just can't be sure where it is. Fortunes have been lost on surer bets than this."

Adam started to speak, but Ben held up his hand. "I'm a stubborn man, Monville. I made my fortune following my instincts and taking risks now and then."

Pyburn mumbled his agreement.

Eppler pushed a steel pen and inkwell across the table. "My heart's not in this, Ben. You pick up the pen and you could be destroying the Ponderosa."

Deliberately, Ben took the pen, studying its steel point a moment, then dipped it in the reservoir of ink. As he touched the pen to the paper, a chill ran down his spine. Was this the end of the Bristlecone and the beginning of the end of the Ponderosa? He signed his name with a flourish, though it was a gesture empty of enthusiasm.

Pyburn coughed into his fist. "Ben, you've got to think about options, in case the Bristlecone doesn't produce before you must repay the loan."

Ben carefully placed the pen on the table and shoved the signed papers to Eppler. "I'm overdue for a trip to San Francisco," he replied. "I'll check the waters among my monied acquaintances there, see if I can pull together backing enough to pay off the loan and buy us a little more time."

"You're running out of time, Ben," Eppler warned.

"I understand," Ben said, "thank you both for coming here. Adam or I will stay in touch with you."

Eppler gathered the loan agreement and gingerly placed the papers in his satchel. "You best make sure Hoss and Little Joe know the importance of keeping these discussions secret. No offense, Ben, but those two don't understand the business like you and Adam."

"No offense taken," Ben answered, standing up from his chair to escort Eppler and Pyburn to the door.

Pyburn stood up and stretched as Eppler snapped his satchel shut, then arose. Ben shook hands with both men, who departed without another word.

After they left, Ben and Adam silently contemplated the risks they faced. "Your brothers don't have your head for numbers and business, Adam," Ben chided. "You've got to be patient with them."

"I don't have time to explain everything to them, Pa."

"Then you best make time while I'm gone to San Francisco, because I don't want to return and find my sons squabbling among themselves so that it breaks up the family. That's more important than even the Ponderosa."

At dusk Little Joe called on Holly Lucas at her boardinghouse. The landlady eyed him suspiciously and impatiently tapped her foot while she worked her knitting needles furiously in the yellow glow of the coal-oil lamp. When Holly Lucas emerged from the hallway, Little Joe smiled. She was wearing a new dress, a soft yellow gingham that highlighted her green eyes and the crown of her long golden hair. She acknowledged the landlady and quickly joined Little Joe on the porch.

Stepping outside, she twirled around, the hem of her dress billowing out. "What do you think?"

"Only thing prettier than the dress is you," he said. She took to the flattery like a kitten to a saucer of milk.

Holly giggled and grabbed his arm. "Where are you taking me to dinner?"

Little Joe gently touched her cheek. "I'm taking you to the International Hotel, the restaurant there."

"I've never eaten there, but I have heard it is so good. And," she whispered, "expensive."

Little Joe slipped his arm around her waist. "Now don't you worry about that."

"It must be nice to have money and never to want for anything," she said, snuggling against him.

Holly stopped and Little Joe turned to face her.

"What's the matter?" he asked.

"Just this," she answered, standing on her toes and kissing him on the cheek, then they continued walking. "How are things at the mine?"

"I'm ready to get out of mining, so's Hoss. We're ready to sell the mine. Problem is, our fifth shares don't add up enough to beat Adam's one-fifth share and Pa's two-fifths shares when they vote together as they always do."

"And you voted on it today?" Holly asked.

"Sure did, and me and Hoss lost three-two."

"Oh, Little Joe, mining is so fascinating, you'll have to tell me more."

Little Joe was pleased at her interest and at the kiss she had planted on his cheek. He had high hopes for the evening.

From the gym, Adam walked to the courthouse and waited on the front steps for Lucia Sinclair, who was working late. When she joined him outside, he saw in her eyes that she was tired. They had talked about going to the opera house for a performance, but the attraction of that had dwindled with their energy.

Adam took her hand and directed her toward the International Hotel. "Thurston Smalley do anything affecting the Bristlecone that you heard of?" asked Adam.

"Didn't see him today, though I hear rumors about title problems with the Bristlecone claim. I figure he's the one behind them. How'd your meeting go with your father and brothers?"

Adam shook his head.

"That bad?"

"Yes, ma'am, that bad," Adam answered. "Hoss and Little Joe want to get out of mining, the sooner the better."

Lucia glanced around, making sure no one on the walk could overhear them. "You're not giving up, are you? Selling out?"

"We're running out of time, but for now we're still in the mining business. My single vote and Pa's two votes beat theirs."

They walked silently for a block toward the International Hotel. When they went inside, Adam pulled his hat down over his face so as not to attract every rumormonger who wanted to jaw about the latest speculation.

At the entry to the dining room, Adam paused and studied the occupants, then retreated back into the lobby.

"What's the matter, Adam, lose your appetite?"

"Not exactly."

"Then what is it?"

"Little Joe," Adam replied. "He's here with that Holly Lucas."

"So?"

"Tonight I don't feel like eating under the same roof with Little Joe."

CHAPTER 9

"Where is she?" Big Jim Fowler bellowed from the meeting room over the engine house of Zephyr Engine Company. The company's fifty volunteers shifted awkwardly in their chairs, gauging Fowler's hot anger. Fowler stalked from behind the front table, where the secretary nervously straightened a single page of minutes from the last meeting. "She knows as belle of Zephyr Company that she's supposed to be here for our monthly meeting."

From the back row a skittish volunteer lifted his arm meekly.

"What is it?" Fowler growled.

The volunteer stood up slowly and grabbed the back of the chair before him. "I saw Holly eating at the International Hotel." He took a deep breath. "With that Cartwright boy, she was."

Fowler's face reddened and he shook for an instant like a boiler about to blow. Then his face suddenly relaxed and he spoke calmly. "After we finish our business, I'll remind Miss Lucas of her responsibilities as 'belle.' "

Retreating behind the table, Fowler seated himself beside the company's recording secretary and called on the treasurer for an accounting of the dress ball and its profits.

The treasurer, a spindly man with thinning hair, stood up, a single sheet of paper in his hand. He smiled awkwardly and his voice cracked as he started to read. Some volunteers snickered until Fowler banged the gavel. The treasurer wiped a film of perspiration from his face. "Income," he called out, "of $4753.38."

The volunteer firemen cheered mightily, yet the treasurer shifted nervously on his feet.

"Expenses," the treasurer said softly, and gave a figure that few heard over the murmuring crowd.

"What?" yelled several.

The treasurer turned around and stared at Fowler, who nodded curtly at him. Clearing his throat, the treasurer looked at the report and with sudden courage shouted, "Expenses of $4397.44."

Stunned, the volunteers sat silent for a moment, allowing the treasurer to continue.

Now his voice was subdued and embarrassed. "Profit of $355.94."

Pandemonium exploded in the room. Volunteers jumped to their feet, jabbering, yelling, and shaking their fists at the front table.

"Order, order," shouted Big Jim Fowler. "This meeting should come to order." He stood up, shoving his chair in anger, tipping it back over onto the wooden floor. He grabbed his gavel and pounded the table. "Order, I say, order."

The noise subsided, but not the anger. The volunteers growled among themselves, staring with defiant eyes toward Jim Fowler. The treasurer slipped to the side of the room, folded the financial report and shoved it in his pants pocket.

"We want answers," shouted a stocky volunteer.

"A couple thousand dollars or more we've made on every past dress ball," yelled another volunteer. "Why not this one?"

"Yeah, yeah," thundered others.

Fowler waved the gavel in the air, signaling for silence, but the angry din continued. Defiantly, he thrust his chin forward and pounded the palm of his hand with the gavel. He had the right, as captain, to decide how to spend money for the good of Virginia City and for the good of Zephyr Engine Company No. 7.

The clamor gradually diminished, but the silent anger rose like the temperature on a hot day.

Fowler stood contemptuously before the men who had voted him their leader less than a year ago. He waited until all the whispering stopped, until the room emptied of noise, but not of tension or suspicion. "Now that I have quiet, I'll explain," he said.

"There's plenty of explaining to do," yelled an angry volunteer.

Fowler slammed the gavel onto the table. "It's been bad since the big fire. We all know that."

The volunteers mumbled agreement.

"We all know the move's afoot to disband the volunteers and create a paid department," Fowler continued.

Every head in the room nodded.

"I figured to put on the grandest ball ever on the Comstock. Most people agreed it was just that. It left a good feeling among city folks toward the volunteers."

A fireman jumped from his seat and pointed at Fowler. "But we promised folks we'd raise money enough to buy a steam pumper for Virginia City. We didn't raise near enough money." The men shouted agreement.

"Dammit," shouted another, "you just —"

Fowler shot a finger at the volunteer. "A five-dollar fine for profanity. You know it's prohibited by our constitution." Turning to the recording secretary, Fowler had him note the offender.

Planting his hands on his hips, Fowler glared at the volunteers. "I'm trying to help us survive as a fraternal organization we can all enjoy," he stated.

A burly volunteer stood up, shaking his fist at Fowler. "Nobody else'll say this, but I'm not scared of you. There's a lot of talk you don't care about this company and all you're doing is winning favor with citizens so you can head a paid city department."

"Yeah, yeah," came a chorus of agreement, then applause.

Fowler stepped toward the miner, who moved for the aisle until nearby men grabbed his flexed arms. The volunteers on the front row jumped up to prevent Fowler from advancing. Fowler backed away behind the head table and picked up his overturned chair, sliding it under the table. He leaned forward on its backrest. "I dare any man to say he has worked longer or harder for this engine company than I have over the last five years." He scanned the room and was pleased with the number of agreeing nods. If defiance didn't work, then perhaps supplication would. "I worked for me, yes, because I wanted to be a part of Zephyr Engine Company Seven, the best damn engine company in all of the West."

A couple of men raised their voices at his profanity.

Fowler grinned. "I know what I said, but that's how I feel." He turned to the recording secretary. "Mark me for a five-dollar fine."

His action again drew supportive nods. Fowler relished his ability to manipulate the men. "I intended to make this year's dress ball the most memorable in Comstock history. I succeeded, but not without a cost, the loss of your trust. In trying to restore the faith of Virginia City in the volunteer departments as capable fire-fighting units, I have lost your trust in me as your leader. I regret that deeply."

Fowler watched the volunteers as they whispered among themselves now, no longer so adamant or suspicious. He paused for them to gossip. Finally he spoke again: "Like you, I wish our fancy ball had made more money, but at the time I approved the costs I thought them necessary to restore the town's faith in us. I have two more months left on my term, and I had planned to run for captain again, but I shall not if that is your wish. I respect all of you too much to go against what you think is best for this engine company. And if it be the wish of this company tonight that I resign, I shall. I only ask that you take a public vote on it."

Fowler picked up the gavel and offered it to the first assistant, who was seated on the front row. "Take charge of this meeting, and I'll leave the building so you can freely discuss whether you desire my continued service," Fowler said.

The surprised first assistant moved reluctantly forward, Fowler patting him on the back as he took the gavel. Then Fowler marched confidently down the center aisle, accompanied by a smattering of applause, not enough to alleviate the fear that they might oust him, but enough to let him hope he might keep his position. His ploy would allow him a graceful exit from a heated meeting that could last until midnight or later. Now he could go to Holly Lucas's boardinghouse and see if she was indeed out with Little Joe Cartwright. The thought stoked the anger already simmering within him.

Fowler went down the stairs and through the room where the hand pumper and hose cart were polished and ready for the next alarm. Outside, a sliver of a moon hung overhead as he walked away from the engine house. The gas lamps offered halos of light along the walk, but he avoided them, preferring not to be seen.

At the boardinghouse, he knocked on the door.

Through the window, he saw the landlady waddling toward him. The door swung open and she squinted until Fowler stepped into the shaft of light seeping from inside. When she recognized him, she shook her head and clucked her tongue. "She ain't here, Holly ain't."

"You know where she is?"

"Nope, just out with some new feller. I'll wait up for her to make sure there's no foolishness that goes on under this roof. Girls that try such, I kick 'em out."

Fowler nodded. "Tell her that I came by and that the volunteers at Zephyr Engine Company missed her at tonight's meeting." With that, he turned and strode off the porch. He walked to the nearest saloon and bought a bottle of whiskey. Uncorking it before he was out the door, Fowler took a hard swig and headed back toward the boardinghouse. He took a position in a vacant lot between two dwellings on the opposite side of the street from Holly's place. Stumbling over an old wooden crate, he turned it over and sat upon it. The weathered wood sagged beneath his weight, but it held. He watched the boardinghouse, gently nursing his bottle from full to empty, then tossed it over his head. It landed with a clink. For more than two hours he just watched.

And finally, after midnight, he spotted a man and a woman approaching, passing through the glow of the streetlamps, laughing and talking loudly. He recognized the giggle as Holly's, and he knew the man to be Little Joe Cartwright. Fowler felt the anger rising in him, and he arose on wobbly knees. He would whip Little Joe right now, he thought, taking a half step toward the street. He lifted his arms and knotted his hands into fists. A moment before, the couple had seemed so far away, and now they were standing on the porch, kissing.

Fowler wanted to speak, but his mouth was filled with liquor's bile and he realized he didn't know what to say. He staggered toward them. He would take care of Little Joe right now and whip Holly Lucas tomorrow. They seemed to kiss forever, and Fowler could stand no more. With two big steps he charged them, then went sprawling onto the earth.

When Fowler managed to push himself up from the cold ground, he shook his head to clear it of the muddle. On his hands and knees, he studied the boardinghouse. Now he was confused. The porch was empty and the front parlor was dark. It didn't make sense to him anymore. Dammit, why had Holly Lucas betrayed him for Little Joe Cartwright? Maybe Little Joe had money, but he didn't have a chance in hell of becoming chief of the paid fire department in Virginia City. Didn't Holly Lucas understand that?

Holly Lucas awoke with the sun shining through a break in the curtains. She felt as if she had slept with a smile on her face all night. Little Joe had treated her like a queen. For the

137

first time in her life, she had ordered lobster. And Little Joe had complimented her several times on how she looked in her new dress.

Stretching in bed, she hoped Little Joe would call upon her tonight like he said he would. Oh, it must be nice to be rich like a Cartwright, to order anything from a restaurant menu, to have fine clothes, to sleep all day if you wanted. Holly dressed, knowing she should have gotten up earlier and gone to the eatery to work breakfast and lunch where hash and beans, not lobster, were the staple. She felt so common, working the tables, but last night Little Joe made her feel rich and beautiful. This morning she wanted to live the dream just a little longer.

At length, she arose from bed. She had been up but a moment when she heard a knock on the door. "Holly, Holly Lucas," came the landlady's gravelly voice, "someone to see you."

A morsel of terror lodged in her throat. Was it Jim Fowler? She prayed not. He would hurt her for seeing Little Joe. "Is it Jim Fowler?"

"No," answered the landlady, "it's that runt of a man that came by the other night."

It was Thurston Smalley. Holly felt both relief and fear, relief that it was not Fowler, but fear that Smalley was dangerous in his own way. Even so, she enjoyed the money Smalley had given her because it bought clothes with much less work than waiting tables. And it helped hold Little Joe's eye. "Just a minute," she called.

When she was properly dressed, she stepped

into the hallway, where her landlady stood with her arms crossed across her wide breast. "I thought you worked today?"

Holly smiled. "Yes, ma'am," she replied triumphantly. "I just decided I deserved a little more rest today."

"That's your business, Holly Lucas, as long as you remember that rent's due the first of every month."

"Yes, ma'am," she said, squeezing by and walking down the hallway for the front door.

Thurston Smalley stood just inside the door, a narrow smile upon his lips, a gold toothpick clamped between his yellowed teeth.

Holly glanced over her shoulder, down the hall at her landlady. "You shouldn't be inside her parlor," she whispered.

Smalley shook his head. "She makes an exception for me."

"No," Holly replied, "she makes an exception for no one."

Nonchalantly, Smalley pulled a handful of gold pieces from out of his pants pocket. "She does for me. Now, tell me about last night."

For an instant Holly was taken aback. "What about last night?"

"You were with Little Joe."

Holly's mouth dropped open. "How'd you know?"

"I know everything that goes on in Virginia City."

"Did you follow me?"

Smalley laughed. "My time's too important to waste following you and your men friends."

"Was your man across the street last night? I heard some strange noises when I got home."

Shrugging, Smalley stepped closer to Holly Lucas, reaching out to touch her cheek where Fowler had hit her. "You must be careful to avoid a man that would do you this way. And I must warn you that Fowler's in a bit of trouble with the Zephyr volunteers."

Holly flinched at his touch. "Why are you telling me this?"

"I don't want you to get hurt, my dear, and we both know Fowler's got a nasty temper. He'll be madder today. Seems the volunteers voted to remove him as captain last night. Wild stories are going around about him spending too much money at the fancy ball. They didn't like that. He didn't like it that you weren't there."

"Jim Fowler doesn't own me," Holly snapped.

"No," Smalley replied, "I do." His comment was as serious as his malevolent eyes.

"I don't have to tell you anything." Holly backed away a step, crossing her arms over her chest. "I don't want to do anything that will hurt Little Joe."

"You have taken money from me already, money you've doubtless already spent, money that you can't repay me in two months working tables at an eatery. We had an agreement that you would supply me information. I intend to see that you carry it out."

"And if I don't?"

"My dear, you are so naive. If you don't, the first thing I will do is let Little Joe know you are passing along information to me. Then I'll see that rumors start about you, that you are no better than the whores who work the red-light district on D Street. My dear, you just don't have any idea the terrible things I can do to you without ever laying a finger on you."

Holly felt the high optimism she had awakened to deflating with Smalley's every word. Her eyes began to flood with tears and she buried her head in her palms. She shivered at the touch of his clammy hand and felt nauseated.

"Now, now, my dear," he said, stroking her hair, "you've nothing to worry about if you just live up to our agreement. And remember, I'm still paying you for the information."

"It won't hurt . . ." She paused to get control of her emotions. ". . . Little Joe, will it?"

"Oh, no, my dear, not at all. Maybe it'll help him settle a score with his father."

Holly brushed a tear from the corner of each eye and tried to stand with head erect and shoulders straight, but she had never felt more miserable. "What do you want to know?"

"That's better," Smalley said, his voice sinister rather than soothing. "The Cartwrights met yesterday afternoon in the office of the Bristlecone. What did they discuss?"

Holly shook her head, then caught her breath

and closed her eyes. "They voted on selling the Bristlecone."

Smalley rubbed his hands together. "How'd the vote go?"

"Three to two. Little Joe and Hoss voted their fifth shares to sell. Adam voted his fifth and the old man his two-fifth shares to keep mining."

"Excellent, my dear." Smalley took her hand and closed her fingers around coins as cold as he himself.

When Holly opened her eyes, Smalley was gone. In her hand she held a hundred dollars in gold.

CHAPTER 10

Whistling a tune, Little Joe sauntered up the stairs of the Bristlecone office. Things couldn't get much better for him. Sure, the Bristlecone had some problems, but that was Adam's worry. Meanwhile, on his father's orders, he was staying indefinitely in Virginia City. He had a room of his own at the International Hotel, and a lady friend who was enamored of him. With nothing but time on his hands, he would have plenty of occasion to escort Holly Lucas wherever she wanted. And on top of that, Big Jim Fowler had not shown up at Little Joe's court hearing that morning. Rumor said the volunteers of Zephyr Engine Company had replaced Fowler as captain last night. Without Fowler, the judge quickly dismissed the case and Little Joe was free to attend his business or his pleasure. He preferred the latter. As he had exited the courtroom, his father had given explicit instructions. Be at the mine office at five o'clock!

Little Joe was a little late, but he had run into Holly. They had begun to talk, and time had just gotten away. At the top of the stairs, he removed his hat, stopped his whistling and flashed his most charming smile at the closed door.

Twisting the doorknob, he entered with a broad grin. Little Joe felt his smile wither under his father's hard gaze.

Ben, dressed in a three-piece broadcloth suit over a starched shirt with bat-wing collar and string bow tie, picked up his key-wind gold watch, the watch he always carried on business or travel. He glanced at the timepiece, then at his son. "I thought you knew how to tell time, Joseph." Ben's voice had an edge to it, an edge honed by exasperation.

Little Joe glanced from his father to Adam and Hoss, but found no support in their eyes. "Pa, you know I can tell time," he offered, holding the brim of his hat in both hands.

"If that's so, I take it as willful disobedience when you don't follow my instructions," Ben replied, snapping the watch cover shut.

"Pa, I'm not a kid anymore."

"Then prove it, Joseph, by assuming the responsibility that's your birthright as a Cartwright." Ben pointed to a seat. "It's five-twenty, and I've a train to catch at seven o'clock."

"A train?" Little Joe asked.

"For San Francisco," Ben said with disgust. "Weren't you listening yesterday?"

Little Joe sighed. Now he remembered, now that it was too late to save himself embarrassment. Pa was going to San Francisco to seek Bristlecone investors from among his monied acquaintances.

"In my absence," Ben said, looking straight at

Little Joe, "Adam will be in charge. He will be my proxy, but will telegraph me of any significant changes in our situation. Likewise, I will keep him informed in coded telegrams of my luck in San Francisco."

Little Joe could feel anger pulsing in him, anger at himself for being late, anger at his father for always making it hard on him, anger at Hoss for not coming to his support, and anger at Adam for getting them and their fortune so deeply intertwined with the success or failure of the Bristlecone. Mired in his anger, Little Joe did not realize his father was addressing him.

"Joseph," Ben called with a firm voice, "are you listening?"

Little Joe sighed. "Sorry, Pa, I had my thoughts on something else."

"As I said, Joseph, I've checked out of the International Hotel, and have had you and Hoss checked out as well."

"What? Why?" Little Joe sputtered and looked from his father to his brothers. Again he received no looks of encouragement.

"The presence of all of us in town gives the appearance the mine is taking all our energies and our monies," Ben replied.

"It is," Little Joe responded.

Ben's eyes flashed again. "Boy, do you intend to anger me or do you just not think when you speak?"

Little Joe gulped. There was no greater fury in his father than when he addressed one of his sons as "boy."

Ben leaned forward sternly. "From this point on, you'd best listen without comment."

Little Joe felt his shoulders slump and his spirits sag. He was just trying to defend himself and find out what was going on. Why did this antagonize his father so?

"Joseph, you and Hoss will use the two bunks in the room back of the office downstairs. I want one of you three boys here all the time in case the miners discover something promising, and just to keep an eye on things. We've got armed guards, water barrels, and water wagons at crucial places in case someone tries to burn us out."

"But Pa," Hoss interrupted, "with all the precautions, ain't the Bristlecone safe?"

Ben pursed his lips, then shook his head. "Thurston Smalley can dangle enough money in front of an honest working man to corrupt him. I want one of you boys here at all times to keep an eye on things."

Hoss nodded. "I hadn't thought about that."

Little Joe lifted his hand meekly, like a schoolboy embarrassed to ask a question of his teacher.

Ben studied Little Joe a moment. "Yes, Joseph."

"What about Adam, where will he stay?"

Crossing his arms over his chest, Ben answered with a steady voice. "In his suite at the International Hotel."

"It's not fair," Little Joe half whispered, "him getting to stay at the hotel all the time, and us having to room on hard bunks in the back of the office."

"You're right," Ben said, "it's not fair, Adam putting so much of his time and effort into this mine, trying to bring it in, trying to making it a success, while his kid brother's out gallivanting about town. You're right, Adam's entitled to more than a hotel suite for all he's tried to do for us."

Little Joe slumped deeper in his chair. He couldn't win, not with his father, not with the mine. He was glad to know he would be seeing Holly this evening. At least she appreciated him.

"If anyone asks," Ben said, "I've returned to the Ponderosa for a few days to deal with ranch business. We'll buy a train ticket to Carson City in case anyone checks here. I'll buy one from there to Reno and then get one there on into San Francisco. Maybe that'll keep folks here and in Carson City from learning my true destination. My success may well depend on secrecy so I can talk to potential investors before they hear Smalley's rumors."

Ben asked Adam for the latest assay reports. Adam picked up a clipboard and flipped over a couple pages, then identified the reports by the laterals. "In the Nina, $19.75 a ton. The Pinta assays at fifteen dollars even, and the Santa Maria comes in $9.50."

Ben clucked his tongue.

"I've been thinking," Adam continued, "about shutting the Santa Maria and putting all our crews in the other two laterals."

Ben nodded. "Give the orders."

"I already have," Adam replied.

Little Joe could only shake his head. Adam and Pa agreed on everything, while he and his father could agree on nothing.

"In my absence," Ben said, looking straight at Little Joe, "Adam'll be in charge of things. Did you hear that, Joseph?"

"Yes, sir," Little Joe replied, his face flushing with embarrassment. He straightened in his chair, trying as best he could not to look insolent and not to antagonize his father any more.

The hardness in Ben's stare softened a little. Digging into his pocket, he pulled out a couple of silver pieces and slid them across the table to Hoss. "I want you to go over to the Virginia and Truckee depot and buy me a ticket to Carson City. If anyone asks, tell them you're figuring on going back to the Ponderosa. Once you get back, I'll time my departure for the depot to get there just before the train leaves, to decrease the likelihood of many folks seeing me at the station."

"Yes, sir, Pa," Hoss said, taking the money.

"Little Joe, go with Hoss and work out the times you're staying here tonight, and then go to the International Hotel and collect your things."

Little Joe stood up with Hoss and both moved for the door.

"One last thing," Ben called. "I know tensions are running high. It'll be a greater tragedy to lose the family than to lose the mine."

"Yes, sir," the three sons said in unison.

Adam heard the cry of the steam whistle as the Virginia and Truckee locomotive chugged away from the station, carrying his father on the first leg of his trip to San Francisco. Behind Adam, the Bristlecone works rumbled in Virginia City's thin air. Adam walked briskly to Bill Davis's gymnasium. He was anxious to see Lucia Sinclair, but it was Friday evening and the conscientious Lucia always worked late on Fridays so as not to start out behind on Monday mornings.

Adam knew he would have time to work out then reach the courthouse before Lucia called it a day. In the distance, he could see the passenger train disappearing toward Gold Hill. He wished his father luck and himself even more. It would be a heavy burden if his bad business judgment cost the family the Ponderosa.

At the gym, Adam changed quickly into his boxing tights and jogged around the gymnasium a few times before heading to the punching bag. The bag bounced rhythmically as his fists alternated back and forth. It felt good to pummel the bag and relieve some of the frustrations of running a mine. For thirty minutes he danced around the bag, hitting it steadily with long smooth strokes. His breath, like his muscular arms, was controlled and steady. As he tired, his arms grew heavy. His body glistened with perspiration when he stopped, bending over and resting his hands on his knees.

"Tough workout?"

Adam looked up into the face of John W. Mackay, the richest of all Virginia City's silver kings. "Evening, John, it's been a frustrating day."

"Mining can do that to you! And you, being so close to the Big Bonanza and not striking it yet. Confounds a man, doesn't it?"

Adam nodded. "If I don't find it quick, I know you'll be getting all of it from your direction."

Laughing, Mackay shrugged. "You know mining laws as they are, Adam Cartwright, and that's sure a possibility." Then Mackay's tone changed from jovial to serious. "How are things with the Bristlecone these days?"

"Not bad, but could be better," Adam said, straightening up and stretching his shoulders and arms.

Mackay shook his head. "That's not what I hear."

Adam froze, his arms hanging stiffly in the air. He lowered them and his voice. "What is it that you hear, John?"

"Your brothers want to sell out, get out of mining entirely. That's the word going around town, around the Washoe Club."

Trying to disguise his own surprise, Adam studied Mackay closely. Was the silver king trying to bluff him, trying to scare him into selling out? Mackay was as honest a man as walked the streets

150

of Virginia City, so Adam doubted he had ulterior motives. Further, by mining law, Mackay could follow the mother lode wherever it led him and as much as two hundred feet into an adjacent claim; he had little to gain from starting rumors about the Bristlecone.

Mackay seemed to read Adam's suspicions. He held up his hand. "I'm passing this information along to you as a friend, Adam."

"Thurston Smalley's behind this," Adam said with a deep breath.

"He must be getting good information, then, because the word is you four Cartwrights voted on it yesterday — Little Joe and Hoss voting to get out, you and your father opting to stay with the Bristlecone longer."

Mackay's report struck Adam between the eyes like a bare-knuckle fist. His gaping mouth betrayed his surprise.

The silver king nodded. "I won't spread a word of it, Adam, but others will. Fact is, Smalley's getting solid information from your confidants. You better be careful."

"I appreciate that, John," Adam said. He reached out and grabbed Mackay's hand, pumping it slowly.

Mackay smiled. "I best not be seen talking too much to you or another set of rumors will crop up about your Bristlecone or my Consolidated Virginia." With that, the millionaire walked to another punching bag and began his own workout.

Like a beaten gladiator, Adam walked slowly to the dressing room. He bathed and dressed, all the time going over the people who had been in his office yesterday when the vote was taken. His father, his two brothers, Clarence Eppler, Monville Pyburn, and himself had witnessed the vote. Never would it be Ben Cartwright. Hoss was slow on occasion, but as honest as nature. Such treachery seemed out of character for him. Little Joe! Now, he might be the culprit, being nineteen and of the age when he had more braggadocio than sense. But he was not so crazy as to jeopardize the Ponderosa. Eppler and Pyburn possibly were at fault, but they had been trusted advisors to Ben Cartwright for years. Neither was a greedy man and both despised Thurston Smalley. Adam could not point a finger at them. That left only himself, but Adam knew he had told no one. Except Lucia Sinclair!

He caught his breath and shook his head. Throughout his friendship with her, Lucia had always been honest about everything, from her likes in poetry and opera to her thoughts about marriage and work. He admired her as much for her independence and intellect as he did her beauty and temperament.

Adam left the gym and walked quickly to the stone courthouse. He dashed up the steps and down the long hall toward the county clerk's office, almost running for the door that was ajar. Then he slowed. What a fool he was to suspect Lucia. He stopped in the hallway, collecting his breath and his thoughts. He would trust Lucia with his innermost secrets, as he had on numerous occasions. She had never betrayed him.

Reassured, he moved down the hall, figuring himself a fool for doubting her. He grabbed the doorknob, then froze at the sound of Lucia's voice and another he recognized but could not immediately place. Slowly, he cracked the door wider until Lucia came into view behind the counter. As the door moved a fraction more, Adam saw Thurston Smalley standing opposite her!

Adam's mouth went dry. Should he believe what he was seeing? Was Lucia betraying him?

Smalley extended his hand as if to shake hers, but Lucia stood perplexed, hesitant. She moved out of Adam's line of sight and he pulled gently on the door, but a hinge squeaked softly. Adam caught a glimpse of Lucia turning her gaze slowly from Smalley to the door. Adam jumped back, then retreated to an intersecting hallway where he slipped out of sight. He waited a couple minutes, which seemed to drag by like a bad sermon, before he heard the moaning of the hinges as the door swung open, then shut. Peeking around the corner, Adam saw Smalley exiting onto the street.

Adam moved down the hall and leaned up against the wall opposite the door, watching the office dim as the lamps were snuffed out.

The door rattled and Lucia stepped into the hallway. Holding her keys up to a hall lamp, she saw Adam and gave a small cry. "You startled me," she exclaimed. Then her eyes narrowed and she stared squarely at Adam. "How long have you been here?"

"Arrived," Adam lied, "as you started killing the lamps."

Lucia seemed relieved. She turned and locked the office door.

Adam stepped across the hallway and took her arm as she checked that the door was secure. "Where for dinner?" he asked.

She leaned her head against his. "I'm awfully worn-out tonight, could you take me home, Adam? It was a long and bad day."

"Too tired for poetry? I'll read you your favorite," he offered.

She shook her head. "Not tonight."

Adam didn't know what to make of it. She seldom turned down a poetry reading. Could she have betrayed him? He could not ask her because she would never tell if she had, and she would be incensed if she hadn't. She could never have betrayed him or the Bristlecone, Adam told himself. He was a fool for even thinking it. He should have just asked her about Smalley's visit. Instead he had lied to her about not seeing them together. It was no secret that Smalley had been looking for a flaw in the Cartwright claim to the Bristlecone. He may well have been studying the county records after hours, knowing that continued rumors of a flawed claim would weaken even more the Cartwright hold on the Bristlecone.

It was foolish of him to ever doubt Lucia, Adam thought. She could be trusted with every secret he had ever had, and at times could almost read his thoughts, like now.

She squeezed his arm and leaned her head against his shoulder. "We're both quiet tonight. Did things go badly for you?"

"Bad day for me too. We shut down the Santa Maria because it was assaying only $9.50 a ton. We're putting all our crews into the Nina and the Pinta. At $19.75 a ton, the Nina's the best hope we've got. The Pinta's only at fifteen dollars a ton. It's so bad, Pa's gone to San Francisco to search for investors."

"I'm sorry to hear that, Adam."

It was if she were preoccupied with something else. Or wanted him to think that! Now Adam was uncertain if he should have given her the latest figures and news on the Bristlecone. He had never felt more perplexed or awkward around Lucia Sinclair.

"I've got to be at the mine by ten o'clock," Little Joe reminded Holly Lucas.

"Oh, Little Joe," Holly answered, "I do enjoy being with you." She leaned over and kissed him as they walked along the street.

"I've so much business to attend at the mine, I wish it weren't so," Little Joe said, trying to impress Holly.

She squeezed his arm even tighter.

"And now with Pa off to San Francisco, I've

had to move out of the International Hotel, just to be closer to things at the mine."

"Are things going well, Little Joe?"

Now was his chance to impress her, thought Little Joe. "Mining goes up and down. Right now things are down for us, but I've a suspicion that's about to change. We've been working three laterals near the bottom of the mine, the Nina, Pinta, and Santa Maria. I named them for Columbus's three ships, since they found a new world for Spain and I'm trying to find a new world for the Cartwrights."

"You're so smart, Little Joe."

"Well, the Santa Maria was assaying at only $9.50 a ton, so I shut it down to concentrate our work on the Nina and the Pinta. The Nina's assaying at $19.75 a ton. The Pinta assays at fifteen dollars."

"Oh, Little Joe, you know so much. I wish you didn't have to be back so early so we would have more time together."

"That's the mining business," he answered.

CHAPTER 11

Vorley Deaton lifted his battered felt hat, which was stiffened with resin to deflect the falling debris occasionally dislodged by the Burleigh compressed air drill. Leaning against the momentarily idle drill, he wiped the sweat off his forehead. No sooner had he done so than his face was moist with more perspiration. The mines were hot at the 1200-foot level, reaching temperatures as high as 140 degrees without ventilation. Even the candle flames that illuminated Deaton's work space seemed sluggish in the heat. Deaton's muscled arms glistened in the flickering light. The patches of his chest not covered by the straps of his overalls were grimy from the dust and grit the Burleigh drill blasted from the hard quartz that separated a mine owner from his fortune and a miner from his wages. With the Burleigh drill, work was easier on the muscles but harder on the lungs. The fine dust and debris loosed by the drill made breathing hard at best, painful at worst.

Deaton smiled. It was just a few minutes until shift change. He would ride the hoist cage from this earthen Hell and breathe the fresh mountain air to cleanse his lungs. Until today, Deaton had been working the lowest lateral, but for some reason the foreman had closed it off and reassigned crews to the two laterals above it. Deaton knew the bottom lateral likely wasn't showing assays as good as its closest neighbors, but he also knew a miner's instincts were sometimes better than all the principles of the assaying sciences. He had a hunch about the bottom lateral. The closing would interest Thurston Smalley, but Deaton planned to avoid the stock manipulator for as long as he could. He knew that mine wages at four dollars a day would hardly compare with the hundreds of dollars Smalley paid for information, but he also knew it was tainted money, and tainted money pained his conscience these days as much as the dust from the drill hurt his lungs.

When Deaton's chuck tender returned, offering him a drink from a bucket of ice water, Deaton took the pail and drank deeply. The water felt as if it soaked into every pore of his body. Putting the bucket aside, he held up his candle and looked at the pattern of holes he had drilled into the hard rock. As the drill man, Deaton gave the orders for this two-man crew. "It's time to take her down," he said, slapping the Burleigh drill.

Both men pitched into the drill. They released the thirty-six-inch drill bit and stacked it with the others of varying lengths to be turned over to the Bristlecone's blacksmith for reconditioning. The two men lifted the drill from its mount wedged between floor and ceiling by screw jacks, then carried it back to the side tunnel. When they returned, they quickly loaded an ore cart with the remainder of their drill equipment and hand tools. As they pushed the ore cart over its iron rails to a side tunnel, Deaton nodded at the blaster and his assistant as they passed, each holding a rope handle at the end of a dynamite crate.

Deaton caught his breath. It was Jesse McMatt, perhaps the best blaster in all the Comstock, a man so good with dynamite he could make a murder look accidental in the mines. McMatt was a dangerous man, especially if in the employ of Thurston Smalley. Deaton cursed beneath his breath. No good would come of McMatt's presence. Pushing the ore cart into the side chamber, Deaton told his chuck tender to relax.

Deaton, though, stood in the tunnel, watching McMatt and his helper drop the dynamite crate where he had just worked. The assistant pried the lid off the crate and began to pull out sticks of dynamite, slicing a gash in the side of each. McMatt then let several loops of Bickford fuse slide down his shoulder to his hand while his other hand fished out a wad of blasting caps from his pocket. Deaton shook his head. A careful blaster usually moved blasting caps in a padded box or even a special ore cart with spring suspension and a padded bottom. McMatt was indeed a dangerous man.

Squatting over the discarded crate lid, McMatt dropped the blasting caps and then the Bickford fuse. He stared impatiently at his helper, then stood up and pulled his pipe and tobacco from his pocket. Nonchalantly, he filled his pipe and fired it with a match he tossed at his helper. The apprentice gasped and swatted at the flaming match to knock it away from the dynamite crate. McMatt laughed, his voice deep and sinister, then fished a pocket-knife from his britches and began to cut lengths of Bickford fuse by rote.

The fool, thought Deaton. Tossing the match at the dynamite was more show than threat, but smoking in a mine, that was something else. Smoking was prohibited. Nothing — not a cave-in, not a crate of dynamite going off, nothing else — set a miner's heart to pounding like the worry of a fire in the mine.

McMatt squatted over the discarded wooden lid, inserting varying lengths of fuse into the blasting caps, crimping the cap ends with pliers. As he finished each blasting cap, he grabbed a stick of dynamite and slipped the detonator into the slit. With a length of jutelike cord, McMatt wrapped the dynamite stick and then pulled the cord tight, closing the slit and encasing the detonator inside.

Once the dynamite was primed, McMatt began to tamp each stick into the holes Deaton had drilled into the quartz. A bit of fuse brushed against McMatt's pipe. As the fuse began to spit and sputter, the apprentice gasped and grabbed the crate of dynamite to make his escape. McMatt tossed the spare length of lit fuse at him. Laughing, McMatt finished tamping the charges in place, then ordered his helper to tote away the crate.

From the back wall, fifteen lengths of Bickford fuse drooped like the tails of giant rats. The apprentice looked nervously from the box of dynamite to McMatt, who was calmly cutting a final length of Bickford for the spitter he would use to light the fuses. The spitter had to be cut just shorter than the shortest of the fuses so the blaster would have time to escape.

"Signal the hoist," called McMatt, and a miner at the signal station by the shaft rang out two bells, then three bells, signifying the lateral level. Shortly, after the whir and grinding of cables, the hoist cage appeared at the shaft. The miner responded with five bells, the signal that blasting was about to occur. The cage lifted a moment, then settled back to the level of the tunnel floor, the signal that all was okay for the blasting to proceed.

McMatt touched his pipe to the spitter and it began to pop flame. "Fire in the hole!" he shouted as he touched the spitter to the first of the fuses. "Run, boy, run," he yelled.

Wide-eyed, the apprentice lurched forward, stumbling under the load, gained his balance, then tripped over the track. The crate flew from his hands. Dynamite sticks scattered like an armload of kindling. The youth scrambled to his knees, lunging for the box and grabbing for the dynamite. Behind him, McMatt laughed and the fuses hissed. "You never run, boy," McMatt cried out.

161

"You walk calmly like this." He lit the last fuse and turned around, striding past his assistant. "You better hurry," he taunted, then passed his scrambling assistant.

Deaton grabbed a candle holder and dashed to help the apprentice.

"You fool," McMatt yelled as Deaton ran by, "it's the boy's responsibility."

Deaton fell to his knees to pick up the dynamite. He looked at the back wall. The flame on one of the fuses had disappeared into the hole. "Come on, let's run," he shouted, but the boy was paralyzed with fear. Pushing himself up, Deaton tossed aside his candle and, with his muscular arms, grabbed the boy under the shoulders and jerked him up. He had but seconds to make it to cover.

Deaton plowed ahead as best he could in the darkness, dragging the boy with him. He stumbled over the tracks, but somehow managed to keep his balance. The glow of the side chamber drew nearer and he knew he was going to make it in time. Then the boy's dragging feet snagged on something. Deaton lost his grip and the boy fell in a heap upon the mine floor.

McMatt, unseen behind cover, loosed a sinister laugh that echoed through the tunnel.

Deaton spun around and bent down, grabbing the apprentice by his arms and dragging him toward the crosscut. Deaton thought he would make it. Then the world exploded.

It happened so fast, Deaton could not sort it

out in his mind. The concussion knocked him off his feet and threw him into the far wall. Something was ripped from his hands. He heard a scream but he was so confused he did not know whose. His lungs were bursting with pain and every breath was tainted by suffocating fumes. He seemed to bounce on the floor and his head threatened to burst with pain. He opened his eyes. The world was dark and murky, broken only by a glow of a distant light. Then he felt two hands grab him under his shoulders and pull him away; he did not know where to, only away, only into the distance. He was dropped onto something cool and flat and he was alone. Instinct, not his senses, told him this. Wherever he was, it was lonely and forever.

After an eternity he felt something dropped atop him. He heard bells, and even in his stupor he counted them because bells were the signals that miners depended on to survive. Three bells, a pause, three bells, another pause, and then three more bells rang out. It was the miner's dirge. It meant a body was being hoisted from below.

Deaton felt the strange sensation of rising in the sky and the heat of the mine give way to a rush of cool air. He could not explain it, and his eyes were suddenly flooded with a light that he could not comprehend.

Deaton passed out.

Someone was running up the stairs. Adam jumped from his chair and raced to the door.

Could it be the assaying reports? Could it be they had finally uncovered the lode they had been looking for? Adam jerked open the door to see a wide-eyed clerk about to knock.

"Trouble in the shaft, sir," the clerk said.

"What kind?"

"Don't know, sir, just that nine bells sounded after an explosion in one of the laterals. Likely a blasting accident."

Adam brushed past the clerk and bounded down the stairs, past the front desks and down the hall to the back door. At the bunk room, he saw Hoss poke his head out.

"What'sa matter?"

"Accident," Adam replied, motioning for Hoss to follow. Adam flung open the back door and darted outside, Hoss behind him on the plank walk leading to the hoisting works.

Adam burst inside the hoist works, skirting the machinery and sprinting toward the shaft where a clump of men were bent over something. "Get a doctor," one of the men yelled, and a man peeled away from the crowd, running by Adam for the exit.

"Make way," Adam said, wading into the crowd. "What's wrong?"

"One dead," called the shift foreman, "one injured. Premature detonation!"

"Who handled the explosives?"

"A new one for us, Jesse McMatt. Supposed to be one of the best."

"Where is he?"

"He stayed below to look for dynamite."

Adam pushed his way to the injured miner. Cut, bruised, and bloodied, the miner shook his arms feebly at the air. "Back up," Adam shouted, "give him room to breathe."

His order was ignored until Hoss plunged into the throng. "You heard him. Make way, give the man room to breathe."

"The other one's over here," the foreman said, pointing to a lump beneath a tarp. "He ain't a pretty sight."

"Have a wagon ready to take this one to the hospital as soon as the doctor gets here," Adam commanded, and a couple of men scurried away.

Hoss kept the crowd back and ordered someone to bring water. Shortly, a pail and dipper appeared. Squatting over him, Adam lifted the miner's head and helped him sip at the water.

The man's eyes fluttered at the touch of water against his lips and he blinked at the strong light.

Something about the man was vaguely familiar, Adam thought as he pulled the dipper away from the miner's bloodied lips. Then Adam remembered the brewery fire and sealing up the Bristlecone. He remembered, too, reopening the mine and how one miner, this miner, had worked twice as hard as any other man on the crew. "Can you hear me?" Adam asked as he tried to recall the miner's name.

The miner nodded slightly, a trickle of blood draining from the corner of his mouth.

"Your name?"

"Vorley . . . Deaton," the miner managed.

"Don't worry, the doctor's coming and we'll get you to a hospital," Adam reassured him. "You'll be taken care of."

The miner nodded and closed his eyes.

Damn the luck, Adam thought, glancing around the hoist works. What else could go wrong at a time when so much had to go right for the Bristlecone to make it and the Ponderosa to survive? A flurry of activity at the back entrance announced the arrival of Dr. Paul Martin, black bag in hand, serious expression upon his face. Martin walked quickly to Deaton and squatted beside him, spending a few minutes to feel Deaton's extremities for broken bones, then checking the bumps and bruises on his head.

"He's lucky," Martin finally announced. "Appears to be just a nasty bump on the head. We'll keep him in the hospital. A day's rest and he should be fine."

"My men are bringing a wagon around for him," Adam said. "You want to check the one that wasn't so lucky?"

Martin nodded. "It's part of the job."

Adam motioned to the tarp, and Martin stepped reverently in that direction. Bending down, he lifted a corner of the tarp to inspect the apprentice's face. "Always a shame when it's a young one like this." The doctor gently touched the dead man's face, noting the bloody pulp on the side where debris had struck. He covered the body. "Anyone know if this boy had family?"

Everyone shrugged.

"Shame, isn't it," Martin said, "some people have more family than they need and some don't have any when they need them."

"The Bristlecone'll be his family," Adam answered. "We'll cover his burial and Deaton's hospital stay."

Some men fashioned a stretcher for Deaton, and a few others wrapped the blaster's assistant up in the tarp. Then both were carried to the wagon, Martin taking a place between them as the wagon pulled out of the building.

Adam instructed the foreman to send the men back to work or home if their shift had ended. "Hoss," he said, "come with me." Adam walked over to the hoist operator. "Next cage, we're going down to the level of the accident."

Hoss balked. "Dad-blame-it, Adam, you know I don't trust all this equipment."

"Even at your weight, Hoss, it'll hold." Adam took two candles from the supply near the hoist operator's station. He lit the candles, placed them in holders, and gave one to Hoss.

The bell clanged as the hoist operator moved the cage from level to level. Finally it reached the top, disgorging miners from the previous shift. They were a sweaty and grimy bunch as always, but the mirth that usually accompanied the end of a shift was missing, word of the death having reached them. They nodded at Adam, then went their way. Adam and Hoss took their places on the cage. Hoss stood by the corner where he could tightly grab a rail. He clenched his jaw as the cage started to descend into the bowels of the earth. Instantly they were immersed in a darkness broken only by the flickering glow of their candles. The cage dropped dizzily down the shaft, allowing only occasional glimpses of men at work in the laterals. At last the cage stopped at the Pinta.

Adam then Hoss stepped into the tunnel which still smelled of dynamite fumes. "Boy, I hate it down here, Adam."

At the end of the tunnel, Adam and Hoss saw another crew of miners shoveling into a cart the debris from the fatal explosion. Another man walked around, kicking at rocks. As they approached with their candles, Adam realized the man was holding sticks of dynamite.

"You McMatt?" Adam asked.

"Yeah," the blaster answered, waving a stick of dynamite. "Who are you?"

"The owner of this mine," Adam replied.

"That a fact?"

"How'd the accident happen?"

"My helper stumbled and fell after the fuses were lit, then panicked. That fool miner ran back to help him and almost made it before the charge went off. Damn shame."

A coiled rattlesnake had more sympathy in its buzz, Adam thought, than McMatt did in his words.

"Now if you fellows don't mind, I've got to keep looking in case any more dynamite's buried around here. I'd hate for us to lose another miner." McMatt laughed and turned his back on Adam and Hoss.

The two brothers returned to the hoist landing. Adam rang the signal bell.

"You know," Hoss said, "I trust that man less than I trust Big Jim Fowler, and I don't trust Fowler at all."

CHAPTER 12

The corner table at the Washoe Club was set
with the finest bone china, the finest crystal, the
finest silver on the Comstock Lode. The food on
Adam's plate was untouched, even though it was
fresh-smoked salmon, one of his favorites. The
crystal decanter of brandy, too, was undisturbed.
Adam had lost his appetite. The kid was the first
fatality ever for the Bristlecone. There had been
injuries before; that was to be expected in a dangerous business like mining, but no deaths. At
times Adam wondered if the pursuit of silver was
worth the risks. It sure didn't seem like it now.

And today's assay reports had not brought any
better news. They had been nominal, as before
in the Pinta and the Nina. Nothing solid enough
to attract investors, only vultures like Thurston
Smalley. Adam carried in his pocket the first telegram from his father in San Francisco. Even
among Ben's friends things didn't look promising.
No one wanted to risk pouring money down an
empty hole. Even in San Francisco bad rumors
were floating that the Bristlecone was draining
the Cartwrights. The rumors seemed too pronounced for Thurston Smalley not to be involved
in them.

Adam's thoughts kept returning to the accident, a strange set of circumstances. Was it an accident or was it Smalley's sinister reach extending all the way into the Bristlecone? Adam could understand a blaster's assistant being injured in an explosion, but why was a miner, rather than the blaster himself, the other man injured? Maybe it was one of the vagaries of mining that just couldn't be explained, but perhaps it was more than that.

Adam was lost in his thoughts when he realized someone was standing over his table. He looked up into the owlish eyes of Monville Pyburn. The stockbroker's expression was as somber as that of a preacher at a funeral. "Sorry to hear about the accident," Pyburn began, "but I need to talk to you about something else."

"Have a seat, Monville," Adam said, nodding toward a chair.

"Not here, Adam, too many people around," Pyburn replied.

Adam picked up his napkin and tossed it on the table.

"It can wait until after your meal."

"My stomach's churning, Monville, but I'm not hungry."

Wordlessly, Adam followed Pyburn outside and down the street to his office. Unlocking the door, Pyburn held it open for Adam, then locked it behind them. Both men retreated into the back room, where they could not be seen through the windows.

"Sit down, Adam," Pyburn suggested, though he himself paced the room. "Word's getting out on the street, accurate word, about the Bristlecone."

Adam slumped in his chair and released a heavy sigh. As if there weren't enough problems — now this. He remembered catching Lucia with Thurston Smalley. "What's the rumor?"

"Everybody knows Ben went to San Francisco."

That bit of information Adam had passed to Lucia, but many along the railroad might have seen Ben. That could be explained away.

"Word is you closed your lowest lateral and have started concentrating on the upper two, the Nina and Pinta, as I recall."

Adam nodded. He had told Lucia they would be closing the Santa Maria, but he could not pin that one on her since the closing of a lateral sets miners to gossiping below ground and above. "Is that all?" Adam asked.

Pyburn sighed, then shook his head.

Adam swallowed hard. He knew what to expect next, and he knew who to blame. Lucia, damn her!

"You did not advise me of yesterday's assays, did you, Adam?"

"No, sir."

"I didn't think so. Of course, I'm getting old and my memory's not what it used to be."

"You're just shrewd, Monville."

The stockbroker smiled slightly. "Tell me if

172

these figures are near the actual figures. In the Nina, $19.75 a ton, fifteen dollars in the Pinta, and $9.50 in the Santa Maria. Those close?"

"They're not close, Monville, they're right on the money."

"Damn," said Pyburn. "I feared that."

Adam thought of Lucia Sinclair and let out a heavy breath. "Me too!" Adam could still see Smalley with Lucia after closing time in the county clerk's office. Had she betrayed his trust in her?

Big Jim Fowler trudged to the engine house, anger rising in him like pressure in a steam pumper. He was returning the silver megaphone the Zephyr captain used to issue orders at fires. He cursed. His chances of heading a paid city fire department were dwindling like his moments with the trumpet. Much as it galled him, he would maintain his allegiance to Zephyr Engine Company No. 7. At the engine house, he went inside, where his successor as captain sat at a table playing poker with a half dozen other volunteers.

When Holly Lucas had turned against him, the engine company had as well, Fowler figured. And who was responsible for that change of heart? Little Joe Cartwright. He would get Little Joe for that.

The men at the card table greeted Fowler, but not with the same respect they once had. That galled him too. "I'm passing this to the new captain of Zephyr Company," Fowler said, placing the megaphone on the table. His successor acknowledged Fowler with a nod.

Fowler lingered a moment, hoping for an invitation to play cards. When he received none, he looked at the hand pumper, spotting a couple smudges on the brass fittings that needed to be polished. He would never have allowed card games in the engine room. Maybe upstairs in the meeting room, but not here where the equipment was kept and maintained. The men should be working instead of playing. This wouldn't be a problem with a paid staff in a city department, not if he ran it.

He waited a few more minutes, but no one spoke to him. Finally Fowler gave up and slipped from the building into the darkness of night. He wandered aimlessly around, winding up in a saloon he had never visited before and drinking jigger after jigger of whiskey. How could he ever head Zephyr Company again? The only way was to prove himself a hero, to show he was the best fire fighter in town. He could do that. He might need to start a few fires to do it, but he could. And if Little Joe Cartwright died in one of the fires, all the better. That way he would win Holly Lucas back for sure.

A terrible thought bothered Lucia Sinclair. What if Adam had seen her talking to Thurston Smalley? Surely not, but could it be? Adam was never this late for their standing Saturday night trip to the opera house. She had not sought out

Smalley, and he had been careful to let no one see him — unless Adam had — in the county clerk's office.

Smalley knew how to trap people with his duplicity. He was, she now thought, a master of offering people their dreams. For most it was money. For her it was to become Nevada's first practicing female attorney. Smalley somehow knew this and had detailed how it would be within his grasp and resources to arrange just that, if only she would provide him inside information on the Bristlecone. The irony, though, was that if she accepted that bribe, she would be betraying the law she so desperately wanted to defend. She could never do that, nor could she betray Adam. He was as tolerant and accepting a man as she had ever met. He was not threatened by her, and that was a rare quality in a man.

Lucia paced about her modest parlor, its back wall covered with bookshelves, each overflowing with books of poetry and history, literature and law. Her personal library was the envy of several unions and volunteer fire companies which maintained libraries for their men. Her house was small but adequate for her needs, with a nice parlor, small kitchen, tiny dining room, and adequate bedroom. Except for Adam, she rarely received visitors, and was content to read her books or sit on her porch in a rocking chair Adam had given her. The house was freshly painted white with dark blue trim, and it stood on Stewart Street on the gentle slopes of Mount Davidson, which towered over all of Virginia City. Her house was nestled among a few mansions and a few shacks. For all its wealth, Virginia City had no rich neighborhood nor none exclusively poor. Instead, people of all walks of life, of all occupations and of varied incomes, lived side by side, if not in total harmony, then at least in mutual acceptance.

As she passed a mirror on her parlor wall, Lucia hesitated and brushed back a lock of hair. She had combed it out as Adam preferred, and had rouged her cheeks and colored her lips for the occasion. Adam had been under so much pressure the last few weeks with the Bristlecone, she worried for him. Her concern was so deep that she was startled at the knock on the door. Checking her hair a final time and flashing her most inviting smile, she strode to the door and opened it.

Adam shocked her by his appearance. Instead of the fancy suit he usually wore to the opera house, he was dressed in work clothes. He had not shaved since morning, a rarity for him, so his face was stubbled with a day's growth of beard. When he took off his hat, his tousled hair needed combing. Lucia felt her smile slide away into oblivion. His appearance was so odd, she half expected him to have liquor on his breath. She was relieved when he stepped wordlessly inside, and she detected only the odors of the mine, not the smell of whiskey. Lucia closed the door and turned to him, at a loss for words. She had never seen him like this and didn't know what to say, or, maybe more importantly, what not to say.

Adam stared straight into her eyes, his black eyes simmering like coals. His stubborn jaw was cocked with doubt and he made no effort to address her.

"Are you okay, Adam?" she managed, uncertain what to expect. "We can still make the opera house in time for the first act."

"We lost a man at the mine," he responded.

"Oh, Adam," she said. She stepped to him and wrapped her arms around him. "You can't blame yourself." She attempted to kiss him.

Adam turned his head, avoiding her lips, then breaking free.

Lucia sagged from his rejection, but Adam seemed not to care, which was unlike him. This was the mine's first fatality, and she knew Adam would struggle with it. During her acquaintance, Adam had always been quiet and serious. Ben Cartwright had once told her that Adam had been more carefree as a child, but when he was sixteen he had released the Ponderosa's prize bull, against orders of the ranch foreman. When the foreman tried to return the bull to the corral, the animal had gored him, killing him before Adam's eyes. Ben Cartwright said Adam that day turned suddenly serious and deeply introspective. Lucia could imagine how hard Adam must be taking this miner's death. He would blame himself.

"If we're going to the opera, let's go," Adam said abruptly.

"We don't have to, if you'd rather stay here," Lucia offered, but Adam marched past her to the door.

"You coming or not?" he called over his shoulder.

Lucia scurried around the room, gathered her shawl, blew out the lamp and followed Adam onto the porch. She locked the door without him making an offer to assist. She sighed, then jogged to catch up with him. When distracted by mining problems before, he had at least been courteous.

Side by side they walked to Piper's Opera House, where all Virginia City's best theatrical productions were staged. Adam neither spoke to nor touched her. At the opera house, Adam nodded curtly at acquaintances as he directed Lucia down the aisle to their front row seats. They arrived only moments before the curtain lifted. A traveling troupe was presenting Shakespeare's *Romeo and Juliet*. As the play started, Lucia thought it might distract Adam from his worries, but as it progressed, he only seemed to grow angrier and more fidgety in his seat. At the end of the first act, Lucia leaned over and whispered in his ear. "Would you prefer to return to my home?"

"Fine," Adam said curtly.

Before Lucia could wrap her shawl around her shoulders, he stood up and glared down at her impatiently. He offered her neither a hand nor an encouraging smile. Lucia could feel her own anger building. She had done nothing to deserve

178

this treatment. She was sorry a miner had died, but she had had nothing to do with it.

Adam led Lucia from the seats, not even waiting for her at the aisle. Her face red from embarrassment at his rudeness, she marched behind him to the back of the opera house and out the door into the cool night air. He never paused for her to catch up.

"Please, Adam," she called, "wait up for me."

Adam slowed a moment, allowing her to slip her arm under his, then marched wordlessly toward Lucia's home. Lucia never remembered a more agonizing walk.

"What's the matter, Adam?" she asked softly.

"I told you I lost a miner today," he growled.

"But why are you treating me this way?"

Adam ignored her question and seemed to flinch from her touch.

When they reached her house, she stepped up on the porch, pulling her arm from his as she found her key and unlocked the door. Adam slipped away to the rocking chair and sat down. The chair and the porch creaked as he began to rock. Lucia went inside and lit a lamp. Retreating to the open door, she watched him. He said nothing, just rocked in the chair.

"You are welcome to join me inside, Adam, if you care for me," she said.

"I'll join you in a moment. I've got to think something over."

"Okay," Lucia said, leaving the door open as a standing invitation for Adam. Never had she felt more helpless. She fought back her emotions, knowing if she didn't, her eyes would tear up and she would cry in frustration. This was a side of Adam she had never seen, a side she did not like. Had the mine finally ruined him? She marched into her bedroom, found a kerchief, and wiped the coloring from her lips. Looking in the mirror over her dresser, she flipped her hand through her hair, mussing it, regretting the time she had spent primping for Adam.

In the parlor, she heard the door shut and assumed Adam had entered. With a sigh, she turned around and walked into the parlor.

Adam was slumped forward on the sofa, his elbows resting on his knees, his chin cradled in his upturned palms. "Can we talk?" he asked with resignation.

"Sure," Lucia answered softly, "if it will help."

"Nothing will help this," Adam said, suddenly bolting up from his chair and pacing about the room.

Lucia marched to the sofa and sat down. She felt like a little girl about to be scolded by her father. She watched Adam stalk around the room. When he finally spoke, he did so without looking at her.

"The mine has been a burden, Lucia, you know that," Adam started. "The death was a terrible thing to add to my problems."

"I would like to help, Adam. Whatever I could do for you."

Adam now stared at her, his eyes making silent

180

accusations. "What you can do to help, Lucia, is just listen and don't make this any harder than it is."

Lucia had a sinking feeling that Adam had indeed seen her with Thurston Smalley.

"I'm battling the earth and Thurston Smalley to save the Ponderosa. We are in desperate straits unless I find the mother lode within the next ten days, Lucia."

"I know it's been —"

Adam held up his hand to silence her. "All sorts of rumors are getting out about the Bristlecone and the Ponderosa, Lucia."

Lucia squirmed beneath Adam's withering gaze. She did not like the way Adam was approaching this.

"The rumors, though, haven't all been rumors. Some of them were true, information I had told you."

Lucia felt her lips tighten across her clenched jaw. She could not believe Adam was accusing her of betraying his trust.

"What do you have to say for yourself?" Adam crossed his arms over his chest.

"You're accusing me?"

Adam nodded.

Lucia's face flushed with anger. She clasped her fingers together, taking several deep breaths to control her emotions. "Maybe you've reached a hasty conclusion, Adam. I know you've been under a lot of pressure."

"That's beside the point," Adam shot back,

pointing his finger at Lucia. "I want an answer."

Jumping from the sofa, Lucia paced the room. "In a court of law, you're innocent until proven guilty. It seems I'm guilty already."

"I told you Pa was going to San Francisco to find investors. That's going around Virginia City today. I told you we were shutting down the Santa Maria. That's going around Virginia City today."

Lucia shouted back, "Your father's a well-known man, so what if people know he's in San Francisco? Every miner in the Bristlecone knew when you shut down the Santa Maria."

Shaking his finger vigorously at Lucia, Adam continued, "But they didn't know the assay findings to the penny. I told you, and today word gets back to me those figures are being circulated."

"I'm the only one you told?"

"You and my brothers, no one else."

"Maybe they told someone?"

Adam cocked his head. "Hoss doesn't have a head for figures, and Little Joe's only interested in women. And I haven't seen either of *them* talking with Thurston Smalley."

Lucia felt her shoulders fall. He had seen her with Smalley.

Adam strode across the room and grabbed her arms. "Explain that!"

Even if she explained, he would not believe her. Lucia had no reason now to clear up his confusion. If he could not trust her word, she could not enjoy his company. "I can't explain it."

Adam released her arms and shook his head in disgust. "You betrayed me, Lucia."

Instinctively, Lucia drew back her arm and swung for his face, striking him full across the cheek. "You betrayed yourself, Adam. Now get out and don't ever come calling again."

CHAPTER 13

It was a fitting cemetery, carved and hewn out of the slopes of Mount Davidson. The assorted tombstones bled long shadows which lapped one another in the morning sun. Adam, Hoss, and Little Joe stood with hats in hand, heads bowed, as the preacher finished a short prayer over the open grave. Then several miners lifted the coffin while others slipped two ropes beneath it. With the ropes, they positioned the coffin over the open grave, then lowered it silently, reverently, into the earth.

Adam lifted his head and tugged his hat in place, looking among the miners for Jesse McMatt. He didn't spot him. Perhaps McMatt couldn't handle the funeral of a man his accident had killed. Funerals weren't good for a man's nerves, and men who handled explosives had to keep sure nerves. Or perhaps McMatt was just a callous man with no remorse.

The coffin settled into the grave and a couple miners pulled the ropes free. Others picked up shovels and began to cover the grave. For men whose muscles had removed tons of ore from the bowels of the earth, this was easy work and a final tribute to one of their own. Adam stood transfixed as shovel after shovel of dirt and stone landed atop the coffin, gradually covering it. Feeling a strong grip around his arm, Adam looked around at Hoss.

"There's nothing more you can do than buy him a fine stone, and I know you've done that. Let's head back to town," Hoss suggested.

Adam stared down the mountainside. Beneath him Virginia City was spread out like a grimy blanket. His eyes focused on the Bristlecone mine works, the buildings standing like dark tombstones over an unfinished grave. Each day his hopes were buried deeper in the ground, just like this miner's coffin.

Nodding, Adam followed Hoss and Little Joe around the grave, through the throng of miners lingering in clumps about the cemetery. The brothers climbed into the rented surrey, Adam and Little Joe taking the front bench seat, Hoss the back. Adam untied the reins and loosened the brakes, maneuvering the surrey around the hearse and down the dirt road toward Virginia City.

"What do you say we drop off the surrey and eat us a little lunch?" Hoss said.

"You never eat a little of anything, Hoss," Little Joe replied.

Hoss and Little Joe looked at Adam. For a moment he seemed lost in his thoughts. "Before we return to the stable, I need to stop by the International Hotel, pick up my belongings."

Little Joe glanced from Adam to Hoss, then

back at Adam. "We ain't that broke yet, are we? Are we?"

Adam shook his head.

"Then why you moving out, Adam?" Little Joe persisted. "Your conscience bothering you since Pa kicked us out?"

Adam shrugged.

"Dad-blame-it, Adam," Hoss said, "we've got a right to know, even if Pa did leave you in charge."

"I don't need the suite anymore," Adam finally said. "I figure it'll make it fair for me to bunk in the office with you."

Little Joe folded his arms across his chest, a smirk working its way across his face. "Don't need a suite, do you? It can't be that you and Lucia Sinclair've had a falling out, now can it?"

Adam slapped the reins against the rump of the horse, and the surrey lurched ahead faster down the sloping road toward Virginia City.

Little Joe laughed. "Don't need the room anymore, do you?"

Hoss grabbed Little Joe by the shoulder, his iron grip imparting the message that now was not the time to pester Adam.

Little Joe hushed.

When Adam broke his silence, he spoke not of Lucia, but of the mine's latest assay reports. "The Nina's down to $18.25 a ton and the Pinta's dropped to $13.80 a ton."

Hoss whistled. "Think it's ever gonna turn around?"

Adam shrugged. "If I knew that, I'd still be staying at the International Hotel," he replied with a trace of bitterness. He drove the rest of the way to the hotel without another word. He parked the surrey and asked Hoss to accompany him. They rode the hydraulic elevator, one of the first west of the Mississippi, up to the top floor and went wordlessly to Adam's room. Sitting in the middle of the floor was a trunk and two valises.

Hoss shook his head at Adam. "Now I know why you invited me up, instead of Little Joe. He couldn't wrestle this trunk to the wagon."

Adam smiled and clasped Hoss on the shoulder. "Thanks for calling Little Joe off, Hoss. Lucia and I came to a parting last night."

Grunting as he squatted down, Hoss grabbed handles on each end of the trunk and hoisted it waist level. "Not bad for a trunk. Toss those valises on top."

"Nope," Adam said, "too much of a load for you, Hoss."

"Not like the load you've been carrying, Adam." Hoss gave Adam a gap-toothed grin as he moved to the door.

"I appreciate that, Hoss," Adam replied. He picked up his two valises and marched out into the hall, closing the door behind him.

They rode the elevator down to the first floor. While Adam settled his account, Hoss dropped the trunk and sat atop it. Adam paid his bill quickly, then exited with Hoss through the crowded lobby, drawing the questioning stares of several speculators.

Outside, Hoss threw the trunk on the floorboard, then took the valises from Adam and tossed them on the seat. The surrey tipped as Hoss climbed aboard, but settled on its springs as he collapsed in the seat. Adam went around the wagon and climbed up. He slapped the reins against the horse's rump and turned the wagon around in the middle of the street, then put the animal into a lope for the Bristlecone.

Little Joe crossed his arms and glanced in the direction of Holly's boardinghouse as Adam maneuvered down the streets of Virginia City at a brisk pace. "After we unload your belongings at the mine office, Adam, you want me to return the surrey?" he asked.

Adam looked over at Little Joe. "It'd be a help."

Little Joe grinned broadly, knowing he could impress Holly Lucas with a ride in the surrey. He felt Hoss's paw slap his shoulder.

"What about that food?" Hoss asked. "Aren't we gonna eat?"

"I'm not as hungry as I thought I was," Little Joe replied.

Adam eased the surrey around the corner on F Street and headed for the Bristlecone offices at the end of the street. Little Joe saw a pair of armed sentries patrolling the perimeter of the mine property. Both men tipped their hats as

Adam passed. Little Joe wondered if the extra guards were really needed. Adam was just too cautious about some things, particularly at a time when Cartwright Enterprises had less and less money to spend.

Before Adam drew the surrey to a complete stop, the vehicle convulsed as Hoss jumped to the ground and grabbed the trunk from the back. "I don't know about you fellas, but I'm hungry as a bear!"

Little Joe just shook his head. "If the Bristle-cone goes under, how will we afford to feed you, Hoss?" Twisting to check Adam's reaction to his joke, Little Joe choked on his own smile. Adam's face was clouded with a scowl. "Didn't mean any harm, Adam."

Adam's slight nod was accompanied by the faint smile of his tight lips. "Maybe it's best we don't eat together," he said as he tied the reins of the surrey.

Hoss lugged the trunk around the front of the team, calling over his shoulder, "Come on, you two, let's get this thing unloaded so we can go eat."

Little Joe jumped from the wagon. Adam twisted around and took one of the valises from the seat, tossing it at Little Joe. The valise plopped a little too firmly against Little Joe's chest as he scrambled to catch it. Then, just as he got it under control, he looked up to see the second valise coming toward him. Little Joe fumbled the first valise, which tumbled to the ground as he caught its mate. "Watch it," he called to Adam.

"You're the one that dropped it," Adam replied, sliding from the buggy and bounding up the steps into the Bristlecone office.

Mumbling to himself, Little Joe dusted off the abused valise, then carried them both inside and up the stairs to Adam's office.

"I'll have a cot brought up here," Adam said to Hoss, who stowed the trunk into the corner of the room.

Tossing the two valises atop the trunk, Little Joe spun around and headed back out the door. "You two coming with me? If so, you better start moving your feet."

"Sure thing, little brother," Hoss answered.

Little Joe laughed. "Too late, Hoss!" He bounded down the stairs and out the door. He heard Hoss call for him to wait, but by then he was out the front door. He hopped into the surrey, untied the reins, and slapped the leather against the rump of the horse, which lifted its head and pranced forward, then made a wide turn in the street. He tipped his hat as he passed the two armed guards, but neither acknowledged him as they had Adam. Little Joe smiled to himself as he thought of Holly Lucas. She would like the surrey and the fact that he was all dressed up. He didn't have to tell her he was wearing a suit because of a funeral Adam insisted he attend.

Little Joe turned up Union Street and then over to C Street and the commercial district, an eclectic mix of saloons and mercantiles, restaurants and law offices. As he passed the International Hotel, he wondered what had happened between Adam and Lucia Sinclair. If ever a pair had plenty in common, it was Adam and Lucia, both enjoying too much from books and too little from life's grand adventure. Now that they had had a falling out, Little Joe only wished Adam had given up the room for him.

Just down the street from the Wells Fargo office was the Nugget Restaurant where Holly Lucas worked. The service was fast, the prices low, the food acceptable, and the owner sober, making it one of the more appealing eateries for working men, and a place where women could eat without their virtue being suspect. It was the slow time of the day between breakfast and lunch, so Little Joe expected to have time to visit with Holly. He pulled the surrey up in front of the door and stared through the grimy window. He thought he saw Holly pass by with a tray of dirty dishes in her hands, so he tied the reins and leaned back in the surrey's spring seat, hoping she would pause and see him. His impatience outweighed his hopes, so he finally crawled out of the seat and straightened his string tie and the lapels on his suit coat before marching inside.

A few customers were scattered about the room, a couple reading the latest edition of the *Territorial Enterprise*, others staring idly at their food. Holly Lucas scurried from the back, holding a pot of coffee, and made the rounds, filling the cups at each table. She passed within ten feet of Little Joe without seeing him.

"Ahem," Little Joe started.

"Be right with you," Holly answered as she grabbed a couple of silver coins from a dirty table and advanced on the next empty coffee cup. After filling that cup, she slid by the dirty table, dropping off the coffeepot and heading for Little Joe. She lifted her head at him and smiled perfunctorily, then realized who it was. The insincerity disappeared from her smile. "Why Little Joe," she said, patting in place a lock of hair which had fallen from the white scarf she wore around her head, "what a pleasant surprise."

"Came to take you for a ride if you can get off work," he said, pointing to the surrey outside.

Holly clasped her hands in front of her full breast. "Oh, Little Joe, you're so dear. And I've another new dress. I think you'll like it." She stepped to him as if to kiss him.

Just as Little Joe reached for her, he saw the owner of the restaurant enter from the kitchen. Little Joe let his hands fall nonchalantly to his sides and Holly stopped.

"No visiting," the owner called, "unless he's a customer. If not, clean that table off and bring those dishes in back. Everything needs to be done before the noon rush begins."

"Yes, sir," Holly called over her shoulder. Then she whispered to Little Joe, "I'll tell him I'm not feeling well, and you can meet me here in an hour and a half."

"I'd just as well eat, and this place is better than most."

"The food's nothing like the International Hotel's."

Little Joe cocked his head and smiled, the curve of his lips accentuating the dimple in his chin. "It's not just the food I'm interested in."

Holly giggled and pointed him to a table. "You're making me blush, Little Joe, now stop it." She offered him a menu, but he waved it away with a brush of his hand. "Bring me what you think I'd like most, as long as it isn't liver."

"Yes, sir," she said, heading back to the kitchen under the watchful eye of the owner. Moments later she returned with a cup of coffee and a tray to clear the adjacent dirty table. As she moved away from his table, Little Joe admired the way she filled out her white blouse and dark blue skirt, and the way curls of blond hair kept falling out from under her scarf. She was easy on the eyes.

He leaned back in his chair, occasionally sipping at the cup of coffee. A few minutes later Holly appeared in the kitchen door, drying her hands on a towel. Little Joe winked. Holly blushed, then retreated into the kitchen. A pair of customers at the back table stood up and wiped their faces with napkins which they tossed atop the skeleton of their meal. The pair strode outside, holding the door open for another customer.

Little Joe caught his breath when he saw who it was. Lucia Sinclair stood motionless a moment,

193

surveying the room, looking from one occupied table to the next, her gaze finally settling on Little Joe. She smiled politely, but seemed at a loss about what to do. Her appearance surprised Little Joe, not that anything was wrong with it. Her dress was neat and proper, her hair, as always, in place, but she fidgeted more than normal and seemed uncomfortable.

"Good day, Lucia," Little Joe said, rising from his seat, "care to join me?"

She sighed slightly. "Thank you, but I mustn't bother you."

"Oh, no, not a bother at all," Little Joe replied confidently.

Lucia Sinclair forced a smile. "Thank you, Little Joe."

Little Joe slid a chair out from the table and seated her opposite him. "How are you doing?" he asked as he settled into his seat.

"Could be better," she said. Her eyes avoided his.

"Something come between you and Adam?"

Her lips tightened and her eyes stared hard at the calico tablecloth. Little Joe thought he saw a ghost of a nod, but he could not be sure and he did not intend to discomfort her.

"Adam's taking it bad too, moving out of the hotel."

Lucia looked up suddenly, hope flickering in her gray eyes for an instant, then disappearing like a candle flame in a stiff breeze. "Adam's got more important worries, like the Bristlecone."

"But not any prettier worries," Little Joe answered softly.

Lucia smiled sadly. "Adam always said you were the charmer in the family."

"Adam knows business and I know flattery."

"Both have their place," Lucia said.

Little Joe nodded. "But flattery's more fun."

Holly Lucas appeared from the kitchen holding a tray with Little Joe's meal. She stopped for a moment, startled to see a woman with Little Joe. Approaching the table, Holly frowned until she recognized Lucia Sinclair. "You're Adam's girl, aren't you?"

Lucia blushed and shrugged.

"This is Lucia Sinclair," Joe said. "She escorted Adam to the fancy ball. Lucia, you remember Holly Lucas?"

Lucia smiled, then pushed her chair back from the table. "Good to see you, Little Joe. Give my regards to your family."

Holly moved beside Little Joe and slid his plate on the table. Little Joe started to move his chair and stop Lucia, but Holly blocked the way. Lucia was at the door before he could do much more than call after her. "Lucia, wait."

The door closed and Little Joe saw Lucia stride away by the window.

"She's not as pretty as I am, is she, Little Joe?"

Shaking his head, Little Joe turned to Holly. "Not at all," he offered halfheartedly, then looked at his plate. Holly had brought a bowl of clam chowder and a plate of steak and potatoes. She had piled so much on the plate, he figured even Hoss would be satisfied.

Holly refilled his coffee cup. "I told my boss I wasn't feeling well, and he said I could leave in about thirty minutes. Then," she whispered, "I'll let you take me for a ride in your surrey." She retreated to the kitchen, leaving Little Joe to attack the victuals.

He ate until he was full, and there was still half a plate of food left. He kept thinking about Lucia and Adam. He always saw Adam as emotionless, never succumbing to the fun and vitality of life. To see that he could affect a woman such as Lucia gave Little Joe a bit of begrudging respect for his oldest brother.

When Holly emerged from the kitchen, she had removed the scarf and her blond hair cascaded down her face. She approached the table in a hurry. "You ready to go?"

"All I need to do is pay."

"I took care of that for you, Little Joe. I'm ready to go, but first take me home so I can put on my new dress."

"I'd be obliged to," Little Joe said, shooting up from the table and slipping his arm in hers to steer her outside.

Holly giggled as Little Joe helped her into the surrey. He dashed around the wagon and bounded into the front seat, the whole wagon vibrating with his enthusiasm as he settled in beside her.

"Oh, Little Joe, this is so much fun," she

squealed as he turned the gelding loose and let him trot away.

Little Joe relished her enthusiasm and her habit of leaning her head on his shoulder.

After the surrey rounded the block, Holly tightened her grip on Little Joe's arm. "How'd things go at the mine today? Any sign things are picking up?"

"Nope," Little Joe replied, "they're getting worse. Assays are $18.25 in the Nina and $13.80 in the Pinta." He liked tossing out those figures to impress Holly.

"That's too bad, Little Joe. I hope things turn around for the mine."

Little Joe smiled. "At least things are going good with us."

CHAPTER 14

Holly Lucas giggled as the surrey disappeared in the darkness. Their afternoon ride had lasted into the night. She patted her hair, straightening it as best she could without a comb, then turned around and stepped onto the porch. Through the window's lacy curtains Holly saw the glow of her landlady's knitting lamp and her landlady slumped forward in her chair, her chest rising with each breath. This was so unlike her, Holly thought as she slipped her shoes off. Holding her breath, she twisted the knob and the door moved the breadth of an eyelash. The hinge groaned softly as she pushed the door open and slipped inside, closing it behind her. Holly tiptoed by her landlady and down the hall to her room, past the darkened doors of the other boarders. At her own door she saw a fringe of light. Her landlady had lit a lamp for her. Again, so unlike her, Holly thought.

Quietly, Holly slipped into her room and shut the door. Leaning against the door, she tossed her shoes on the throw rug by her bed.

"Evening, Miss Lucas."

Holly jumped from the door, too scared to scream. Her hand flew to her mouth as she glanced to her side.

In the corner sat Thurston Smalley, staring hard at her, his yellow teeth exposed between his sinister lips.

Holly spit out her words. "Get out. You're not supposed to be here. I'll scream for the landlady."

Smalley stood up slowly and pursed his lips, gauging her like a snake preparing to strike.

"Get out," Holly repeated. "The landlady doesn't allow it."

Smalley shook his head. "Tonight she did."

"She wouldn't do that."

"She'd never been offered the money I gave her."

"Damn you! I don't want anything to do with you anymore."

"What are the latest assay reports?"

Holly stepped defiantly toward him, waving her fist. "Get out of here. I'm not going to help you." She swung at his jaw.

Snake-quick, his hand flew up and caught her wrist. She was surprised at his reaction and his grip. He squeezed her wrist until it felt as if he would break the bone. He twisted her arm and she gritted her teeth against the pain.

"I'll not tell you," she managed, then gasped as he twisted her arm behind her back and began to shove it toward her shoulder blade. His other hand flew to her mouth, smothering her scream.

"You'll tell me or I'll ruin you, young lady."

She bit at his hand, but he jerked her arm

higher up her back and pain shot like fire along her arm, up her shoulder and into her brain. "I don't want to hurt Little Joe," she mumbled in agony.

"It's too late for that. I'll tell him what you've been telling me." He shoved her arm higher up her back. "I'll break your arm."

She gasped, fearing he would rip her arm from its shoulder socket. "The Nina's at $18.25 and the Pinta's at $13.80," she mumbled through her clenched jaw.

Smalley eased off her arm. "Again."

Holly took a deep breath. "It's $18.25 in the Nina and $13.80 in the Pinta."

Smalley released Holly and shoved her toward the bed. "Don't defy me again. I can hire men to take care of you, men who can make this seem like child's play."

Grasping at her arm, Holly felt her eyes flood with tears. Smalley seemed a blur, even when he stood over the bed. He dug into his coat pocket and Holly flinched, afraid he would bring out a gun or a knife to kill her. Through her blurred eyes she watched him remove his hand and open his palm.

He tossed coins on the bed beside her. "Buy yourself another pretty dress. Remember, I'll be back."

With a disdainful sweep of her hand, she knocked the coins onto the floor. They sounded like hailstones as they hit. "Get out, get out!" she sobbed.

Smalley sneered. "You'd best keep providing me information."

Holly wept as he strode into the hallway, leaving the door ajar. She stood up at the sound of the front door banging shut. She staggered from her room into the now darkened parlor and latched the door. As her eyes adjusted to the darkness, she realized her landlady had gone to bed. Holly suspected her landlady had feigned sleep at her arrival. Then, knowing that she had returned, she had blown out the light and slipped to her own room, leaving Holly to the mercy of Smalley. His money had bought the landlady.

Damn her!

Damn him!

Holly sobbed loudly as she pushed herself away from the door and started for her room. Most of all she damned herself for being such a fool to fall in with Thurston Smalley and for falling in love with Little Joe.

Big Jim Fowler stared at his reflection in the bottom of an empty whiskey glass. It had been late when he marched to Holly Lucas's place. Holly was gone, her landlady wouldn't say where or with whom. Fowler had crossed the street to hide and await her return, but he had grown impatient; the boardinghouse received but one male visitor in all that time, and him a spindly little old man who the landlady, after a long conversation at the door, had admitted into the parlor.

Finally Fowler had given up and gone to the

nearest saloon. Purchasing a bottle of whiskey, he consumed but three jiggers. He had plans for the rest of the bottle, plans that would help revive his reputation as one of the best fire fighters on the Comstock.

Well after midnight Fowler grabbed his bottle and headed outside. The night was still and the mountain air cool. The moon was a dim ivory sliver, dodging the clouds that meandered across the sky like grazing sheep. When the clouds blocked the moon, he would start his fire.

But where? He had considered the Bristlecone mine works, but armed guards patrolled the premises. Around the mine, water wagons were positioned as if others knew his plans. He looked elsewhere, wandering the busy streets for an hour, waiting for the crowds to disperse and the clouds to cover the moon just right. As the number of pedestrians gradually diminished, Fowler found himself on D Street among the brothels and saloons where whiskey and life were cheap.

He shook the whiskey bottle with one hand and patted his pants pocket with the other to feel the bulge of the match tin. Glancing over his shoulder, he saw no one behind him, so he darted between two buildings. Overhead, the clouds seemed to avoid the moon, but that no longer mattered, so confident was he. In the soft moonlight he moved carefully, looking for a wooden footing or a pile of scrap lumber he could douse with the whiskey then set afire. Between the two buildings he found nothing that would work, but behind them he found a lean-to built against the back of the two-story structure. By the noise seeping down from upstairs, Fowler knew it was a brothel.

He looked around, then up at the building to make sure no one was watching from a window. Satisfied, he opened the shed door and slipped inside. He fished the tin from his pocket and extracted a match, flicking it to life against his thumbnail. He smiled at piles of sheets. This was a brothel laundry shed. A black wash pot stood in one corner, the rumpled and stained sheets in another.

The match spent itself, leaving an odor of sulfur which stung Fowler's nose. Uncorking the whiskey bottle, Fowler took a swig, then dumped the remainder on the sheets and added the bottle to the pile. He retrieved another match and scratched it against the shed's weathered wood. The match flared up and Fowler let it grow. Leaning toward the sheets, he tossed the match onto the whiskey stain. Flames swooshed across the sheets and Fowler jumped from the shed, then walked as fast as he could between the two buildings toward the street. At the walk, he looked both ways to make sure no one was watching, then dashed across the street.

He walked briskly halfway down the block and waited. It seemed to take forever for someone to notice the blaze. Fowler could see the glow from his handiwork. Then someone else saw the flames.

"Fire! Fire!" came the yell. Others took it up, and quickly men and women began to pour out onto the street. When a tongue of flame shot up from behind the brothel, the crowd gasped, men and women running to alert others and to sound the alarms. Shortly, the clang of fire bells reverberated through the thin mountain air.

From the torched building, men and women began to run in all states of undress. A few drunks applauded a particularly buxom woman who left her top and her modesty in the flaming structure. Fowler worked his way toward the building, knowing he would be inconspicuous among the crowd now.

Flames began to lick at the roof, and from down the street came the cry of an approaching company of volunteer firemen. "Clear the way," called the leader through his megaphone. Fowler could hear the huffing of a steam pumper, and he knew the fire wagon would likely not have enough steam for several minutes yet to put water on the building. Then he heard the clang of the bell from another approaching fire cart. It was Zephyr Engine Company No. 7 with its hand pumper. The Zephyr boys were shorthanded, as Fowler knew they would be this time of night. Until other volunteers were roused from bed, Zephyr's skeleton crew would need help from everybody. Fowler laughed. Everything was working perfectly. If only the entire block didn't burn down before the night was over.

Fowler rushed from the crowd for the approaching cart and grabbed the wagon tongue to help the volunteers position the hand pumper. The men on the hose cart stopped at a nearby water wagon — one of dozens parked throughout town for fire control — and ran the hose to the pumper. Other volunteers strung hose from the pumper to the fire. The night air was acrid as smoke and embers floated on the fire's draft, carrying with them the potential to burn down all of Virginia City. Fowler took a position at one of the hand brakes and, on the signal from the captain, began to raise and lower the rail. The firemen worked the rail quickly until pressure built. The hose nozzle squirted, spurted, then blew a stream of water.

"First water for Zephyr Company," yelled Zephyr's new captain. Fowler felt resentment raging within him and he pumped harder. Those words should be coming from his mouth.

The two firemen handling the hose followed the captain's instructions, moving closer to the conflagration, trying to steady the powerful hose but seldom succeeding. As more men joined those at the hand pumper, the increased pressure made the task harder for the two hose men. The reinforcements worked the pumper smoothly, so Fowler gave his position on the rail to a late-arriving volunteer, then ran for the hose, grabbed it behind the two volunteers and worked his way toward the nozzle, the stream of water steadying as he advanced. The volunteers glanced over their shoulders, grinning at the sight of Big Jim Fowler.

Fowler braced his legs, then squeezed his powerful hands around the neck of the hose. Behind him the length of carbolized hose writhed from the pressure, but the nozzle was steady upon the building, thanks to Fowler's brute strength controlling the gigantic serpent. A cheer went up from the crowd. Under Fowler's steady hands the water hit the roof and the flames popped and snapped at the steady stream. Another cheer arose as the steam pumper finally sent a weak, then strong funnel of water at the building.

Other volunteer companies arrived, including a hook and ladder team, its men grabbing axes and pole hooks and attacking the building itself, knocking out windows and doors, then scurrying into the flaming building and returning with armloads of furniture and clothing. In a minute enough furniture was piled across the street to fill two houses. Then the hook and ladder volunteers began to knock the building in on itself. With quick action maybe the fire could be contained to this one building. To be safe, the hook and ladder volunteers scoured the buildings adjacent to the brothel, relieving them of their furnishings. If a neighboring structure took fire, these men would dismantle it ahead of the flames.

Other fire companies added their water to the fight, and the fire proved stubborn but manageable. Had even a slight breeze blown in over the mountains, the fire could have devastated Virginia City's entire commercial district. Up and down the street citizens walked with buckets of water and sand, ready to douse or smother any escaping ember.

As the flames receded, the volunteers closed in on its remnants and the crowd began to advance for a closer look. Sheriff Roy Coffee marched among them, ordering them back to give the volunteers room. Coffee assigned a couple deputies to guard the piles of belongings removed by the hook and ladder volunteers.

"Stay back," he shouted. "You best be checking your own places to make sure no sparks have fired your property." The crowd, though, mostly ignored Coffee. Billy Makovy, an abrasive reporter from the *Territorial Enterprise*, tipped his derby at the sheriff and strode past, toward the smoldering rubble that only two hours before had been a busy enterprise. Coffee shook his head. He'd just as soon deal with crooks as newspapermen.

A few minutes later Coffee saw the newspaperman talking to an abundant red-haired woman. He knew her well. "Fat Minnie" she was called, the proprietor of a clean and honest brothel for working men. Nothing fancy about Fat Minnie's place, but her girls were as honest as they came in the trade, and Fat Minnie changed the sheets regularly and didn't let drinking get out of hand among her clientele. As Coffee watched, the reporter pointed at him.

Fat Minnie waddled Coffee's way. She was out of breath when she reached him. Wiping her hand across her smoke-smudged face, she tried to smile, but her eyes were red and watery from smoke or tears. Coffee suspected tears when she tried to speak.

"Ruined, Sheriff, I'm ruined."

Coffee hated this part of his job, trying to console someone who had lost a loved one or property that could never be replaced. "All your girls and customers got out, Minnie. And the volunteers got some of your furniture and things out," he said.

Fat Minnie sobbed, reaching for Coffee's shoulder. "Money, Sheriff. I had more than thirteen thousand dollars in my trunk. It's gone. Nobody got it. The savings from three years work, lost like that."

"Wish there was something I could do to help, Minnie."

Fat Minnie wheezed as she spoke. "There is. You can find the son of a bitch that started this fire."

"You saying this was arson?" Coffee asked.

"My colored boy says he saw a big guy carrying a bottle slip into the sheet shed. He just figured he was another drunk looking for a place to sleep off his liquor. Next thing he knows, the shed's on fire."

Coffee shook his head. "An arsonist. A windy day and there won't be any more Virginia City. Let me talk to your boy."

Fat Minnie grabbed Coffee's arm and pulled him back toward the blackened shell of her brothel. "All gone, all gone," she kept repeating as she steered Coffee toward a neighboring building. There on the steps sat a black youth, maybe fourteen years old. Beside him with his leg propped up on a step was Billy Makovy, his notepad resting on his thigh as he took notes.

"Well, Sheriff, it looks like the *Enterprise* got to the lone witness first," Makovy said.

"If all I had to do, Billy, was pester people, I'd been here before now."

Makovy had a beak for a nose and wide eyes that gave him a hawklike look matching his personality. Coffee, though, preferred to think of him as a buzzard, feasting on the carrion of others' misfortune. Makovy's breath reeked of cheap whiskey and inferior cigars.

"It's part of the *Enterprise*'s never-ending search for the truth, Sheriff."

"Billy," Coffee laughed, "if the *Enterprise* is so interested in the truth, why do you print so many lies?"

"Because those lies," Makovy grinned, "sell a lot more newspapers than the truth."

"First honest thing I've ever heard you say."

"Let me assure you, Sheriff, it will be the last." Makovy took off his derby and bowed to the sheriff.

Coffee pointed toward the volunteer companies. "Why don't you let your search for truth carry you over there?"

As Makovy straightened up, Coffee heard the crowd roar behind him.

"Three cheers for Big Jim Fowler," came a voice amplified through a fire captain's megaphone.

"Hip, hip horray! Hip, hip horray! Hip, hip horray!" chanted the crowd.

A dozen firemen hoisted Big Jim Fowler up on their shoulders and paraded him around the hand pumper of Zephyr Company. "First water for good old Zephyr Company," the volunteers shouted.

"There's your story, Billy," Coffee said.

Makovy laughed. "Sheriff, if you just had a touch more larceny in your soul, you'd make a pretty good newspaperman yourself."

"Get going, Billy, before I make an arrest."

Makovy thrust out his chest. "For what?"

"Public drunkenness."

"Oops," Makovy replied. "I'll see you, Sheriff, but don't forget to read in tomorrow's *Enterprise* about your prominent role in protecting the brothel furniture." Makovy ambled away whistling.

Makovy was equally annoying, drunk or sober.

Fat Minnie had taken a seat by her hired hand and was patting him on the shoulder. "It'll be okay."

"But my books, Miss Minnie?" He leaned his head against Fat Minnie's ample shoulder.

"Son," Coffee said, "I'm sorry about your belongings, but can you tell me what you saw?"

The black youth looked from Minnie to the star on Coffee's vest. "Miss Minnie's teaching

210

me to read real good."

"What did you see?" Coffee asked.

"It was dark, but there was a big man carrying a bottle. He got in the sheet shack, stayed a bit, then he run away. Next time I look, the shack's on fire. I yell and run folks out."

Coffee nodded. "You figure he started the fire."

"Yes, sir, I do. I take too good care of the sheets for it to be an accident."

"He's a good worker and honest," Fat Minnie vouched.

"Can you tell me what this fellow looked like?" Coffee asked.

"It was dark and I couldn't see much, except that he was big, real big."

Coffee looked at Fat Minnie. "Any of your girls entertain any big men tonight?"

"Not that I recall, Sheriff."

"Any of the girls spurned a proposal from a big man?"

Minnie shook her head.

Coffee turned back to the youth. "Look at the crowd. Any of them appear this man's size?"

The youth studied the crowd, then nodded and pointed at a man by the hand pumper, the one the volunteers had been carrying on their shoulders.

It was Big Jim Fowler.

CHAPTER 15

Adam stared at the telegram. His father was having no luck. Even the Cartwright name couldn't attract investors as long as accurate word on the Bristlecone reached San Francisco almost as soon as Adam received the assay reports. Adam wadded up the telegram, shoved it in his pocket and headed for the door. He walked briskly from the telegraph office to the Bristlecone. The moment he walked inside the office, one of his clerks shot up from his seat and pointed upstairs. "Mr. Pyburn and Mr. Eppler are in your office awaiting you."

"Did I forget a meeting?" Adam asked. The way things had been going, something could have slipped his mind.

The clerk shrugged. "They just said it was urgent."

Adam caught his breath and dashed up the stairs two steps at a time. His heart was pounding. They never came unannounced. This could only mean one thing — bad news.

At his office he caught the handle and pushed the door open. Their eyes stern, their lips tight, both men sat at his table, holding copies of the *Territorial Enterprise*. It was trouble.

"Gentlemen." Adam nodded, tossing his hat on the table.

"Have you see today's *Enterprise*?" Pyburn asked from behind his wire-rimmed glasses.

"Not yet," Adam said. "Bad news?"

"You better sit down, Adam. If it's accurate, it's bad news."

Adam was stunned. Taking the paper, he saw an account of a fire that destroyed a brothel and made a hero of Big Jim Fowler.

"Under the fire story," Eppler said.

Adam caught his breath when he saw the headline over the two-paragraph story. B'CONE ASSAYS DOWN read the heading. "Where are they getting this?" Adam asked.

Eppler shrugged. "That's what we'd like to know."

Shaking his head, Adam read the story to himself as the two men looked on.

Times are getting tougher for the Bristlecone Mine and some are speculating it could be the end for Cartwright Enterprises, managed so successfully by Cartwright patriarch Ben since the California Rush of 1849.

Latest reports show ore assaying out at $18.25 a ton at the 1100-foot level and $13.80 at the 1200-foot level. Already, at 1320 feet, the deepest level, mining has been suspended due to the death of a blaster's assistant and even poorer assay returns. The reports are so bad that the Cartwright's beloved Ponderosa may be lost before all the Cartwright debts and liabilities are resolved.

Adam clenched his teeth and dropped the paper.

Pyburn was the first to speak. "Are the figures accurate?"

Adam nodded. "To the cent."

"Damn," said Eppler.

Pyburn folded his arms across his chest. "Could your assayer be doing this?"

"No," Adam said emphatically, slamming his fist on the table. "The samples are blind samples. The assayer can't match them with the level so precisely."

"You have a serious problem, Adam," said Pyburn.

"If any more reports as damaging as this one get out, it'll take the Bristlecone down and the Ponderosa with it," Eppler intoned. "Have you talked to anyone at the paper lately? A newspaperman named Billy Makovy wrote the article, we found that much out. Some say he takes money from Thurston Smalley."

Of all his problems, Adam felt worst about blaming Lucia when the previous figures had gotten out. Lucia could not have known the latest figures. But why had she been talking to Thurston Smalley in the courthouse? He resolved to answer that question later. For the time being, he had to identify who was leaking the information. It could be one of only two people. As much as it pained him to think this, Adam knew it had to be either Little Joe or Hoss. They were the only two he had told the latest figures.

"I'll talk with Billy Makovy," Adam said. If that did not work, he had to set a trap to catch the brother with the loose tongue.

The Enterprise Building was a prosperous structure of red brick trimmed in gingerbread, with a wooden awning that shaded the front walk. Passing through the tall glass door, Adam was assaulted by the odor of printing ink and cheap cigars.

At the front counter a lone clerk was selling an advertisement to a spindly lady and fielding a miner's complaint about a story that ran two days back. Behind them were a half-dozen cluttered desks stacked with papers and pencils and back copies of the *Enterprise*. At one desk, a man had leaned back in his chair, his feet propped up on the desk corner, his hat pulled down over his eyes and a cigar smoldering between his fingers. Beyond the desks, Adam could see into the composing room, where men in ink-stained aprons moved from type case to type case, setting advertisements for the next day's editions. The *Enterprise* bragged that it maintained the first steam-activated press in all of Nevada.

The clerk took silver coins from the woman, who turned up her nose at the rude miner and walked out. The clerk deposited the money in a cash drawer beneath the counter, then clasped his hands together and leaned over the counter at the miner. "I told you yesterday and I'll tell you again, I don't write the stories so I don't make any mistakes. Billy Makovy will be back tomorrow. Today's the day he spends in the hills with target practice. You'll recognize him when you see him, big strong fellow. I'll tell him you didn't like his story, so he'll be real happy to visit with you. Just don't get too close to him. Last fellow that complained too much to Billy Makovy, they found him the next day at the bottom of a mine shaft."

The miner gulped and pushed himself away from the counter.

"All our competing papers said it was an accident." The clerk smiled. "We at the *Enterprise* had our doubts."

The miner turned on his heels and retreated out the door, not even bothering to shut it in his wake.

The clerk snickered a moment, then turned his attention to Adam. "What can I do for you, sir?"

"I gather Billy Makovy's not in?"

The clerk's smile disappeared, and the man reclining at the desk behind the counter pushed the brim of his derby up with the soggy end of his cigar. He had a prominent nose and large eyes.

"It depends," the clerk answered.

"On what?"

"On who's wanting him."

"Adam Cartwright."

The man at the desk dropped his feet, knocking a stack of old newspapers on the floor, and twisted his swivel chair around until he faced Adam. He stuck the cigar in his mouth. "Adam Cartwright, superintendent of the Bristlecone Mine, eldest son of that Nevada patriarch Benjamin Cartwright, the intellectual among the Cartwright boys." The man stood up, doffed his derby and made a bow. "Billy Makovy, the Diogenes of the Comstock, at your service."

Taking in the slender man with thin birdlike features, Adam shook his head. "I was expecting a bigger man after what I just heard."

Makovy unbent his thin frame. "On the pages of the *Enterprise* there is none bigger, Mr. Cartwright, and that is all that counts in my world. None other than Samuel Clemens, Mark Twain himself, worked at the very desk I now call my own. One day the name Billy Makovy will be as world-renowned as his. Need I say more?" Makovy moved from his desk to the postern in the mahogany railing that separated customers from the newspaper staff. He opened the gate. "Please join me."

Adam took off his hat and walked past the newspaperman, who pulled a swivel chair from behind another desk and rolled it to his visitor. Sliding into the seat, Adam waited for Makovy to finish digging around for something on his desk. The journalist pulled out a cigar box and opened its lid to offer Adam one. Adam waved it away.

"Good choice," Makovy said. "The box is imported, but the cigars are not. You are as discriminating as your reputation, Mr. Cartwright. Now, how can I help you?"

"The Bristlecone story in today's paper. What made that news?"

Makovy laughed. "I made it news, Mr. Cartwright. Let me explain. If a dog bites a man, that's not news." He paused to suck on his cigar. He exhaled a cloud of smoke. "Unless, of course, that dog bites a newspaperman. Now, that its news, and yesterday I was bit by a dog with that information."

"Does this dog have a name, Mr. Makovy?"

"Why, yes, he does have a name, and I suspect you'd like to know that name. Of course you realize it would be a serious breach of journalistic ethics" — he flicked his cigar so that a spot of ash fell on the floor — "were I to divulge the name of this particular dog, but I can assure you he is a big dog, and I can also assure you I have no ethics if the price is right."

Adam lifted his hat and started to rise. "I don't pay bribes."

Makovy grabbed his arm. "Mr. Cartwright, you underestimate me. Were I one to sell my soul solely for money, do you think I would've started newspapering?"

Adam settled back in his seat.

"If the Bristlecone comes in, I want to be the first reporter to know about it. Give me the exclusive and I'll give you the name. It's that simple." Makovy shoved the cigar between his teeth.

Adam stroked his chin, gauging whether Billy Makovy could be trusted. The offer was simple, and Makovy would have to show his hand first. Adam nodded. "Agreed. Who was it?"

Makovy leaned back in his chair, studying Adam as if making his own assessment of his integrity. "You won't be surprised. It's Thurston Smalley."

Adam's hands tightened into fists. "Where'd he get the details?"

"Remarkably accurate, were they?"

"Accurate to the cent!"

Makovy shrugged. "I can't help you there. Smalley controls people and information in more ways than I can imagine. Too much money and power and too little integrity, that's Thurston Smalley." Makovy smiled.

Adam no longer suspected Lucia Sinclair. He wished he could be as certain about Little Joe and Hoss. As much as he hated to do it, he knew he must set a trap to snare one of them.

Adam strode down the back hall of the Bristlecone office and pushed open the door to his brothers' bunk room. The door opened silently and he spotted Hoss on his bed reading a tabloid. Hoss shifted in his bunk, the paper rattling in his hands, its corner falling down, exposing his eyes. When he realized he had a visitor, Hoss lowered the paper, then slapped it shut and shoved it under his pillow. He shot up from his bunk.

Adam eyed his brother suspiciously, then closed the door. "What you reading?"

"Just a newspaper, dad-blame-it," Hoss sputtered.

Adam circled the table in the middle of the room and walked to the bunk. Hoss fidgeted with each step. Then his face reddened as Adam pulled the tabloid from under the pillow. Unfolding the paper, Adam took in the lurid line drawings and the sensational headlines. *"Police Gazette,"* he said. "I'm glad you read something, Hoss."

Hoss's shoulders sagged in embarrassment. "It's nothing like the highfalutin literature you read all the time."

"It doesn't matter what you read, Hoss, as long as you read something. If you don't work your body, your muscles'll go weak on you. Same with your brain."

"Boredom'll drive a man to do things out of character, like reading, even the *Police Gazette.*"

Adam tossed the tabloid on the bunk and pulled out a chair from the table. He turned the chair backward, straddled its seat and folded his arms on the backrest. "You miss the Ponderosa?"

"More than anything," Hoss nodded. "City life is fine in small doses, and the bigger the city, the smaller the dose it takes." He circled the table. "That's what's worrying me about this mine. We could lose the Ponderosa. I don't mind a good game of poker, Adam, but the stakes are too high with this gamble."

"Life's a gamble," Adam replied. "You and I know Pa had to take risks to build the Ponderosa. But many times it's harder to keep something together than it is to build something from scratch."

"That's true for your type," Hoss agreed, "but I'm no builder. It's not so easy for my type."

"We're both Cartwrights, Hoss, and that says a lot."

"It won't if we loose the Ponderosa." Hoss stopped in front of Adam. "How are the latest assays?"

Now Adam stood up, moving to the window that looked out at the hoist works and stamp mill. Until now he had never had reason to mistrust his brothers. He knew what he must do, but still it hurt to lie to Hoss. Adam suspected Little Joe was the culprit, not Hoss. Anticipating the figures he would give Hoss would be repeated to no one, Adam would tell Hoss numbers that could be the most detrimental to the Bristlecone. If he were wrong about Hoss, the damage was potentially great, especially if the bogus figures reached San Francisco, where his father was trying to raise money. Adam shook his head and turned to face Hoss, eye to eye. He would tell no one the truth until he could identify the leak. "Both the Nina and the Pinta have dropped below ten dollars a ton," he lied.

Hoss knotted his hand into a fist and pounded his palm.

"The Nina's at $9.65 and the Pinta at $8.10. It's draining us faster than I thought possible. If Pa can't find investors soon, we . . ." Adam let the sentence and the implication go unfinished.

Hoss looked up at the ceiling. "We should've never gotten into mining, Adam."

"Maybe not, Hoss, but mining's so unpredictable that one day you're broke, the next day you're rich."

Hoss pinched the bridge of his nose and squinted at Adam. "I think I could use some air," he said, as much to himself as to Adam. "Maybe I'll go for a walk."

Adam nodded. "I'll stay around the office the rest of the day, so take your time. And one other thing, Hoss."

"Whatever I can do to help."

"I appreciate that, Hoss. I want to break the bad news to Little Joe myself, so don't you be talking to him about it."

"I don't see Little Joe that much now that he's taken to squiring Holly Lucas around. He's more interested in her than in the Ponderosa." Hoss retreated to his bunk, grabbed his boots and wrestled them onto his feet. Standing, he picked up his hat from the overhead bunk and trudged out the door. "Our only luck's been bad luck lately," he mumbled, then disappeared down the hall.

Little Joe poked his head inside Adam's office. "They told me downstairs you wanted to see me."

Adam smiled. Indeed he did. Adam suspected Little Joe much more than Hoss. He doubted it was malicious or intentional, just that Little Joe hadn't grown up as much as necessary to handle sensitive details of the mining business. "Little Joe, I've business to discuss with you."

Little Joe entered cautiously, as if he expected trouble. His fingers wriggled nervously at his waist. "I can't stay long, Adam, I'm to meet someone in a half hour. I need to get cleaned up first. This is Hoss's night to stay here."

Frowning, Adam motioned for Little Joe to take a seat. "Seems Hoss has been staying here most nights."

"Just as well. He ain't doing nothing else, like me." Little Joe settled stiffly into a chair.

"This won't take long," Adam said, "because it looks like things are turning around for us."

Little Joe's nervousness melted and he leaned forward, a slight smile tugging at his lips. "Pa got investors?"

Adam grinned. "Better than that. The ore's grading out high."

"Yeah!" Little Joe shouted, clapping his hands.

"The assay reports today have provided what we've been looking for, in the Nina at least. It assays out at $253 a ton. The Pinta's up, but still under twenty dollars, at $19.75. It looks like we're on the edge of the Big Bonanza."

Little Joe rubbed his hands together. "When do we celebrate?"

Adam held up his arm as a caution. "Not for

a while. In fact, tell no one, and leave it to me to tell Hoss."

"Whatever you say, Adam. I guess you were right about the Bristlecone all along."

Adam hoped he was wrong about Little Joe.

Big Jim Fowler stood on the boardinghouse porch. Many times in the past he had stood here, either picking her up or dropping her off after an evening usually centered around Zephyr Company.

Today he knocked on the door and stood shuffling his feet, awaiting the landlady's scowl. Under his arm he held a copy of the latest *Territorial Enterprise*, with the account of the fire and his part in it. The volunteers of Zephyr Engine Company No. 7 had welcomed him back, not as fire captain, but at least as a member in good standing. He could work his way up to the top again. For now, though, he wanted Holly to go back with him.

The door swung open to reveal Holly's hefty landlady. "Ain't seen you in a while."

Fowler answered with a hard stare.

"I don't suppose it's me you came to see," the landlady said. "I'll see if she wants to talk to you." Before retreating down the hall, the woman latched the door.

It seemed forever before the door swung open. Holly Lucas stood before him, and the landlady, her arms folded over her chest, towered behind Holly. "Could I have a minute with you, Holly,"

Fowler asked, "out here?"

Holly's eyes were awash in confusion. She seemed to have changed so much since the last time they had been out together. Between them, Fowler thought he could still feel some of the old magnetism they had shared, but it was weakening.

"I brought something to show you, Holly."

Holly looked over her shoulder and nodded at her landlady, then stepped toward Fowler. She ignored his proffered hand.

"Did you see the *Enterprise*'s account of the D Street fire? I thought you'd want to hear about it." He pulled the paper from under his arm and pushed it toward her.

Holly shrugged. "I'm not interested."

"What about me? Are you interested in me? I handled the hose that got first water on the fire, maybe even saved Virginia City from Hell's fury. The engine company's invited me back. It'll be like old times, me and the men and you, the belle of the engine company. We'd be the talk of Virginia City, not a better-looking couple around. Please Holly, give me another chance."

"Another chance to hit me, is that what you want?"

Fowler lowered his hand with the newspaper. "I was angry, lost control of myself that night."

"No, Jim, and that's final."

"I could take you out tonight, show you a good time."

"No, Jim."

"Why not tonight?"

"I've got other plans."

"Tomorrow night?"

"No, I'm going to the opera house," Holly said emphatically.

"Damn you," Fowler said, drawing his arm back. Realizing his mistake, he left his hand fall to his side.

"Good evening, Jim, and don't come calling me again."

Big Jim's spirit collapsed. There was no hope. He retreated to the street. As he walked, he ripped the day's paper into shreds and tossed the pieces into the breeze, scattering the fragments of his accomplishments across Virginia City.

There was one man responsible for Holly's rejection. Little Joe Cartwright! Holly couldn't let go of Little Joe. Unless, of course, something happened to him.

CHAPTER 16

Thurston Smalley left the Nugget Restaurant, his mind racing. He usually avoided inferior eateries, but breakfast was his first chance to catch Holly Lucas after her evening with Little Joe. Smalley had choked on his eggs when she whispered the latest assay reports — $253 a ton in the Nina. It was as Smalley feared. The Bristlecone did skirt the mother lode, and time was running out for him to ruin the Cartwrights.

Until yesterday Smalley might have doubted Holly's figures, but that was before Billy Makovy of the *Enterprise* had come calling with a report of Adam Cartwright's visit. Makovy was a cheap one to bribe, a bottle of whiskey, a few dollars, and the promise of a story usually worked. "Accurate to the cent," Makovy had quoted Adam Cartwright in evaluating the figures Smalley had gotten from Holly.

Still, Smalley wanted to confirm those figures through Vorley Deaton, even though Deaton had lost his stomach for this kind of work. Deaton was a man of principle, driven to duplicity to provide a better life for his family. Sometimes, men like Vorley Deaton got eaten up by too much principle. Too much principle could threaten

Smalley, and that's why he strung along a few unprincipled men like the dynamite expert Jesse McMatt to do his dirty work.

Smalley would pay McMatt to kill Deaton, who had spent a night in the hospital after the explosion that killed McMatt's assistant, and was back working the day shift. Smalley left the Nugget and headed to the one-room office he rented in a brick building just down from the Washoe Club. He wrote a note to Deaton. "Tonight at Piper's or else — T.S.," he scribbled, then folded the paper and shoved it in an envelope. He dripped candle wax to seal the missive and addressed it to Deaton at the Miners Union Hall. He stepped out onto the plank walk, watching the passersby until two schoolboys, likely playing hooky, came his way.

"Boys," he called, motioning them over with his index finger.

They studied him suspiciously.

"You want to make two bits apiece?" Smalley asked, and their faces lit into smiles.

"Yes sir," they called in unison.

"Do you know where the Miners Union Hall is on B Street?"

They nodded.

"Deliver this and bring back a receipt. I'll give you a quarter now and a quarter when I get the receipt."

"Sure thing, mister," the bigger of the two boys answered.

Smalley gave them the envelope and a silver

coin from his pocket. The boys darted up the street and Smalley retreated to his office, settling into his overstuffed chair and staring at his uncluttered desk.

Until now he had leaked the accurate assay reports. As long as the assays were declining, they served his purposes in weakening the Bristlecone and plaguing the Cartwrights with accurate reports they could not counter. Now, though, with the Bristlecone turning the corner, the mine's potential price would rise with expectations. To depress the potential price, at least in the public's eyes, Smalley knew he must now disseminate false information. As long as the public thought the Bristlecone a loser, its price would stay low. He could have let false information trickle out all along, making up declining assay figures each day, but that did not suit the cruel streak that coursed through his soul like blood through his veins. Not only did he want to take over the Bristlecone, but he also wanted to break the fortune and the spirit of Ben Cartwright in this game of financial cat and mouse.

Smalley heard the clatter of feet on the plank walk outside, then the door swung open and the two youths rushed in, both out of breath and one waving a slip of paper.

"Here's your receipt," said one. "Where's our quarter?"

Smalley reached into his pocket and extracted a small silver piece, flipping it on the desk. One boy dropped the receipt, the other grabbed the coin. "Thanks, mister," he said as both spun around, then darted outside to spend their new fortune.

It should be an interesting meeting, thought Smalley, tonight at Piper's Opera House.

Big Jim Fowler left the firehouse at dusk. All day he polished the brass fittings on the hand pumper because tonight the city would need it. Tonight a great tragedy would befall Virginia City. Since Holly Lucas had spurned him yesterday, Fowler had waited for this moment. If he couldn't have Holly Lucas, neither would Little Joe or anyone else. It was a shame that so many others would have to die with them once he set fire to the opera house.

Fowler patted the tin of matches in his pocket as he walked into a saloon on the way to Holly's boardinghouse. He bought a bottle of cheap whiskey for later and a jigger of a better brand for now. The whiskey went down easy. He slammed the jigger hard on the bar, then spun around and was out the swinging doors before the bartender could reprimand him for taking his frustrations out on the counter.

Outside, the evening air was cool and a brisk breeze was blowing from over the Sierras. Fowler laughed. It would be a dangerous fire in this breeze. He avoided the sporadic pools of streetlight puddling around the newly lit gas lamps. He turned up a familiar street, as he had done many times before on his way to Holly's boardinghouse. He skulked to the vacant lot across the street and waited. He wanted to be certain they actually attended the play. After all, it would be a great tragedy to burn the opera house down without them.

Within fifteen minutes Fowler was surprised to see Little Joe standing on the porch. He had expected Little Joe to come in a carriage, but instead he had come afoot, which made it easier for him to tail them to the opera. Little Joe knocked on the door, and Holly Lucas joined him shortly. They hugged, then Little Joe put his arm around her and they ambled down the street. Fowler followed.

Sure enough, Little Joe steered Holly Lucas to the opera house, where they disappeared among the throng of people who had come to see a production of *Romeo and Juliet* by a traveling Shakespearean troupe. Fowler clung to the darkness, planning to wait until well into the first act before setting his fire in back of the theater.

What a tragedy this fire would be. Fowler laughed. He would be as big a hero tonight as he had been at the brothel fire. To celebrate, he uncorked the whiskey bottle and took a healthy swig. This whiskey packed a punch. He wondered how well the building would burn.

It didn't make sense. The perfect trap had failed. Adam was pleased that he hadn't caught one of his brothers giving out information on the Bristlecone. And yet he was perplexed. The latest rumor was that Bristlecone assays had dropped slightly, but were still above ten dollars a ton. He had told Hoss that they had fallen below ten. The rumors had been accurate to the penny previously, but why not today? Hoss wasn't devious enough to figure out the trap and respond with a false trail. Adam leaned back on the cot in the corner of his office.

It still didn't make sense; none of it did. He did know one thing, though. He had been a fool to blame Lucia Sinclair. He must apologize to her tomorrow.

At least the day's rumors tended to vindicate Little Joe. Or did they? Adam shot up from his cot. Wait a minute! Adam clenched his teeth. Thurston Smalley was likely the one behind those rumors, rumors that served his purposes only when they were bad for the Bristlecone. Adam slammed his fist into his palm. That was it! It had to be Little Joe who was talking. But to whom? And why? Little Joe wouldn't intentionally tell anyone. Adam had to talk with him. He grabbed his boots and jerked them over his sock-covered feet. He moved to his desk and blew out the lamp, then strode out the door and down the stairs, past the vacant desks in the darkened office and down the hall to where a light shone around the door rim.

He swung open the door, catching Hoss on his bunk reading his copy of the *Police Gazette* again.

Hoss dropped the paper on his chest. "What's

the all-fired rush, Adam?"

"Little Joe, I need to talk to him," Adam answered.

Hoss grinned. "It'll have to wait. He's not here."

"It won't wait. Where is he?"

"Out with Holly Lucas, I suppose. He said something about going to the opera house," Hoss said. He knocked the *Gazette* on the floor as he sat up. "Trouble? You sound serious."

Adam stared at Hoss, evaluating whether to speak his suspicions. "Little Joe's been telling someone about our assay reports."

"Nah," Hoss replied, scratching his head. "Why would he do that? He wouldn't risk the Ponderosa."

Crossing his arms, Adam nodded. "Maybe not intentionally, but word's been getting out regular, and you're the only ones I've told the last two days. Have you been telling anyone, Hoss?"

"Nope, I ain't spoken to anyone about the mine."

"Then it's got to be Little Joe."

"Sure it ain't the assayers?"

"I've been sending blind samples. No one knows but me and the people I've told."

Hoss's brow furrowed and he stared hard at Adam. "How can you be sure some miner isn't taking samples out and having them assayed?"

"Good question, but it's unlikely that a separate assay would come up with a figure that matched mine to the penny."

Hoss's shoulders sagged. "Not Little Joe?"

"Afraid so," Adam replied, "afraid so. I've got to find him. You think he's at the opera house?"

"Yep," Hoss said, moving to his boots. "I'm going with you."

"Sorry, Hoss, one of us needs to stay here."

"Dad-blame-it, Adam, this can't be right. If it is, he don't mean nothing bad by it. I wish Pa was here to handle it."

"Little Joe's got to grow up sometime," Adam said. He turned and walked out the door.

Vorley Deaton could just make him out, clinging to the shadows near an entrance to the opera house. From years in the mines, Deaton knew something about darkness, but the pitch-black of a silver mine seemed less sinister than Thurston Smalley blending in with the shadows like some ghostly figure. Deaton could not recall when Smalley wasn't something of a ghostly figure amidst the crowd. Odd, Deaton thought, that Smalley craved secrecy but always arranged these meetings in a public place with dozens of people passing by.

Deaton took a deep breath and started toward Smalley, unable to make out the stock manipulator's shadowy face. It was time, Deaton knew, to break with Smalley. The manipulator had ruined several investors on the Comstock, but those men had been as greedy as Smalley himself, never caring for the miners — the very men whose sweat built their fortunes. The Cartwrights, though, had always treated the miners fairly. When some mine owners had talked about reducing wages from four dollars a day, Adam Cartwright had opposed that move, even at a time when it would have helped him financially. Deaton couldn't spy on the Cartwrights, couldn't lead this crooked life anymore. Smalley's tainted money had helped his family, but a man had to live with himself. Deaton was finding that harder to do.

As Deaton reached Smalley, the stock manipulator snarled, "I didn't signal you."

"I'm not taking your orders anymore," Deaton replied.

Smalley's thin lips curled into an evil smile. "You'd better reconsider, Deaton. Nobody walks out on me unless I give them the okay. I want to know which laterals are open and how the ore looks."

Deaton stared hard as bedrock at Smalley, trying to prove he wasn't nervous, but Deaton knew he was scared, scared of what Smalley could do or have done. The ore didn't look good at all, but he would never tell it to Smalley, not that it mattered to the speculator. He had bought so many other people, he could always get the answer. But it mattered to Deaton to finally prove to himself he was honest. "I'm quitting, nothing else to report. I should've never thrown in with you in the first place."

Smalley's smile disappeared. "I made you more money than you'd ever made for yourself," he whispered under his breath.

"Dishonest money," Deaton shot back.

"Money's money." Smalley reached inside his rumpled coat, and Deaton stood frozen, his gaze following his hand as it would a coiled snake. Smalley jerked his hand from beneath the coat lapel and Deaton flinched. Smalley held out a key. "Let me show you one of the privileges money can buy. The key to my box," Smalley said, pointing through the door to a curtained compartment overlooking the stage. "Enjoy Shakespeare from my box. It'll give you time to reconsider throwing away your only shot at wealth." Smalley grabbed Deaton's hand and dropped the key into his limp palm.

Deaton shook his head. "Can't do it."

"You don't have to do it, Deaton, but you will. Otherwise I'll let the word get out that you've worked for me. Who can say that some of the folks I've ruined might not come looking for a little revenge. You'll be ruined on the Comstock, if not dead. Think about what you're throwing away Deaton. Your pangs of conscience could be threatening your only shot at being wealthy, not to mention your safety. And your family's."

Deaton drew a deep breath and looked away from Smalley. He must get his family out of town. He must buy time. He would acquiesce to Smalley's offer and accept the box for the evening. To do otherwise might bring harm to his family before the night was over. He must send his family away tomorrow, then he would join them in a couple days. He nodded at Smalley. "I'll reconsider," he said, waving the key limply at him.

"Good choice," Smalley answered. "I always like to leave a partnership on good terms. The last thing I'll want from you is information on which laterals are open and what the ore looks like." The manipulator seemed to taunt him. "Odd thing, though, people who break a partnership with me never seem to last long on the Comstock." Smalley laughed and walked away, clinging to the shadows as he disappeared against the flow of people.

Deaton entered the opera house, made his way to the stairs, then climbed to the narrow hallway that led to the boxes. He let himself into Smalley's box, which overlooked the right side of the stage. It was a small box with room for four seats. Instead there was but one. Thurston Smalley had no friends. Deaton could understand why as a hush fell over the crowd and the curtain rose on Shakespeare.

The walk had been brisk, his anger building with each step as Adam approached Piper's Opera House. With the house lights down, it would be impossible for him to find Little Joe in the darkness, so he killed time awaiting the end of the first act.

He circled the block once, twice, enjoying the breeze that blew in over the mountains. The streets were quiet. A few men scurried about in the darkness like giant insects.

On his first trip around the block, Adam had seen a hulking shape at the back of the opera house, acting suspiciously. He could just make out the shadowy form of a man. As he turned the corner, he looked behind him and saw the profile of the man against a distant street lamp. The man lifted a bottle to his lips. He would probably be found tomorrow morning dead drunk behind the opera house. Drunkenness was one of the hazards of working on the Comstock.

His second time around the opera house, Adam turned the corner and looked for the drunk. He saw nothing, but heard the sound of shattering glass, then an evil laugh. As Adam looked at the back of the opera house, he saw a match flare as if someone was lighting a cigarette. He could not make out the man holding the match because the match's tiny ball of light did not reach the man's face. The man tossed the match away and the flame tumbled in an arc to the back of the opera house. The match struck close to the building, then whooshed in a great ball of blue fire.

Adam gasped. An arsonist! "Stop!" he yelled.

The arsonist seemed confused for a moment. Then he darted away.

"Stop," Adam cried. "Fire in the opera house. Fire, fire!" he screamed at the top of his lungs. At the back of the opera house he kicked dirt at the flames. "Fire, fire!" he kept yelling, and others took up the cry. In moments bells began to ring throughout Virginia City.

The opera house's wooden wall was as dry as

a Baptist convention, and the ravenous flames licked it wildly, crackling and sputtering and dancing in the breeze. The flames had climbed halfway up the building. Adam ran to the windows, shouting the alarm inside.

From inside the opera house arose the screams of women and the shouts of men. "Fire, fire," they called as they stared at death's red eye. Adam stood at the last window, helping men and women who were climbing out.

Other patrons charged out the front doors, screaming with panic. The tide of humanity overflowed the street with terror. Some women collapsed on their knees, sobbing uncontrollably as they considered what could have been their fate.

From down the street, Adam heard the sound of approaching pumper wagons and volunteer firemen. "Clear the way, clear the way!" came the cry as firemen pulled a steam pumper behind the building, a hose cart following in its wake. Men uncoiled hose and strung it to a nearby water wagon.

Other fire companies soon joined the battle, each moving to the sheet of flames that was the theater's rear wall. Patrons of the opera house still stampeded for the street. Adam did not see Little Joe. He just hoped his youngest brother was safe.

CHAPTER 17

Big Jim Fowler cursed as he sprinted to the Zephyr firehouse. Why hadn't he seen the man who raised the alarm? If the fire had had a better start, it would have been unstoppable, and likely fatal to Little Joe Cartwright and Holly Lucas. Fowler cared less now for Zephyr Engine Company No. 7's reputation than seeing that Little Joe and Holly met the death they both deserved. They might yet die in the stampede for the exits.

Someone must have beaten him to the Zephyr firehouse, Fowler realized, because the distinctive peal of the Zephyr bell carried strong in the breeze. Turning the corner, Fowler raced the final fifty yards to the building. Two volunteers were pushing open the double doors while others took positions on the tongue of the hand pumper or donned their leather fire helmets.

"Big Jim Fowler's here," a volunteer called.

"Good," answered another, "now we can get going."

Fowler felt his chest swell with pride. The volunteers still needed him, still believed in him, still knew a fire wasn't under control unless he was in charge. He grabbed a leather helmet from a hook, tugged it down over his head and tightened the strap under his chin. He scrambled to the front of the hand pumper.

"Men," he shouted, "let's get first water for Zephyr Company."

The volunteers responded with a cheer.

Fowler grabbed the handhold with his large paws and put his massive shoulders to the task. "Pull," he called, and the pumper budged, then rolled forward. Down the inclined ramp from the house, the pumper gained speed and Fowler steered it onto the street. "Pull, men, with your muscles and your heart."

They shouted their response and the pumper accelerated.

"We'll save Virginia City," Fowler yelled, and the men answered with a final cheer, then saved their breath to pull the pumper to the opera house.

Thurston Smalley couldn't believe his luck. As he walked to the International Hotel for dinner, someone ran by saying Piper's Opera House was afire. Smalley glanced over his shoulder. It was indeed. Could he be so lucky that Vorley Deaton would die in the flames? What a tragedy that would be. Smalley laughed to himself. Deaton would die. It was just a question of whether the fire would kill Deaton before he hired Jesse McMatt to do it.

Smalley moved against the tide of curiosity seekers rushing to the opera house. He detested them. Didn't they have better things to do? He certainly did! Dinner.

Tomorrow would be soon enough to find out if Vorley Deaton had survived. Why let something as inconsequential as that interfere with his evening meal?

Smalley walked up the steps into the International Hotel, its lobby and its restaurant virtually abandoned except for employees.

"A table, sir?" asked a mustachioed waiter.

"Certainly," Smalley replied, "away from the window, where I don't have to watch this circus outside."

It was the worst place to be in the whole building, Little Joe thought. He threw his arm around Holly Lucas and pulled her toward him. He could feel her trembling and he knew he must find a way out. At first no one realized what that distant warning was about, only that it detracted from the play. Then suddenly, everyone seemed to understand. Fire! The opera house was ablaze!

All at once the audience rushed the doors, the windows, anything wide enough for a person to slip through. Chairs were knocked over, men and women tumbling atop them, screaming and crying for help. Little Joe and Holly sat in the middle section, near neither aisle. For a moment on stage the actors froze, then a knife of flame cut through the back wall behind the scenery. The actors faced a real-life drama now. They ran from the stage, shouting their warnings and clambering among the spectators to escape. In the commotion, their voices were little heard. The few people who had not panicked up to then did so when the acrid stench of burning wood, long weathered, seeped into the theater.

Holly Lucas trembled, growing limp in Little Joe's arms. "We'll make it, Holly, just hold onto me," he instructed. The aisles were thick with people, people who could have escaped easily in an orderly evacuation but who, in their panic, tripped over one another, becoming thrashing, screaming obstacles for those behind them and increasing everyone's terror.

"Keep your heads!" Little Joe yelled into the human vortex, but no one listened or cared about anything except escape. The aisles were overflowing, and Little Joe knew it was futile to fight the terrified throng. His mind was spinning. Holly was crying. Little Joe swept her up in his arms and looked to the back. The doors were jammed with people, but they were squeezing outside. If he could get to the doors, he could barge through to safety with Holly. The aisles, though, were flooded with people, so he would have to carry Holly through the jumble of overturned seats between him and the doors. He took a deep breath, his head throbbing at the acrid smell of burning wood, then plunged into the tangle of overturned chairs and benches. He climbed over seats, stumbling regularly, banging his shins, weaving around piles of wrecked chairs, gasping for air, hoping his strength would hold out. Holly was limp in his arms.

He walked and climbed and staggered under her weight, but the door did not seem to draw any closer. Then all of a sudden it loomed before him. Little Joe plunged with Holly into the mass of people flailing at the opening. They were caught in a human tide that surged forward like a great serpent caught in a small opening. They made it past the inner door and inched toward the outer door, moving in spurts. Finally Little Joe reached the outer door and the theater seemed to spew them free. He ran, drawing deep breaths of the cool, fresh air, which revived Holly. She sobbed in his arms as he toted her across the street and deposited her on a plank walk where other frightened women sat trembling and crying.

"Thank you," she managed. "I'll be better shortly, and maybe we can go to the back and watch the volunteers."

She confused Little Joe. At first she had been so scared she had fainted, yet now she wanted to watch the fire. Before he could figure it all out, Holly had jumped to her feet, grabbed his arms and started pulling him toward the back of the building where the fire companies had gathered.

A hand pumper and two steam pumpers were already behind the opera house, attacking the burning wall with powerful streams of water as new water wagons arrived. The flames appeared as fiery blades of grass waving in the breeze.

"Look," Holly pointed, "there's the men of

Zephyr Company and Big Jim."

Little Joe grumbled acknowledgment.

"I was belle of the Zephyr Company, you knew that didn't you, Little Joe?" she asked.

Little Joe nodded, but she didn't notice.

"Look," she screamed, pointing at the back door, "someone's on fire."

Vorley Deaton gulped. His knees were jelly and his hands trembled. As a miner, his greatest fear had always been fire, but fire in a mine, not in an opera house. Had Thurston Smalley done this? Likely so, the bastard!

Deaton knocked over the lone chair in the box as he scrambled for the exit and safety. Jerking the door open, he saw the narrow hallway crammed with others, making a human bottleneck at the stairs. Fear bordering on panic rose in Deaton, especially as he caught the odor of smoke, wood smoke. The opera house would become his funeral pyre. Abandoning the door, he looked over the stage and audience below Smalley's box. There was total pandemonium. The spectators scrambled for the aisles, climbing over the chairs, clambering over one another. The exits were clogged with horrified men and women. Clumps of men and women clawed at one another by the windows. The exits were all too far away or too crowded for him to get out.

Below him only the stage was quiet, the actors having deserted it for the exits. It was twenty feet down, but it was his only chance. Deaton climbed to the edge of the balcony and balanced himself by holding a fold of the curtain that draped the box. He took a deep breath and swallowed hard, then leaped for the stage with a scream. It took forever and ended suddenly when he hit the floor. He rolled with the impact, then lay spread-eagled on the stage, momentarily stunned. His ankles hurt and his shoulder throbbed, but nothing seemed broken. He rolled over on his hands and knees, shaking his head of the confusion spawned by terror.

He had to get out! He couldn't die in a fire, not like this. In a mine he knew not to retreat from a fire, but to try and get through it. Behind him he saw doors and windows clogged with people. He did not have time to get out that way. There had to be a back exit. He saw a tongue of flame cut through the back wall. Through the smoke, did he see a door at the back corner of the stage? Was his desperate mind playing tricks on him? He could run through the smoke, but what about fire? Looking hurriedly around the stage and behind the curtains, he found a pile of blankets used for props. He grabbed a couple, shook them to loosen their folds, and draped them over his head, leaving a slit he could see through while covering as much of his body as possible. He took a deep breath and ran for the corner door, driving deep into the smoke. His lungs burned from the acrid fog and his brain was ablaze with fear. Deaton stumbled over the blanket which dragged at his feet like death's sinister

246

train. When he reached the wall, he slapped his hand against it, feeling his way to where he thought the door was. It wasn't there! Was he imagining, had he missed it? Then his hand brushed against the door frame. He grabbed the doorknob and screamed at the touch of hot metal against his flesh. He was growing weak and disoriented from all the smoke. With all his might he threw his shoulder into the door and it gave way.

Deaton stumbled forward in a daze. The heat was intense all around him. He thought he saw people beyond the smoke but he could not be sure. Now he was more confused. He stood there, knowing he was about to die and cursing the day he had started taking Thurston Smalley's dirty money. Then for some reason he could not explain, he felt his breath knocked from him. He tumbled backward onto the ground. Hell could be no more terrifying.

Big Jim Fowler maneuvered the carbolized hose back and forth, dousing the top of the opera house so water ran down onto the flames, keeping the fire from spreading beyond the back wall. So many people had escaped from the opera house, he considered his arson a failure. Little Joe Cartwright and Holly Lucas had likely survived. Now his fire-fighting instincts took over. There was the city to save. Fowler worked the nozzle adroitly, like an extension of his arm. He felt all eyes were trained upon him as if he were the leading actor on the theater's stage.

The crowd gasped, then screamed. From fighting past fires, Fowler knew that sound. He lowered his gaze from the top of the building to the windows and finally to the ground. He saw a door swing open, flames licking at its exterior. In the flaming doorway stood an apparition, a ghostly form with pockets of flame dancing on its torso. The apparition stumbled out of the building, then stood dazed on the ground, its robe afire.

The crowd seemed paralyzed. No one moved to help. With his powerful arms, Big Jim Fowler fought the recalcitrant hose and the muscle of the two men behind him as he lowered the stream of water from the roof to the door, dousing, then knocking the apparition over. Here was his chance, Fowler thought. "Take over," he yelled to the two men wrestling the hose with him. He waited a moment for them to plant their feet and slide up toward the nozzle. Then he let go. The hose convulsed for a moment as the other two men fought it. Fowler dashed ahead, running as hard as he could, straight for the flaming doorway. Behind him he heard a great cry, and then he was amidst the flames, grabbing the form wrapped in smoldering blankets on the ground. He jerked the man up like a doll and slipped his arms beneath the shoulders and knees. Turning, he dashed for safety, feeling the full heat of the fire. The crowd cheered him. He stumbled, then caught his balance, and the spectators shouted even louder. He retreated behind the line of fire hoses spewing water on the blaze, and behind the pumpers and fire wagons to a plank walk. He lowered the man to the walk and shouted instructions for others to take care of him. Then he ran back to the hose and took over the nozzle, directing a steady stream of water against the building.

Fowler smiled to himself. A few more rescues like that and he would be reelected captain of Zephyr Company, or better yet, chief of a paid city fire department.

Even in the darkness, Adam recognized the heroic fireman as Big Jim Fowler, the one who had turned the hose on Little Joe at the brewery fire. Fowler was a big man, like the one who started the fire. Adam wished he had been able to catch the arsonist as well as spread the alarm, but time had been short. The alarm had saved lives, dozens of lives. Somewhere among the milling crowd, Adam expected to find Little Joe. He still had a few questions for his youngest brother, whom he was certain had gotten out unharmed, his younger brother being resourceful, if nothing else. Adam wandered among the crowd, looking for but not finding Little Joe. Instead he saw Sheriff Roy Coffee.

"Stand back, folks, give the volunteers plenty of room," came Coffee's avuncular voice.

Adam advanced toward Coffee, who stood in the middle of the street, motioning for people to get back from the fire equipment.

"Roy," Adam called, waving his arms to attract the sheriff's attention.

Coffee looked around the crowd. His eyes finally settled on Adam. "I need help," Coffee called. "Give me a hand."

Adam stepped out in the street and motioned for the crowd to stay back. Most obliged but several slipped past.

"We were lucky, the breeze like this, that the thing didn't spread," Coffee shouted.

"It was arson," Adam answered.

Coffee's arms dropped to his sides and he turned to stare at Adam, ignoring a couple of men who walked by. "Says who?"

"Me," Adam said. "I saw a big man start it. He broke a bottle of something against the building and threw a match on it."

"You recognize him?"

"No, sir," Adam replied, "and I didn't have time to chase him and raise the alarm at the same time."

"That's just what Virginia City needs, a crazy arsonist and a high wind. He'll kill us all yet."

Behind them the flames were disappearing beneath a steady curtain of water. People in the crowd were carrying lanterns, and a few held torches to help the firemen see. Even with the limited illumination, Adam could see that the back wall of the opera house had disappeared in places and was blackened elsewhere. "Anybody hurt tonight, Roy?"

"A lot of scared folks, and a couple may have broken arms or legs getting out of the opera house. The only other one was that crazy fool that came out the back door. He burned his hands some, but wrapped himself in a couple blankets that protected him from the flames. All told, I'd say we came out pretty lucky."

One derbied man headed straight for the sheriff. Adam recognized Billy Makovy, the reporter for the *Enterprise*. "Sheriff," shouted Makovy, "any truth to the rumor that this was more arson?"

Adam slipped away into the crowd to avoid Billy Makovy and his questions.

"Come on, Little Joe," Holly Lucas said, tugging at his arm to lead him toward the exhausted men gathered in a clump around the hand pumper of Zephyr Company.

Little Joe held firm for a moment, until he saw the pleading in her green eyes. He studied the men around the pumper. Not seeing Big Jim Fowler among them, he stepped begrudgingly in their direction.

"I hope they got first water," Holly said.

Little Joe could only shake his head. Less than an hour ago, he — not the volunteers — had saved her from the stampede and fire. Now she wanted to congratulate the volunteers. That wasn't what he had been anticipating once the fire was out.

Holly dragged Little Joe reluctantly forward.

A couple of the men perked up as she approached. "You boys made me proud," Holly called out. "Did you get first water?"

"Nope," answered a tall slender one. "One of the steam engines did, but they didn't have to come as far as we did."

A half dozen of the Zephyr volunteers mumbled agreement. "You need to come visit us more," another one said. "You're still the Zephyr belle to us, no matter what happened between you and Big Jim."

"I'd like that," Holly said, shyly averting her gaze from the men of Zephyr. "I miss all you boys." Her voice quivered. "You do such good work. Tell Jim how brave he was, rushing into the fire."

Little Joe could sense the true emotion in her voice, an honest feeling he had never noticed between himself and her. She seemed genuinely sad. Little Joe put his arm around her shoulder, perplexed that this deep emotion had replaced her passion for him. "Maybe I should take you home."

Holly nodded and turned away. "Good-bye, boys," she said over her shoulder. Little Joe heard her sniffle as she leaned tight against him. "My parents and three sisters died in a fire four years ago. You don't know what it's like, Little Joe, to see your home burn and know the people you love are inside. In the opera house, I was scared, scared I would die like them."

"I didn't know," Little Joe said.

"It's a hard thing to talk about," Holly answered softly. "It brings back such bad memories. I could only stand there and watch them die. I should've tried to reach them, but I couldn't. Working with the Zephyr volunteers lets me live with myself after failing my family."

Little Joe stopped and turned her face to his. He kissed her forehead, then pulled her to his chest and ran his fingers through her hair. "It's okay." His words seemed to soothe her. The stiffness in her stance softened and her body seemed to mold against his. Her clothes and her normally fragrant hair smelled now of acrid smoke. She could wash the odor from her hair and her clothes, Little Joe thought, but she could never remove the terrible memory of losing her family.

Around them Little Joe noticed some people had stopped to stare. He did not care, until he saw Big Jim Fowler standing in front of him.

Fowler stepped forward, hands clasped in front of his belt. "Holly," he said.

Little Joe felt Holly tighten in his arms, like a rope drawn taut. "I'll take you home now," he said.

"I just want to talk to her a minute," Fowler said. "She's lucky to be alive. If that fire had taken hold while she was in the opera house . . ."

Little Joe stopped instantly. "How'd you know she was in the opera house?"

"What do you mean by that?" There was a

challenge in Fowler's voice. "She always comes out to fires to help. It's her way, and I know that."

"But you said she was inside. How'd you know that, Fowler?"

The fireman shook his fist. "What do you mean by that?"

Little Joe released Holly's arm and brushed her away, planting his feet to meet whatever Fowler came with. "Sounds suspicious to me, Fowler. Suspicious like this fire."

Fowler charged Little Joe, swinging. Little Joe ducked and landed a solid punch in Fowler's stomach, but before he could get out of Fowler's reach, the fireman grabbed him and both men tumbled to the ground, rolling around in a circle of cheering spectators.

What was all the commotion? Adam had seen nothing of Little Joe and he felt the anger welling within him. From the shouts down the street, Adam gathered it was a fistfight. He trotted that way, figuring a fight would attract Little Joe, if he were around.

Adam elbowed through the circle of men and women encouraging a fight. In the dimness it was hard to tell who was fighting. Adam looked around for Little Joe, then heard Sheriff Coffee's voice over the crowd noise.

"Make way for the law," Coffee yelled. "Coming through." The sheriff shoved his way into the circle where the two men thrashed at each other. "Break it up," Coffee yelled, "and come with me."

Adam recognized one combatant as Big Jim Fowler. Then Adam spit. The other was Little Joe. The anger in Adam burst like floodwater through a weakened dam, and he shoved his way to the inner perimeter of spectators just as Coffee waded in between the two men.

Adam jumped beside Coffee, shoving Little Joe backward while the sheriff occupied Fowler.

For a moment Little Joe was stunned, not recognizing Adam. Then he smiled.

Adam grimaced at the smile. It was just like Little Joe to mock him. Adam could contain himself no longer. He drew back his fist and plowed into Little Joe's nose.

Little Joe staggered backward, grabbing at his bloody face. "What was that for?" he yelled, then charged into Adam, punching him in the gut.

Adam gasped for breath. The two brothers grabbed one another and collapsed onto the ground, swinging wildly and unsuccessfully at one another.

"What the hell," called Sheriff Coffee. "Somebody give me a hand. This whole town's gone crazy."

CHAPTER 18

"What's gotten into you two boys?" Sheriff Roy Coffee marched around his desk and stared at Little Joe. "I know there's bad blood between you and Fowler over the Lucas girl." Turning to Adam, he shook his head. "But Adam, I can't figure why you would attack your own brother."

Little Joe rubbed his nose and cocked his head, awaiting Adam's response.

Adam nodded. "One day, Roy, I'll explain."

Little Joe scowled. "Pa's gone and he thinks he's in charge."

Adam took a step toward Little Joe. "I am."

"I wish your pa were here," Coffee said, stepping between them, "because I know he wouldn't put up with this nonsense. And you boys don't know what kind of bind you're putting me in. I'm a friend of yours, a friend of your father's, but if you two don't put this behind you, I'm gonna have to lock you both up."

Little Joe grinned. "Adam's never been in jail."

Adam glared at Little Joe.

Coffee only shook his head. "If you two'll give me your word there'll be no more trouble between you, I'll let you go in a bit."

Little Joe rubbed his tender nose and glared at Adam.

Adam shifted on his feet, nodding reluctantly at the sheriff. The Bristlecone could not afford his absence, not with Pa gone.

"Do you agree with that, Little Joe?" Coffee asked.

"I owe Adam one, but I won't pay him back in Virginia City," Little Joe answered defiantly.

Coffee planted his hands on his hips. "I figured as much. I sent for Hoss. Once he gets here, I'll turn you two over to him, and if I hear of any more trouble between you, I'll give you a couple night's lodging on Storey County."

Adam and Little Joe eyed each other warily as they waited.

The sheriff plopped into his chair and rubbed his eyes. "Things must be going bad at the mine for you two to be at each other's throats." He stabbed his hand at a pile of reports. "Paperwork! If I arrest you, I have to fill out more paperwork, and I'm tired of that." He snatched a pencil from his desk and began to scribble disgustedly. The scratching of Coffee's pencil broke the room's icy silence.

There was the sound of footsteps outside, then the door swung open and a deputy entered, dwarfed by Hoss behind him. Hoss's face was puzzled as he looked from Adam to Little Joe and then to the sheriff.

Glancing up from his desk, Coffee nodded at his deputy. "Did you see Fowler back to the firehouse and advise him to stay away from Little Joe or he'll go to jail?"

"I did," the deputy said matter-of-factly.

Coffee sighed. "Make your rounds and I'll handle it from here."

The deputy touched the brim of his hat and retreated outside.

Scratching his head as he looked at his brothers, Hoss stepped to the sheriff's desk. "Roy, what in tarnation's going on here?"

"Your brothers have been in a fight."

"I'd fought with them if I'd been there," Hoss answered.

"They were fighting each other!"

"Dad-blame-it!" Hoss shot a hard glance at Little Joe, then at Adam. "I knew I should have gone with you, Adam."

Coffee walked around the desk. "Hoss, I'm deputizing you. You're lone responsibility is to keep these two apart and civil."

Hoss flinched, his face contorted with confusion. He scratched his ear. "Dad-blame-it, why isn't Pa here to handle this?"

"If you can't do it, I'll just throw them in jail."

Hoss's face darkened even more.

Adam grinned for the first time since entering the sheriff's office. He could make Hoss accept Coffee's offer. "You'll be in charge of the mine if I don't get out of here, Hoss."

Hoss shook his head, then ran his fingers through his thinning hair. "I don't have to wear a badge, do I, Roy?"

Coffee laughed. "You don't even have to take an oath. Give me your word you'll keep them from settling this problem with their fists. It'll just be a little agreement between you and me."

"I guess so," Hoss said, looking back and forth between his two brothers. "Let's go, you've both got some explaining to do."

They sat on opposite sides of the bunk room, while Hoss prowled the floor between them.

"Why'd you hit me?" Little Joe demanded loudly.

"Easy, Little Joe," Hoss commanded.

Adam stood up and pointed his finger at Little Joe. "You've been hurting the Bristlecone and the Ponderosa."

Little Joe jumped up. "That's a lie!"

"Then how come the assay reports have been getting out to the penny?"

Little Joe shook his fist at Adam, but the anger seemed to melt from his hand. Holly Lucas! He had told Holly Lucas of the assay reports! Had she told others? Little Joe slumped into his chair.

Adam's words sang with anger. "Have you told anyone, I mean *anyone*, about those assay findings?"

"Tell me how you figure all of this," Little Joe challenged.

"I want an answer," Adam demanded.

Hoss held up his hands. "Tell him how you figure it, Adam, if you're faulting him."

"Every day I told you and Hoss the figures,

259

word has come back from the street precisely to the cent on the assay reports. Yesterday, I told you and Hoss different figures."

Little Joe shook his head. He thought Holly Lucas was as taken with him as he was with her. Had she been using him? "Did the numbers you told me get back to you?"

Here, Adam paused and took a deep breath. "Not exactly."

Little Joe shot up from his chair. "Then just what makes you think I'm the one?" Maybe Holly hadn't betrayed him after all.

Hoss scratched his head. "Here's where it gets confusing, Little Joe, so hear him out."

Adam paced the room. "Information was getting out. Precise information." He paused, stopped, stared at his brothers. "I had accused Lucia of spreading the word. I even caught her one night at the courthouse speaking with Thurston Smalley."

Hoss whistled. "That explains you and her breaking up."

Adam nodded. "After that, the only two people I told were the two of you. Still, the exact figures became rumor. One of you had to be telling someone because there was no other way."

Little Joe melted back in his chair. "You told us different stories?"

"I did. I told Hoss the assay reports were below ten dollars a ton, and I told you we'd struck the big bonanza, that we were assaying out twenty times better than that. The rumors came back that we were still losing money."

Little Joe cocked his head at Adam. "Then it isn't my fault!"

"Afraid it is," Adam replied.

Little Joe could only scratch his head.

"Thurston Smalley is trying to drive the Bristlecone into the ground. As long as prices drop, the truth serves his purpose. Had he heard prices were below ten dollars a ton, he would have circulated that rumor quickly. As it was, he had to make up declining figures, which didn't match those I'd given Hoss. Fact is, Little Joe, you're the secondhand source of his rumors."

Leaning forward, Little Joe rested his head in his palms. "I didn't mean any harm telling Holly Lucas. She's the only one."

"Thurston Smalley may have gotten to her. He's an evil man."

Little Joe looked up at Adam. "Why'd you attack me at the fire?"

"I was boiling mad, Little Joe. Things still aren't going well at the Bristlecone, and every day the threat to the Ponderosa grows."

"You can't blame me," Little Joe shot back. "I wanted to sell."

Adam felt his shoulders sag.

"Don't get into that again, Little Joe," interjected Hoss. "What's done is done. We were outvoted so we should accept it and make the best of it. Right now, it's late and I figure we'd all be better off getting a little sleep."

"You're the deputy," replied Adam, striding

to the door. His thoughts were on Lucia. Come daylight, he must make amends with her.

Standing outside the Nugget Restaurant, Little Joe watched Holly Lucas as she carried a coffeepot table to table, filling cups and taking breakfast orders. Little Joe wondered if her looks belied a treacherous spirit. He had thought she might love him, but had she only been pretending so she could use him? He frowned, even after Holly happened to glance out the window and spotted him. The courteous smile she was giving the diners widened into a genuine grin. Little Joe thought he saw her wink at him before she moved on.

After the Nugget's customers thinned out, Little Joe walked inside, taking a chair at a corner table. Instantly Holly was beside him, coffeepot in hand. "Morning," she said, her voice genuine as her smile. "I was wondering if you were ever going to come inside. You look like you survived all the excitement last night."

Little Joe rubbed his nose. "It's a bit sore," he acknowledged.

"Maybe I can help you feel better tonight," she said coyly.

"I'm not sure," Little Joe said, "but let me ask you a question."

"Anything." She smiled, then looked over her shoulder for her boss. Not seeing him, she slid into the chair opposite Little Joe. "I'm buying a new dress this afternoon so I'll be pretty for you."

Little Joe studied her. How could anyone so beautiful be so deceitful? And her dresses? Holly was spending a lot of money on clothes, money she likely didn't earn waiting tables.

Her smile widened more. "You better ask your question before my boss accuses me of loafing."

"Holly, have you been passing information to Thurston Smalley about our assay reports?"

Holly's smile disappeared and she stared at him blankly.

Little Joe had his answer. Adam had been right, damn him. Damn Holly Lucas!

"I did it once, Little Joe," Holly said softly, her eyes watering, "after he came to me to help bail you out. I took his money to buy a new dress so you would like me. I told him I didn't want to do it anymore. He said he'd tell you what I had done the first time if I didn't keep on." Her pleas brimmed with desperation.

Little Joe pushed his chair back and stood up.

"Don't leave, Little Joe. I love you. Thurston Smalley said your father was a mean-spirited man and this would help you against him." Holly's chin sagged and she stared blankly at the coffeepot before her.

Little Joe walked around the table and stopped beside her. With his index finger, he lifted her chin. "The Cartwrights take care of themselves."

Staring at the dwelling of Lucia Sinclair, Adam waited at the end of the block. As punctual as a fine pocket watch, Lucia Sinclair emerged from her home as she did each work day, thirty minutes before the courthouse opened. Lucia seemed preoccupied and did not notice Adam until she was almost upon him. When she spied him, her face lit up for a moment, but the smile faded instantly and she walked faster. Adam took off his hat and moved in step beside her.

"I came to apologize," he offered.

She ignored him.

Adam took her arm in his hand and slowed her. She finally stopped. Adam turned her around until she faced him.

"I should have known better than to think you would have violated a trust," Adam said. "Things were just going badly at the mine, still are, and I should never have been such a fool."

Lucia's eyes softened. "I didn't do it, I promise."

Adam nodded. "I know. Little Joe was letting the information out."

Instantly Lucia shook her arm free and pointed her finger at Adam's nose. "Don't come to me now and apologize, now that you know who did it."

Adam shook his head. "That's not how I meant it. I'm sorry, Lucia, truly sorry."

"If you'd trusted me, you'd have come to me before now. If you can't trust me, Adam, then I can't accept your apology. Our friendship has got to be based on trust." Lucia started for the courthouse again.

"I saw you with Thurston Smalley. I admit I

jumped to the wrong conclusion."

Lucia stopped again to face him. "For information on the Bristlecone, Thurston Smalley offered me something I've always wanted, Adam, the chance to practice law in Nevada, to become the first woman ever to do so. He said he'd pull strings in the legislature in Carson City, make suffrage possible. I'm not fool enough to think he would have carried through on his promise, Adam, but you know how much I've wanted that."

Adam sensed her disappointment in him and in her unfulfilled ambition.

"Good day, Adam Cartwright." She marched toward the courthouse.

Adam scratched his head. He had handled that about as poorly as he had the Bristlecone. He retreated to his office.

Thurston Smalley leaned back in his chair. It was dark outside. Even so, he had drawn the office curtains and adjusted the lamp flame until it was but a soft glow. Too bad the fire last night hadn't killed Vorley Deaton. It would have saved him a thousand dollars, Smalley thought. Despite a few burns, Deaton had reported to his shift at the mine today. Such a pity that he would now have to pay for two deaths.

Smalley heard a key click in the lock, then turn. The door opened slightly and a man with a broad-brimmed hat covering his face slid inside. The door closed with a snap. On time as usual, Smalley thought, as Jesse McMatt relocked the door and came inside.

"Did anybody —" Smalley began.

"Nobody recognized me or saw me enter, Thurston."

"I always like to check."

"You got a job for me?"

Smalley motioned for McMatt to take a seat. "Two jobs!"

McMatt smiled, ignoring the chair across from Smalley, and sat instead on the corner of Smalley's desk.

"A thousand apiece," Smalley offered.

"Depends on who it is."

"Vorley Deaton."

The explosives expert reached for the box of imported cigars in the middle of Smalley's desk and claimed one for himself. He shoved the cigar between his crooked teeth and his hand into his britches pocket, pulling out a tin of matches and a couple of blasting caps.

Smalley flinched at the sight of the blasting caps. "You carry those around with you?"

"This too," McMatt laughed, slipping his hand in his other pocket and pulling out a stick of dynamite. "Don't get nervous, Thurston. It would just make a little bang."

"Don't bring explosives in here ever." His voice rang nervous.

"If I'm to do your dirty work, Thurston, I'll do as I please. Now, we're getting away from why you called me here." McMatt lit the cigar carelessly. "A thousand dollars is a good price for Vorley Deaton. Fact is, I almost got him for you last week for free." McMatt laughed. "Who else do you want me to get?"

Smalley grinned. "Adam Cartwright."

McMatt whistled. "Five thousand for such a prominent man."

"Five thousand it is, but I want both of them killed within the week."

"Sure thing," McMatt said, tossing a blasting cap toward Smalley.

The stock manipulator caught the blasting cap and instantly pitched it back at McMatt, who snapped it out of the air with his snake-quick hand.

"You're the meanest man on the Comstock Lode," Smalley said.

McMatt turned his back and started for the door. "No, Thurston, that honor is all yours."

CHAPTER 19

Adam emerged from the telegraph office as he did each morning since his father had reached San Francisco. In his hand he carried Ben Cartwright's latest telegram. The message was simple, though the implications were not. "No luck, return home tomorrow — B.C." The Bristlecone had gone bad, Lucia had left him, and now his father was coming back empty-handed. What else could go wrong?

Unless the assay reports improved, Adam was running out of options. He had considered dropping from three shifts to two. That would save money but would cost time. The Bristlecone was running out of both, as confirmed by the telegram he crumpled in his fist. Rather than reduce crews, why not add one and reopen the Santa Maria? If they had to sell, buyers would want samples from all levels.

The assay reports from the latest shift would be in by noon. Adam wished for a miracle but knew it was unlikely. He personally had gathered the reports, but they had shown little promise. Adam knew he was deluding himself. It seemed so futile. As he turned toward the Bristlecone, he glanced up Mount Davidson and saw the abandoned works of the Montgomery Mine. It had once been a promising property, but now it was in ruin, like the hopes of its owners. Was the Bristlecone destined for the same fate?

A few clerks had arrived early, opening the Bristlecone office and lighting a few lamps until sunlight took hold. Adam nodded listlessly as he walked past them to his brothers' room. Seeing no light under the door and hearing no sign that his brothers had arisen, Adam figured they were still asleep. Why bother them? Neither cared for mining or its problems. Adam tramped back through the front and up the stairs.

At his office, he saw the glow of a lamp shining under the door. He had forgotten to blow the lamp out before he left. He couldn't remember to do anything right anymore. Opening the door, he was surprised by Hoss and Little Joe sitting at the table.

"Morning, Adam," said Hoss humbly. "We had a talk last night and figured we haven't been the kind of partners you needed. We're here to help."

Adam tossed the telegram on the table.

Little Joe grabbed it, unwadded it, read it silently, then aloud.

Hoss whistled. "It's hard to believe Pa had no luck, as many wealthy folks as he knows in San Francisco."

"It's the reach of Thurston Smalley," Adam said.

Little Joe's head drooped and he bit his lip. Adam took this as acknowledgment that Little

269

Joe had confronted Holly Lucas and confirmed Adam's suspicions.

"Where do we go from here?" Little Joe asked meekly.

"In debt," Adam replied.

"We're here to help," Hoss said, then grimaced. "That didn't sound right."

"Nothing does anymore," answered Little Joe. "Anything we need to do, Adam?"

Adam nodded. "I'm planning on taking the assay samples myself from now on. Other than that, we'll wait until Pa gets back. There's always Smalley's offer."

Little Joe slammed his fist against the table. "No, not him, not now! He ruins everything he touches. I'm with Adam."

"Thanks, Little Joe." Adam pulled his watch from his pocket and checked the time. "I'll be heading into the mine shortly to gather samples."

"Mind if I go along?" Little Joe asked.

"I'd like that," Adam responded.

Another successful shift, Jesse McMatt thought as he dropped the case of dynamite on the rock floor. Some nearby miners quickly retreated from him and his dynamite, not stopping until they had reached the hoist landing and rang the bell for the cage. McMatt had blown dynamite in three locations. Every stick had exploded, and another three or four feet of stubborn rock had crumbled. When dynamite didn't blow, there was always the risk that the next crew would strike it with a tool and detonate it. McMatt didn't mind losing an occasional miner, but he hated it when his reputation was sullied. A blaster who left too much dynamite undetonated soon developed a bad reputation on the Comstock. That was one thing McMatt preferred to avoid, particularly at times like these when he could kill for money. If you killed too many in accidents, it drew attention to you when you killed them on purpose.

McMatt sat his lamp up on the dynamite case, took a candle from his pocket and lit it. He let a little candle wax drop atop the crate, then worked the candle into the wax so it stood upright. He fetched his lunch bucket, retrieved his coffee cup, his tin of water, and a small tobacco pouch containing ground coffee. He filled the cup with water and dropped in a pinch of coffee, then squatted and held the cup over the candle to boil. Over the flame, the tin cup grew hot in McMatt's hand, which had grown callused against fire from years of lighting fuses and handling explosives.

Gradually the coffee boiled and McMatt smiled. He put a patch of stained cheesecloth over the cup's top to strain out the grounds as he drank. As he enjoyed his coffee, the new shift came on, men fresh from a night's rest, men still wearing pants and shirts they would soon discard in the mine's oppressive heat. Several miners looked askance at the candle burning atop the crate of dynamite, then scurried by without a word. McMatt knew dynamite was more stable than most men thought, so he was not worried. Many miners thought the explosives men were as unpredictable as their dynamite. Such a reputation kept miners out of his way.

McMatt leaned his head back to suck the last of the coffee from the cheesecloth strainer. When he pulled the cup away from his lips, he saw a miner standing in front of him. Vorley Deaton. McMatt nodded at the man he planned to kill.

"Put out the candle and get your lamp off that dynamite," Deaton commanded.

McMatt stood up to challenge Deaton, but thought otherwise when he realized that trouble between them would raise suspicions when Deaton was killed. McMatt jerked the cloth from atop his coffee cup, then banged the cup against the tunnel's solid wall, jarring the grounds to the floor.

"That fire's dangerous," Deaton said.

"You should know," McMatt said, bending over and dropping his coffee cup into his lunch bucket. "Ain't you the one that almost got fried at the opry house?"

"I made it okay."

"My my," McMatt said, "I figure a man that didn't know enough not to run through a wall of fire shouldn't be telling me how to attend a candle."

"What I did," Deaton responded firmly, "only risked my life. You're risking every man in this mine. No man has that right."

McMatt fought the urge to strike Deaton, to whip him here and now. It would please him to take care of Deaton later. McMatt bent over the dynamite case and blew out the candle. As he straightened up, he lifted the lamp from the crate. "Now the mine's safe for you and all the others," he said sarcastically.

Deaton shook his head. "The mine'll never be safe as long as you're in it."

McMatt felt his fists tighten. He stepped forward, then pulled himself back. Deaton had exhibited no fear.

From down the tunnel came a voice: "Hurry up, Vorley."

"Coming," Deaton called, and walked away, deeper into the darkness, his lamp casting a yellow ball of light that gradually faded from view.

McMatt watched him disappear. Yes, he would take great pleasure in killing Vorley Deaton. He waited a couple of minutes, until he figured no more miners on the new shift would be along. Then he reached in his pants pocket and pulled out a corncob pipe and a pouch of tobacco. It was against regulations to smoke in the mine, but McMatt regularly disregarded that rule. A good smoke helped steady the nerves. A man who dealt with dynamite could be trusted with a pipe. He filled the pipe and lit the tobacco, inhaling deeply.

At the end of the tunnel he heard the signal bell ring. Someone was approaching. No sense in letting them see a lit pipe. That might jeopardize the $6000 he would get for killing Vorley Deaton and Adam Cartwright. McMatt saw no place to hide the pipe, except for the case of dynamite. He lifted the lid and sat the pipe upright between two sticks of dynamite. After replacing the lid, he propped a foot atop the crate and stared down the tunnel toward the hoist. Shortly, McMatt made out three swinging lamps, then three men approaching. McMatt recognized the shift supervisor, Adam Cartwright, and his brother Little Joe.

As the trio reached McMatt, the shift supervisor, an iron-armed, iron-headed miner of thirty years, held up his hand. Adam and Little Joe stopped too. The supervisor and Adam sniffed at the air.

"Has somebody been smoking, McMatt?" asked the shift supervisor.

McMatt nodded. "A miner passing by here a while back had a cigar he'd got at some saloon. I made him put it out."

The supervisor's eyes narrowed. "You sure it wasn't you and that damned pipe of yours?"

"You're welcome to check around, see if I'm hiding it somewhere." McMatt kicked the case of dynamite. "Why don't you start looking there?"

"Damn you," shot back the supervisor, "don't be doing crazy things like that. You may not know it, but this is Adam Cartwright, who runs this mine."

"I've seen him before," McMatt said, sitting down on the crate.

"You'll be seeing more of him," the supervisor said, "and his brother Little Joe here. Adam'll be collecting samples for the assay reports after most shifts from now on. You do what he says because he's the big boss, you understand?" The supervisor stood akimbo.

"I understand real well," McMatt replied, "but there's one thing he needs to understand. He may run the office aboveground, but down here in the ground, he's a man no different than the rest of us. Down here the earth is in charge."

"Let's go," Adam said to the shift supervisor.

The three men marched on. "Damned hard-headed blasters," the supervisor said, his voice carrying back to McMatt.

"Isn't he the one whose assistant we buried?" Little Joe asked.

"Yes, sir, Mr. Cartwright, that's Jesse McMatt. His apprentice panicked after they'd set the charges. Very unfortunate, that accident, the only man ever to die in the Bristlecone."

Adam interrupted. "You sure it was an accident?"

When he could hear them no more, McMatt got up and cracked the crate lid. He extracted his pipe out and stuck it between his teeth. Leaning against the rock wall behind him, he inhaled deeply on the pipe stem, then laughed strangely. If Adam Cartwright was going to be handling samples every day, he would be as easy to kill as Deaton. McMatt knew the mines from the bowels of the earth, not from the comfort of a plush office like Adam Cartwright. There would be a dozen ways to kill Adam Cartwright, and every one of them would look like a legitimate accident.

McMatt finished his pipe and tapped the burned tobacco out onto the mine floor. Adam would be the easiest $5000 Jesse McMatt had ever made.

Little Joe could not remember his father's eyes ever so deeply etched with worry. When Ben Cartwright stepped off the railroad coach at the Virginia City depot, Little Joe saw something he had seldom seen in his father — failure.

"Pa," Little Joe called, waving his hat.

A fleeting smile moved across Ben's face as he spotted Little Joe and Adam. Ben walked somberly across the crowded platform.

"Glad you're back, Pa," Little Joe said.

Ben shook Little Joe's hand, then grabbed Adam's. "I didn't do us any good," he replied. "Too many bad rumors about the Bristlecone and too few people willing to take a chance on investing."

"They weren't all rumors," Adam said. "Some were true."

Ben shook his head. "Did Thurston Smalley have a plant?"

Little Joe caught his breath. No sense in letting Adam tell on him. "Pa, I —"

Adam held up his hand. "I'm not sure, Pa. All I know is, now I collect the assay samples and tell no one the results, save Little Joe and Hoss." Adam nodded at Little Joe.

Little Joe exhaled slowly. Adam had protected him.

"Where's Hoss?" Ben asked, handing Little Joe his valise.

"Back at the mine office," Little Joe said with confidence. "We're just doing what you ordered, keeping someone at the mine at all times."

Now Ben shook his head. "Now Little Joe, what are you hiding? You're just too accommodating for there not to be something more behind all of this."

Little Joe gulped and he could feel his face reddening. He looked from his father to Adam, who answered his gaze with a slight grin. Little Joe looked down at his boots a moment and shuffled his feet. "Pa, I probably haven't been as big a help as I should've with Adam," he admitted. "I made the mistake of telling —"

Before he could finish his sentence, Adam slapped Little Joe on the back. "Enough of this," he stated. "We had some differences on things, and we got them settled without having to stay in jail but an hour or so."

Little Joe's jaw dropped. He could not believe what Adam had just said. Now they were in big trouble.

Pa looked from Adam to Little Joe, then his stony face cracked into a smile followed by a chuckle. He stepped between his two sons and draped his arms over their shoulders. "That's the only laugh I've had in days. At least you boys still know how to joke."

Little Joe leaned forward so he could see Adam on the other side of his father. Adam just winked, and Little Joe could only shake his head. Adam had told the truth, and yet Pa had taken it as a joke. Why didn't he ever have such luck? Little Joe asked himself.

Adam offered a bemused nod at Little Joe, as if he could read his little brother's bewilderment, but the amusement in Adam's eyes deflated at Ben's next question. "It true you've moved out of the hotel?"

Little Joe grimaced, knowing that his loose tongue around Holly Lucas had driven a wedge between Adam and Lucia Sinclair. He cleared his throat. "Adam figured it was unfair, me and Hoss staying at the office with him in the hotel. He decided to move in with us."

Ben Cartwright nodded. "Maybe you boys don't need me around. There's less friction between you two when I'm away."

"Seems that way, doesn't it, Pa?" Adam said. All three men laughed.

The fuse hissed and sputtered as it made its way to the pockmarked wall at the end of the crosscut. Jesse McMatt watched for a moment, then ducked into a side tunnel as the fire entered the drill holes. The hissing stopped for an instant, before erupting with an explosion. To the un-trained ear, it was one long explosion, but to McMatt it was a series of individual detonations which he could count either by their differing times or intensities. His brow furrowed for an instant. One stick of dynamite had yet to go off. He peeked around the corner just as the final stick exploded. The dynamite's hot breath slapped his face, and a few bits of rock struck his cheek like hot needles. McMatt's laugh was drowned out in the booming echo that bounced around the tunnel.

McMatt drew his finger across a trickle of blood on his cheek, then licked off the red smudge as he stepped out into the crosscut. The air was clouded with dust and haze from the explosion. Now he would just wait and watch. Adam Cartwright would be coming by shortly to gather samples. He would be followed by the next shift of miners, who would clear the latest debris and then begin to drill the new wall.

McMatt ordered his assistant to gather tools while he himself walked to the end of the crosscut, holding his lamp in the air to cut through the haze so he could admire his work. Tomorrow he would set his trap for Cartwright in the Santa Maria, the deepest of the laterals. It had just been reopened, but was being worked by just a single crew.

How best to kill Adam Cartwright? McMatt pondered leaving a few sticks unexploded, but it would be mere chance for Cartwright to detonate them. He must come up with a sure thing. If he could plant a stick or two of dynamite that wouldn't go off in the initial explosion, he could rig them to go off when Cartwright was around.

As he rubbed the rock wall he had just created, McMatt stood proud as a sculptor before a completed work.

He laughed sinisterly. By this time tomorrow afternoon, Adam Cartwright would be dead, and he would be $5000 richer. If Vorley Deaton happened along, he could add another thousand to his earnings. A man couldn't ask for a better day's work.

CHAPTER 20

Holly Lucas was glad to be home after a long day at the Nugget Restaurant. Nothing had gone right, from the breakfast plate she had dropped to the sugar bowls she had filled with salt. She hadn't realized the difference, but her customers did, spitting and sputtering over bitter coffee. Holly had drawn too many of her boss's hard stares and too few of her customers' tips. Nothing had been the same since Little Joe had left her. After entering the boardinghouse and nodding to the landlady, Holly trudged to her room and opened the door. Sunshine poured into the room like water out of a bucket. Her landlady must have done this, she thought; Holly never opened the curtains before work. As she closed the curtains with a jerk of her wrist, she was startled at the sound of the door closing behind her. She spun around.

Thurston Smalley stood there, his beady eyes watching her like prey. Holly scanned the room for a weapon, then picked up her hand mirror from the dresser. "What do you want?" she snarled.

Advancing toward him, Smalley pulled his gold toothpick from between his thin lips.

"I'll hit you," she said as menacingly as she could, but her voice squeaked like a mouse. She lifted the mirror. "I mean it."

Smalley pointed the toothpick at her. "What are the latest assays?"

"I'll scream," Holly said, brandishing the mirror. "Now leave!"

Calmly, Smalley slipped his toothpick into his coat. "Put down the mirror," he said. As his hand cleared his pocket, his fingers held a derringer. "I don't miss many at this range," he said.

Holly hesitated.

Cocking the derringer, Smalley waved it at her nose. "Try me."

Her hand dropped reluctantly to her side and she replaced the hand mirror on the dresser. "Little Joe found out I was passing information to you. He left me because of you."

"Such a pity," Smalley said without emotion.

"I might have been rich, married to Little Joe," Holly said.

Smalley lifted his free hand and held his index finger just a hair away from his thumb. "And I'm this close to destroying the Cartwright empire."

Holly clutched at her throat. "Don't hurt Little Joe."

"I wouldn't hurt him, just like I wouldn't hurt you," he answered, waving the derringer, "unless you did something foolish. And then . . ." He left the threat unfinished.

Holly thrust her chin forward in silent defiance,

but her stomach was aflutter. Smalley seemed but a blur behind the stubby barrel of the derringer.

"Little Joe's not my game, nor you," he said, "unless you see him again. If you do, I'll have you both killed."

Holly hated herself for letting Thurston Smalley into her life with his petty bribes. He had ruined her chances with Little Joe. She hated him for it, yet felt helpless to retaliate. "I don't believe you."

Smalley laughed as he lowered the derringer. "You don't? See if something doesn't happen to Adam Cartwright in the next couple days. An accident, say." Smalley slipped the derringer back in his pocket, retrieving his toothpick.

Seeing her chance, Holly charged at Smalley, her right hand flying for his face.

Smalley twisted his head and caught only a glancing blow from her fingers, but lost his hat and gold toothpick. Rage flared in his eyes and his lips twisted into a grotesque snarl. Cat-quick, his hand grabbed her hair and jerked her toward him.

Holly gasped from the searing pain and his surprising strength. Then he shoved the heel of his palm against her face and pushed her onto the bed.

"You just committed suicide," Smalley said, rubbing at his face.

Though her head pulsed with pain, Holly managed to hide her agony, but not her fear.

Smalley picked up his hat, then strode across

the room to retrieve his gold toothpick from the corner. "I'll send someone to settle our differences," he said, then whirled around and stomped out the door.

Holly flew from the bed to the door and latched it. Her heart raced and her breath heaved with fear. What would she do? Where could she go? Where could she hide? How soon would he send someone? What about Little Joe? Had she endangered him? A thousand questions ran through her mind, but not a single answer. All she knew was that she had to leave, had to find a place to hide, and quick. She fell to her knees by her bed, reaching beneath it to pull out a valise. She threw a few clothes inside, an extra pair of shoes, her hairbrush and hand mirror. She must run away, but where?

Holly stepped to the door. What if Smalley was watching the front? She turned and leaned against the door, her eyes tearing with fear and helplessness, then coming to focus on the curtained window. She could crawl out the window, maybe slip unseen into oblivion.

Jerking the curtains open, she pried the latch free and lifted the window. She tossed her bag out, slid awkwardly through the window, landed on both feet, grabbed her valise and ran.

The sun had disappeared behind Mount Davidson, and the cool of a dying day had set in. She scurried down the street, distancing herself from the boardinghouse. But to where? Zephyr Company, that's where! The volunteers, they would protect her.

Running until she stumbled and almost fell, she caught her breath, but always kept moving, aiming in the direction of the Zephyr firehouse, constantly looking over her shoulder for Smalley. When the firehouse appeared at the end of the block, she ran on fear. Her heart pounded as she reached the door. She gasped for breath as she flung the door open and stumbled inside. It was as she remembered, the pumper all shiny and clean, everything in perfect order. Holly slammed the door and bent over to catch her breath. This was where she belonged. As she straighted up, she saw a form looming behind the hose cart.

It was Big Jim Fowler, his eyes hard and cold.

"I've come back," Holly said meekly.

Fowler stared suspiciously, his silence expressing his skepticism.

"I'm back to stay, Jim." She dropped her valise and stepped past the hand pumper toward the hose cart and Big Jim Fowler.

Tossing his clean rag over a wheel on the hose cart, Fowler advanced emotionlessly toward her.

Holly cried with joy. He wanted her back. Everything would be okay, she thought, until she saw his uplifted arm and the blur of his hand as he struck her across the cheek and nose. She fell to the wooden floor.

He had not meant to hit her so hard, but he

could not control his rage. This was Little Joe Cartwright's fault and one more reason why he had to settle his bad account with Little Joe. Fowler wanted Holly back, but she would have to return on his conditions. He bent over and picked her up, his emotions wavering between rage at her original betrayal and relief that she had returned to him, returned to Zephyr Engine Company No. 7.

His anger diminished with each step as Big Jim Fowler carried Holly to the firehouse's back office. Light seeping through dirty windows revealed a spartan office with a cluttered desk, a wobbly chair, a rough-hewn bunk with straw mattress, a pile of rags in one corner, and a table with pitcher and washbasin by the door. Gently, he placed her upon the bunk. She groaned as she settled on the mattress. He had forgotten her beauty, her blond hair so soft, her lips so pink and full. He would not hit her again, he promised himself. He would care or her, keep her forever.

Over in the corner, he picked up a clean rag from the supply the volunteers kept for polishing equipment, then walked to the washbasin and dampened it. Returning to Holly, he knelt at her side and patted her head with the damp cloth.

She began to moan, flinching occasionally as the soft rag passed over the bruise on her cheek. Her green eyes fluttered open a moment, then closed again.

"I didn't mean to hurt you," Fowler kept whispering. "I won't ever do it again. Just don't leave me."

For a long time Holly seemed oblivious to his words. The room grew dark as night conquered the day outside, the only illumination coming from a distant lamp in the equipment room. She was so still. The only sign she was alive was the softness of her breath upon his hand as he patted the damp cloth against her face.

When she spoke, it startled Fowler. "You've got to protect me."

He scowled. "I'll take care of Cartwright."

"No, no," she gasped, "from another man. Thurston Smalley."

"What? Thurston Smalley, the speculator?" Fowler felt her head nod against the cloth. Was she delirious? "But why?"

Holly held the answer within her. "Don't ask, please. Just protect me. I'm scared. I'll stay if you protect me from him."

Fowler lifted the damp cloth from her face and rubbed his own forehead, which had beaded in sweat. He did not understand this strange plea, but the terror in her voice convinced him she was truly scared. Dropping the damp cloth on the floor, he sat on the edge of the bed and slid his strong arm under her shoulder. He cradled her head in his arms. "I'll protect you," he whispered, "as long as you stay with me."

She burrowed herself deeper in his arms, like a cottontail hiding in its den from a predator. "I'll stay."

Fowler pressed his lips against hers. She returned his affection, and it was as if they had never been apart.

Outside the office door, Fowler heard a noise. He cursed to himself, especially at the call of a familiar voice. "Anybody back there?" It was one of the volunteers.

Gently, Fowler lowered Holly back onto the mattress, then stood up. "Big Jim's here," he called back as he went to the door. He held his fingers up to his lips for quiet. "Holly Lucas is back."

The volunteer cocked his head in a suspicious stare.

"She's back for good, but had a nasty fall and bruised her face pretty bad. I want her to rest, so keep it quiet, especially when the others get here."

Nodding, the volunteer angled for a glimpse into the office of Holly Lucas. Then he moved to the hand pumper and grabbed a rag to attack the brass fittings.

Fowler retreated into the office, bent over and kissed her. "Tomorrow everything will be fine," he whispered.

Exiting, Fowler closed the door and marched triumphantly to the hand pumper. Things were finally looking up. Holly had returned, and now all that remained to be done was to kill Little Joe. Then no one would ever come between him and Holly Lucas again.

"I'll finish it from here," Jesse McMatt told

his assistant. Holding a lamp before his assistant's sweat-stained face, McMatt shook his head. "You look a little weak. Why don't you go on to the surface? I'll gather the tools and be up once the blasting is done."

The youth, barely twenty years old, nodded. "Thank you, Mr. McMatt. It's not true what others say about you."

McMatt placed the lamp back on the floor. "What's that?"

"You being a hard man on your hired help."

McMatt laughed. "You gotta make folks think that so you only get the best — like yourself — for helpers."

"Thank you, sir. I'll wait for you at the top."

"You do that," McMatt replied. "Now go on before you pass out from the heat." His assistant moved down the tunnel, and in a minute McMatt heard him ringing the bell that would bring the hoist. McMatt didn't give a damn about the youth's well-being. He just didn't want any witnesses around.

He bundled two sticks of dynamite together with twine. Then he slit the side of one stick and fished a blasting cap from his pocket. Slipping the bundled dynamite under his arm, he unwound a length of fuse from the roll at his feet and cut off about ninety seconds worth. He inserted the fuse in the blasting cap, crimped the cap with pliers, then retrieved the bundled dynamite and shoved the blasting cap and fuse inside. He worked the blasting cap into the heart of the dynamite, then, with his thumbs, closed the slit around the blasting cap and fuse. Dropping to his knees, he placed the bundle in a depression in the stone floor and straightened the length of fuse to the end of the twin cart rails. He moved to an intersecting tunnel and pushed a partially loaded ore cart back to the bundled dynamite. McMatt unloaded the rocks, placing them first around and then atop the dynamite. If his plan worked, the wall of rock behind him would explode from the regular charges, then cover up the bundle of dynamite he had left on the floor. When Adam Cartwright came for samples, he would knock him out and light the fuse. He could explain away the accident as a stick of unexploded dynamite that Cartwright accidentally set off.

As he finished covering the trap, he called to any miners who might be lingering, "Clear out, clear out." He heard no response, but he had expected none because this was the Santa Maria, the deepest of the Bristlecone laterals. Only one crew was working at this level. Those miners had already departed, except for the one working the signal bell at the hoist landing. McMatt gathered his tools and dumped them in the ore cart, pushing it to the side tunnel where he would await the explosion.

"Fire in the hole!" McMatt yelled as he walked back to light his fuses. He awaited the sound of the warning bells, but heard only silence. "Fire in the hole!" he shouted out again. The miner had passed out or had left this level. "Fire in the hole, dammit," he yelled, "fire in the hole!"

Finally the bell clanged out the signal and was answered from above with a corresponding number of rings.

"It's about time, you slow son of a bitch," McMatt yelled as he struck a match and lit his spitter. As he touched the spitter to the various lengths of fuses hanging from the stone wall, they took fire. When the spitter began to singe his fingers, McMatt finished the last of the fuses, bent over and grabbed his lamp, then walked quickly for the equipment recess.

He awaited the explosion. He had twenty-five regular charges he wanted to go off and two he hoped wouldn't. He held his breath as the first explosion was followed by consecutive blasts that seemed to run together into a great rumble like that of a passing freight train. The earth shook and the hot air slapped McMatt's face. By the noise, he counted at least twenty-four had gone off, and maybe all twenty-five. He waited for more explosions, but none came. Unless the concussion had blown away the two-stick bundle, McMatt figured everything was working according to plan.

While he waited for the dust to clear away, McMatt lit his corncob pipe and enjoyed a smoke. Adam Cartwright would be along shortly. The Santa Maria was now three feet longer than it had been moments ago, and Adam Cartwright was just minutes away from death.

Vorley Deaton didn't understand. He had taken the hoist from the lateral above and was lowered to the Santa Maria, where Jesse McMatt's assistant waited. Deaton looked at the assistant, then at the miner working the signal bell. Jesse McMatt was up to something. "I'll handle the bell if you want to go on up," Deaton said to the miner as the assistant got in the hoist.

"Obliged," came the reply.

Deaton rang the signal bell, and shortly the hoist was jerked away to the sound of whirring and whining cables. As soon as the hoist disappeared, Deaton placed his lamp on the ground by the landing and inched down the lateral, ever careful. When he finally came to a bend in the tunnel, he could see McMatt's lamp at the end of the lateral. The weak lamp gave off a sickly yellow ball of light that made it difficult to see from so far.

What Deaton saw confused him. McMatt was leaving a bundle of dynamite on the floor of the mine, then covering it with a pile of rocks. It was the damnedest thing and was likely something for the worst. Were Deaton just starting a shift instead of just finishing one, he would have figured that McMatt, on Thurston Smalley's orders, was setting a trap for him.

Deaton watched McMatt load his tools in the ore cart and push it to cover. Returning to the end of the lateral, McMatt yelled for everyone to clear out. Deaton froze when McMatt yelled, "Fire in the hole!" He ducked behind the rock wall as McMatt turned and stared down the tunnel.

Deaton retreated slowly at first, then quickly as he remembered that he was working the signal bell.

"Fire in the hole," called McMatt, then again.

Finally Deaton reached the hoist landing just as McMatt called a fourth time. Deaton rang the bell and the yelling stopped. Deaton prostrated himself on the floor, bracing his feet against the hoist landing. He had heard of men getting knocked into the hoist shaft by the concussion of the explosion. He heard the hiss of burning fuses in the distance. Deaton gritted his teeth and waited. It seemed to take forever, then it ended suddenly and the earth shook. The explosion's hot breath rumbled over Deaton and hit the shaft, echoing until Deaton's ears were ringing.

The noise subsided quickly, but the dust and acrid smell of detonated dynamite hung like a death shroud in the air. Deaton waited nervously, expecting McMatt to come his way shortly and take the hoist up, but he waited in vain. He heard no noise, no sign that McMatt was alive. Could McMatt have misjudged his fuses. Did one or all go off before he could take cover? Could McMatt have been blown to pieces? No sooner had Deaton gotten his hopes up than he heard the sound of movement in the lateral. Carefully, Deaton stood up and inched his way to the bend in the tunnel. Looking around the rock wall, he saw Jesse McMatt stooping over the pile of rubble where he had buried the extra dynamite. It still didn't make sense, and it was growing spookier by the moment. That was when he heard the signal bell from above. The hoist was coming down. Deaton ran back to the hoist just as the cage stopped at his level.

A single man emerged with a bunch of empty sample sacks tied around his wrist. Vorley Deaton recognized Adam Cartwright.

CHAPTER 21

Adam nodded absently to the miner at the hoist landing and hiked down the lateral. These days, he gathered samples without hope. On the surface, one of the miners had said the Santa Maria was showing promise, but Adam had discounted that as a miner's perpetual optimism.

Holding his lamp, Adam advanced into the tunnel, which was still murky with dust and pungent from detonated dynamite. When he rounded the bend in the tunnel, he made out a lit lamp sitting atop a case of dynamite in an equipment recess. On the fringe of the lamp's glow stood Jesse McMatt puffing on a corncob pipe.

As Adam drew closer, McMatt made no attempt to hide his pipe, even though it broke mine regulations. Opposite McMatt, Adam pointed at the pipe, the bundle of sample sacks hanging like a growth from his hand. "One spark and these timbers could go up in flames. You're fired."

"Fired, am I?" McMatt answered. "If I'm fired, you aren't ordering me around. I'll smoke when and where I want to."

"When I put word out among the miners that you've been caught smoking in the mines, you'll not get Comstock work again."

McMatt sneered. "I've already found another job, one that'll pay me five thousand dollars for a few minutes work." He stared at Adam, then pulled his pipe from between his bared teeth. Bending over, he hit the corncob against the side of the dynamite crate, knocking the glowing tobacco loose, then ground it into the rock floor with his boots. "That make you happy?"

"It'll do for now," replied Adam. "I want you to be ready to leave when I finish collecting samples. You'll go up then."

McMatt shrugged. "If I'm ready."

This was a dangerous man, Adam thought again as he watched McMatt begin to gather his tools and lunch pail. McMatt was a man capable of murder, the type of man who would push another into the shaft.

"Be ready when I get back," Adam ordered, then strode toward the new diggings at the end of the lateral. He studied the newly exposed back wall, toed at the debris. The rock here was a little different than he had seen before. Maybe the miner he'd spoken to aboveground had been right, maybe the Santa Maria was showing promise. Adam took a mining hammer from his belt and began to chip at debris on the floor. Quickly, he filled five sample sacks, marking them with a code designating their location. When he stood up, he was startled by McMatt.

"I've gathered my belongings," McMatt said.

As he spun around, Adam saw McMatt brandishing a long drilling bit. The iron club sliced through the air at him.

McMatt laughed.

Ducking, Adam took a glancing blow off his arm. He grimaced as he tripped over a large stone, then fell on the sharp debris.

McMatt swung the club again, and it struck sparks from the rock by Adam's head.

Adam dodged another blow, kicking at McMatt. Then McMatt towered over him, chopping at him with the club. Adam fended off one blow with his arm, though pain shot throughout his body, stunning him so he could not dodge the next blow. It struck him on the side of the head. His brain seemed to explode with light and noise. McMatt's demonic laugh was the last thing Adam heard before he blacked out.

Vorley Deaton slipped to the bend of the tunnel, where he watched Adam fire McMatt over smoking. Then Adam advanced deeper into the tunnel, turning his back on McMatt. In the murkiness, Deaton could just make out Adam collecting samples. As Adam worked, Deaton saw McMatt pick up one of the heavier drill bits and stalk Adam. Deaton was scared. McMatt was a dangerous man, an evil man. Deaton knew he had to do something, but fear paralyzed him too long to yell a warning.

McMatt swung the bit at Adam and knocked him down. Deaton made a move to rush McMatt until he saw the explosives expert toss the bit aside. McMatt's hand slipped into his pocket and

Deaton saw the end of his fingers flare up with a match.

Now it made sense. McMatt had planted the dynamite as a trap for Adam Cartwright. McMatt bent over the pile of rubble and lit the fuse, which sputtered and hissed. McMatt laughed. "Goodbye, Adam Cartwright!" Then he spun around and ran for cover.

Deaton's conscience overcame his paralysis. He could not watch a man murdered, particularly when his own dealings with Thurston Smalley contributed to the crime. He forgot the danger to himself.

"Stop!" he yelled, to the fuse as much as at McMatt.

Dashing into the equipment recess, Deaton pushed the ore cart ahead, hoping to run over McMatt. The ore cart gathered speed as McMatt charged down the tracks. At the last instant McMatt jumped aside, banging his head against the wall, but dodging the ore cart. McMatt fell to his knees, stunned, as Deaton raced by, uncomfortable at leaving McMatt behind him, but certain he had only a few seconds to save Adam Cartwright. Deaton jerked on the cart's brake and the iron wagon scraped to a halt at the end of the track. Deaton jumped around the cart to Adam.

While Deaton grabbed and shook Adam, he heard McMatt laughing as he scrambled for cover. "Come on," Deaton pleaded, shaking Adam violently, "I've got to get you out of here."

Adam was out cold. Deaton released him and scrambled for the fuse. His hands clawed at the rock, trying to get to it. But the fuse and the dynamite were buried under too much debris. He could never reach them, not in time to stop the explosion.

Deaton jerked at Adam's shoulders and pulled him off the rock pile, bumping into the ore cart. He was so exhausted from his just completed shift, he knew he could never carry Adam to cover.

The ore cart!

That was his only chance. With his aching muscles, Deaton lifted Adam, turned around and dumped him inside.

Behind him the fuse went silent for a moment. Had it gone out? Deaton gritted his teeth against the expected explosion. All was quiet for an instant, then the fuse sputtered to life again. Deaton shoved the cart. It began to move, slowly at first, then faster. Five, ten, fifteen feet, and the cart began to accelerate. Its momentum would soon carry it to safety. Deaton hopped up on the cart, ready to hide with Adam behind the cart's iron walls.

Deaton yelled with exhilaration, knowing he would make it around the bend and to the hoist, where they could escape McMatt.

Then the dynamite exploded. Rocks showered the tunnel, pinging off the ore cart's iron sides, deadly missiles striking Deaton's back and head. He tumbled in atop Adam, the only sensation the terrible pounding and pulsing in his brain and the wet stickiness of something running down his face. He gasped for breath, but it wouldn't come, and it no longer seemed worth the effort to struggle for it. All about him was darkness and heat and terrible smells. He closed his eyes and died.

Ben sat in Adam's office when the alarm bells rang. A moment later he heard the pounding footsteps of someone racing up the stairs. He expected Adam, but instead a clerk barged through the door.

"Accidental explosion in the mine, sir."

"Adam?" Ben asked instinctively.

"That's all we know now," the clerk replied.

Ben raced down the stairs, through the front office and out the back hallway, Little Joe and Hoss holding the door open as Ben ran past. They raced along the plank walk to the hoisting works and flung open the door. Inside, they darted around the machinery. At the shaft, Ben pushed his way through the crowd gathered around a single man smoking a corncob pipe.

The man shook his head. "Neither of them survived."

"Who?" Ben asked. "Who was it?"

The man pulled his corncob pipe from his mouth. "Some miner and Adam Cartwright."

Ben felt his knees sag and his spirit deflate. "It can't be."

Hoss moved to his father's side. "You sure?"

The man shrugged. "I ain't no doctor."

Ben's mind raced. There had to be some mistake. Adam couldn't be dead. Damn the Bristlecone. Damn himself for not voting against Adam a long time ago. Adam would still be alive had he voted with Hoss and Little Joe. And this man, whoever he was, who spoke so calmly of two men's death, repulsed Ben. He turned to the shift foreman. "Who is this man?"

"Jesse McMatt," the foreman replied, "one of our explosives men." The foreman pointed at McMatt. "Tell Mr. Cartwright what happened."

McMatt studied Ben hard. "You Adam Cartwright's papa?"

Ben nodded.

"He never knew what hit him. One of the charges must not have gone off. He or the miner that was helping collect samples must've detonated it."

McMatt was lying! Ben knew Adam had been taking all the samples by himself. He never trusted anyone to go with him.

"I sounded the alarm, then loaded their bodies in an ore cart, figured another crew could bring them up. I had a close call as it was."

Hoss knotted his fists, stepped toward McMatt. "You're pretty casual for a man that just saw two men die."

McMatt smiled when Ben grabbed Hoss's arm.

"Easy, Hoss, we don't know anything for certain now."

Hoss shook his arm loose from his father's grip.

The hoist bells rang. The cage was coming up. The throng shifted from McMatt to the shaft.

"Get back," yelled the foreman. "We don't want any more hurt."

The flat cable whined mournfully as it lifted the cage from the bowels of the earth. It seemed to take forever for the cage to make it from the 1300-foot level. Ben felt a wrenching knot in his stomach. He had felt it three times before at the death of each of his wives. He was not sure he wanted to see the cage's cargo. He had seen mangled bodies before, but not that of a son.

The whirring of the hoist cables slowed and the top of the cage came slowly into view. Gradually the full cage appeared. Two miners stood beside a battered ore cart; a mangled arm hung limply from the top, bouncing as the hoist cage stopped. A pair of men lifted the bar on the side of the cage and the two somber-faced miners pushed the cart out onto the landing. A dozen miners crowded in to lift the bodies gently from the cart. Ben recognized the first only as a miner, his head bruised and battered, his body caked with blood which had quickly dried in the mine's oppressive heat.

Ben's throat tightened at the sight of the second limp body. He recognized the bloodstained clothes. It was Adam. Ben bit his lip. He could feel his eyes moistening. He must be strong for Hoss and Little Joe as much as for himself. Gently, the miners placed Adam on the planked deck, and one by one they removed their hats.

Ben knelt beside Adam. Fortunately, his body was not mangled, but that was a small consolation at a time like this. Ben brushed his hand against Adam's face, still hot from the heat of the mine. He looked at the bloodied clothes that Adam wore, and he noticed the sacks of ore samples still tied around Adam's left wrist. Slowly, Ben stood up and turned around. Little Joe wiped his eyes and Hoss stared blank-faced at Adam.

"Get up, Adam, get up," Hoss repeated.

Ben only shook his head and moved between his two surviving sons. "Somebody needs to tell Lucia Sinclair."

Hoss resisted his father's touch.

"Get up, Adam, get up," Hoss whispered.

"Let's go, Hoss."

"Wait, Pa," Hoss said, bending forward, squinting at his older brother. "He moved, Pa, he moved!"

Ben shook his head. He knew it was wishful thinking.

"The man's right," shouted a miner. "He's still alive."

Ben spun around in time to see Adam's hand quiver. "Get the doctor," Ben shouted, "he's alive!"

"He's what?" shouted a voice from behind.

Ben recognized it as the voice of Jesse McMatt.

"He's alive?" McMatt shouted incredulously. "Impossible."

"Somebody get a doctor," yelled the foreman, "and let's get him to the hospital quick."

Ben squatted beside Adam, grabbing his hand. Adam groaned feebly.

This was enough, Ben thought to himself. No mine, no amount of money, was worth losing a son over. The time had come to sell the Bristlecone, even if it meant turning it over to Thurston Smalley at an incredible loss.

"Time will tell," said Dr. Paul Martin. "Concussions are strange. He may wake up in a few hours, or a day or two. Sometimes they never wake up, just wither away and die."

Ben shook his head and looked around the hospital ward. By the wall sat Hoss and Little Joe, their heads in their hands.

"How long do you think it will be, Doc?" Ben asked.

"In forty-eight hours we should know if he's going to recover."

Ben mumbled his thanks.

Dr. Martin stared at Adam for a moment, then shook his head. "I've never seen an explosion wound like this. Even with his concussion, he's lucky."

"What do you mean, Doc?"

Martin rubbed his chin. "He took a couple blows to the head, which is not unexpected in an explosion, but there's no other marks on the body except for a bruise on the arm and shoulder. Usually they're peppered with bruises and cuts. That's the way the miner was they brought up with your son. It just doesn't make sense."

304

"A lot of things don't make sense," Ben responded.

The doctor walked away to check other patients in the twelve-bed ward. At the door, he paused, holding it open for a slender woman with long black hair.

Ben stared. He had see her somewhere but was unable to place her. As she stared back, Ben realized he was being rude. He averted his glance toward the motionless Adam, whose head was bandaged in white gauze. Then Ben realized the woman was Lucia Sinclair with her hair down. He offered a smile as best he could.

Lucia seemed tentative and ill at ease. He stepped toward her and she ran to him.

"Oh, Mr. Cartwright, I came as soon as I heard." She hugged Ben. "I'm so sorry about this, sorry for Adam."

Ben nodded. "I wish we knew he'd be okay, but we don't know."

Lucia pushed Ben away. "Don't talk like that. He'll be okay."

She moved to Adam's bed. Hoss and Little Joe both stood as Lucia bent over Adam. "It'll be okay, Adam." She kissed him softly on his bandaged forehead.

Ben smiled. A man needed a good woman at times like these.

"I'd like to sit with him, Mr. Cartwright, if you don't mind?"

"Lucia," Ben replied, "we'd appreciate it, and Adam would too."

Lucia seemed pleased. She moved a chair to the bedside.

Ben looked at Little Joe and Hoss. "We should try to get some sleep, boys." Both nodded, staring a final moment at Adam before slipping wordlessly away. Their heavy steps echoed off the ward walls and down the hall to the exit. As they reached the door, Ben heard the doctor calling after him.

"Mr. Cartwright, Mr. Cartwright," shouted Paul Martin, "wait just a minute." The doctor ran into his office. When he came back out, he held a bundle of sample sacks in his hand. "I cut these from around Adam's wrist when I brought him in."

For a moment the sacks repulsed Ben because they were so closely linked to Adam's injury. "Thank you," Ben managed, taking them. He headed out the door with Hoss and Little Joe.

From St. Mary's Hospital they walked silently in the darkness. Mount Davidson loomed over them, huge and silent. The sound of merriment from the saloons on C Street and the brothels on D Street floated on the cool breeze as if from another world, a world where accidents never happened and sons were never injured.

Turning on F Street toward the Bristlecone, Ben was startled to see lamps still burning in the main office. It was well after ten o'clock now. Surely no one had stayed that late. Ben picked up his pace, and Little Joe and Hoss kept by his side. At the office, Ben twisted the knob and the door slid right open. Stepping inside, he found a couple dozen employees and miners waiting, their eyes wide with concern. "How is he?" a clerk asked.

"He took a bad blow to the head and isn't conscious yet," Ben answered. "That's all we'll know for the night."

Another man asked, "Anything we can do to help?"

Ben shook his head. "The only thing you can do now is get some rest. And pray for Adam."

Each man nodded somberly as Hoss picked up one of the coal-oil lamps and the three Cartwrights marched upstairs to Adam's office. Little Joe opened the door, allowing Hoss and then his father to enter ahead of him. Ben tossed the samples on the table, then pulled out a chair. Hoss placed the lamp in the center of the table and slumped into a chair. Little Joe paced back and forth between the table and the window.

After a long silence Ben finally spoke. "Boys, I settled in Nevada with nothing but my good name and two sons. I added a son and still have my good name. I built the Ponderosa and made a fortune along the way. I can build another ranch or make another fortune, but I can't replace a son. The Bristlecone's not worth the price, even if it costs the Ponderosa. It's time to sell the Bristlecone."

Hoss bolted up from the table. "No, sir."

Shocked, Ben jerked his head toward Hoss. "I know you don't like what might happen to the

Ponderosa, Hoss, but you wanted to sell last time."

Hoss nodded slowly. "I did, Pa, but I figure we owe it to Adam to bring in the Bristlecone."

Little Joe agreed. "I'm still with Hoss. Whatever he says."

Ben shook his head. "You boys confound me all the time. I know Adam would be pleased, but he understands mining, understands business. You can't make it work on emotion."

"We can't give up now, Pa," Little Joe pleaded.

"We're not giving up, Little Joe, just changing direction. The Bristlecone's left us with debts we would've had to pay even if we'd never taken out the loan. I'll repay those debts to save my good name and yours." Ben's shoulders sagged. "We'll lose a good deal of the Ponderosa, though I can't say right now how much."

"The Ponderosa won't be the same without Adam anyway," Little Joe replied.

Ben shook his head, toying with the bundle of sample sacks, his eyes moistening for a moment. "Losing the ranch is like losing the button off a shirt. You can replace it. Losing a loved one — and I lost all three of your mothers — is like losing your arm. You can't replace it and you can't forget it. I'll spend what's left of my fortune to save Adam, but not another cent to save the mine."

Both Little Joe and Hoss stared at their father.

"I'm closing the Bristlecone and will start Clarence Eppler handling the legal work to get us out from under our debts."

"What about voting our shares?" Little Joe protested. "Hoss and I vote to stay in the Bristlecone, for Adam's sake."

With a vigorous nod of his head, Hoss affirmed Little Joe's declaration.

"It comes out the same," Ben answered. "Without Adam's proxy, my two votes and your vote apiece comes out in a tie, and I have the prerogative to break ties. We're getting out of the mining business as soon as we can sell the Bristlecone. The mine won't bring in enough to repay the loan, and our other assets have been overextended to keep the mine going. The Ponderosa is all we've got left to repay the loan. I'd rather lose it than our good name . . . or Adam."

CHAPTER 22

Through the closed door, Holly Lucas heard the gossip among the firemen. One of the Cartwrights had been injured in a mining accident. The fragment of conversation sent her mind and blood racing. She prayed for Little Joe's safety and wondered if Thurston Smalley's threat against Adam Cartwright had been carried out. She placed her ear against the door and heard Adam's name. She sighed. At least Little Joe was safe, but would he remain so? She must warn him of Thurston Smalley's threat, see him once more. Big Jim Fowler would be enraged. He must not find out.

Holly moved from the door, rubbing her cheek where Fowler had struck her, wondering what he would do if he found out she had seen Little Joe once more. Holly would write Little Joe a note, pleading with him to meet her. But where? She moved to the dirty window, pondering her dilemma. As she thought, her gaze moved up the slope of Mount Davidson, then focused on a clump of mine structures, abandoned like worn-out shoes. The Montgomery Mine! She could have Little Joe meet her there, in the remains of that hard-luck mine.

She moved quickly from the window to the

desk and picked up paper and a pencil. Hurriedly she scribbled a note to Little Joe. "Please meet me today at two o'clock at the Montgomery Mine building. It's a matter of life and death. Please believe me — Holly Lucas." She folded the note and inserted it in an envelope, writing Little Joe's name on it. Then she looked about the room for a place to hide it, finally slipping it beneath her pillow. Now she had to find an excuse to get it delivered.

She was patting her pillow when she realized Fowler had opened the door. She lifted her hand like a child stealing cookies.

Fowler only smiled, holding a folded flag. "Care to help me run up the flag?"

Holly nodded.

"And we need to let the restaurant know that you're sick and won't be in for a few days," Fowler said.

"As long as another volunteer carries the message," Holly answered, "and you stay nearby to protect me."

"Sure," he replied, unfolding the flag.

Holly smiled to herself. Big Jim had just opened the door for her to get the message to Little Joe.

They raised the flag, and it hung limp in the early morning air. Fowler enjoyed it as Holly sidled up to him, taking his hand. Even so, he wondered what she had hidden beneath her pillow.

"You hungry?" he asked.

She nodded.

"Let me get my money from inside and I'll take you for a bit of breakfast."

"I'd like that." Holly moved with him to the door.

Fowler smiled. "You'll be okay out here for a few seconds. Enjoy the cool."

She smiled.

Leaving her outside the door, Fowler moved quickly to the back office. He shoved his hand under her pillow and pulled out the envelope. He saw Little Joe's name. Rage flamed to life within him, then flared when he read Holly's note, telling of a life-and-death situation. Could Holly know he planned to kill Little Joe? Surely not. Confusion plagued him, but he knew he must hide his anger. Then he realized this was the opportunity he craved to catch Little Joe alone and kill him.

The abandoned Montgomery Mine at two o'clock, he noted. He hurriedly folded the note and slid it back in the envelope. He shoved it back under the pillow and retreated toward the front door and Holly. Fowler smiled at his good luck and at Little Joe's bad.

They sat around the table in Adam's office. Ben Cartwright, his jaw stubbornly set, listened to the stockbroker, Monville Pyburn, and lawyer Clarence Eppler pleading with him to continue mine operations until they found a buyer for the Bristlecone.

"Shut down the mine and it'll knock the bottom

out of the selling price, Ben," said Pyburn.

Eppler nodded. "It's a fact, Ben, you know that."

Little Joe had never seen his father so obstinate. What Eppler and Pyburn were preaching made sense, but Pa was adamant. He wanted out. Little Joe toyed with the sample sacks Ben had brought back from the hospital after Adam's accident. It was almost noon, and all morning Little Joe had kept thinking about Adam in his hospital bed, still unconscious, Lucia Sinclair at his side. Absentmindedly, Little Joe took to lifting the sacks and dropping them on the table, the cloth-shrouded rocks clacking against the wood.

Annoyed, Ben cut a disgruntled glance at Little Joe, then began to tap his fingers on the table. "Joseph, you're a distraction," he said with a withering gaze.

Little Joe dropped the sacks a last time, his fingers scrambling too late to catch them and strangle the noise.

Ben hit his balled fists against the table. "It's settled," he said, staring hard at Pyburn and Eppler. "I know you think it's unwise, but I'm closing the mine and selling out."

Pyburn stared through his thick glasses. "Even if Thurston Smalley's your only choice?"

Ben swallowed hard and nodded.

Eppler shook his head. "That's not the Ben Cartwright I've always worked with."

"That Ben Cartwright didn't have a son in the hospital, Clarence," Ben answered emphatically.

"I'm turning the miners loose at the end of the day shift."

Eppler and Pyburn looked from Ben to Hoss and Little Joe.

Pyburn grimaced. "We'll need samples from each level for a final assay, give us a way of figuring out a reasonable price."

Ben pointed to Little Joe's hands on the table. "There's the samples Adam got from the Santa Maria before the accident. We'll get samples from the other levels, then shut down the mine."

Eppler pulled his gold pocket watch from his vest pocket. "There are a lot of details we'll need to work out. We —"

A loud rap at the door interrupted the lawyer.

Ben looked over his shoulder. "Come in."

A clerk from the office entered meekly. "A message was delivered here, said to be important."

Ben shot up from his chair. "About Adam?"

"No, sir, a firemen brought it for Little Joe."

Little Joe cut a quick glance at Ben. The clerk dropped the envelope on the table in front of Little Joe, then backed out of the room. Taking the missive, Little Joe recognized Holly's handwriting.

"Some young lady, I suppose," said Ben.

Little Joe shrugged as he opened the envelope and read the message from Holly Lucas.

Little Joe refolded the letter and stuffed it in his pants pocket. "Some business I need to attend to, Pa."

Ben eyed Little Joe skeptically. "This isn't one of your tricks, is it?"

"No, sir! I don't know what it is, just that it's something I need to attend to."

Ben nodded. "You've been jittery all morning. You can go, if you must."

A smile worked its way across Little Joe's face as he pushed himself away from the table. "Yes, sir."

"What about me, Pa? It's getting to be lunchtime," pleaded Hoss.

"I need you to stay, Hoss," Ben replied.

Hoss's smile shrank. "What about lunch?"

"After a while," Ben said.

Hoss's receding smile melted into a frown. "Yes, sir."

Little Joe nodded his regrets around the table. "I'll see you later," he said.

"Not so fast," said Ben.

Little Joe froze.

"Why don't you take those samples by the assay office and tell them you'll wait for a sealed report? Pay cash for the testing so they can't be certain it's from the Bristlecone," Ben commanded.

"Yes, sir," Little Joe said. He grabbed the sample sacks from the table and took his hat from the hook by the door. He escaped into the hallway, shutting the door and hearing Hoss's complaint that "Little Joe has all the luck."

Quickly, before his father changed his mind, Little Joe exited the mine offices and headed toward the nearest assayer's office. As he walked, he looked up the side of Mount Davidson to the abandoned works of the Montgomery Mine. Odd place for Holly to request a meeting. Could it be a trap? He thought about running back to he office and getting his gun, but decided he didn't need it. Holly wouldn't set a trap for him.

The assayer's office was a tiny building of weathered planks and dirty windows. Little Joe stepped to a counter, not two paces from the door. A wizened old man with a stained apron strode up to the front, past tables overloaded with scales, bottles of chemicals, beakers, and other tools of the trade.

"How long for an assay, five samples?" Little Joe asked, plopping the sacks on the counter.

"A couple hours, me being behind and such."

"I'll give you double your regular charge if you can get it done within an hour."

The assayer studied Little Joe a moment. "You're no regular here. Payment in advance."

Little Joe dug into his pants pocket and pulled out some silver pieces. "Will that cover it?"

The old man picked up the coins and dropped them in a pocket in his apron. Taking the samples, he took a step toward his workbench along the side of the room.

"One other thing," Little Joe said, "give me a written report in a sealed envelope."

The assayer eyed Little Joe suspiciously. "You don't want to know the results?"

"I'll learn later."

Shaking his head, the assayer slid onto the stool

at the workbench. "You're the first man ever brought in a sample that didn't want to know the findings as soon as I figured them out."

Little Joe sat down and leaned his chair against the corner where he could see outside. He kept wondering what Holly Lucas could want. Perhaps it was a ruse to see him again. Little Joe admitted he still held an attraction for her, but he could not court her, not after her betrayal.

With payment in his pocket, the assayer worked quickly and efficiently. Occasionally Little Joe got a whiff of the chemicals as the old man mixed. When he was done, the assayer tossed the sample sacks back on the front counter, then moved to his desk and began to write out his findings.

"You sure you don't want the results?" the assayer asked again.

"Nope, just seal them up and let me have them. You can keep the samples too."

"You're the customer," he answered as he put the report in an envelope and folded the flap. He rummaged on his desk for a stick of wax, then lit a match under the wax, allowing it to drip atop and seal the envelope.

As the assayer approached the front, Little Joe hopped up to the counter. The assayer slid the report to Little Joe. "Mind if I ask you where you found those samples?"

"The Bristlecone," Little Joe replied, taking the envelope and tucking it in his pants pocket. "Now I've got a young woman to meet."

"Buy her something pretty," the assayer said.

317

"You ought to be able to afford it."

Little Joe ignored the old man's comment and walked briskly out the door and down the street, then turned west toward Mount Davidson and the abandoned mine works. In the years since the Montgomery Mine was abandoned, its equipment and innards had been stripped and put to use in other mines. The windows had either been removed or broken by vandals. The gray coat of paint the building had worn during optimistic times had cracked and chipped during the hard Nevada winters. Peeling and flaking away, the paint had exposed weathered wood that had begun to rot in places. When the great winds blew over Virginia City, the abandoned buildings set off an eerie wail, unnerving many women and children and not a few men. It was the bad-luck mine.

Little Joe approached the mine works cautiously, but he saw nothing suspicious as he circled the main building. He entered through an opening where a door and its hinges had been removed by scavengers. "Holly," he called, but only his echo answered. The building was dark, lit only by intermittent shafts of light streaming through holes in the roof and uncovered windows. Gradually Little Joe's eyes adjusted to the dimness and he made out a stairway leading to a second level. A third floor rose above it to shelter the hoist works. Though bits of the hoist still survived, most of it had been removed for spare parts in other mines.

Little Joe started up the stairs, figuring to watch the entrance in case Big Jim Fowler showed up instead of Holly. The once sturdy stairs creaked with each step, the boards loose in several places and broken in a couple. At the top of the stairs he moved about the second level, which was nothing more than a wide platform traversed by rails over which ore carts had moved tons of rock from the shaft to a chute that sloped down to a railroad spur. The floor was pockmarked with holes where accidents had gouged into the wood. Little Joe walked about the platform, stopping and staring down the battered chute, scarred from tons of ore.

As he gazed across Virginia City, he heard Holly's voice. "Little Joe! Are you here?" Little Joe inched to a corner of the platform, peeking from behind a thick post. Holly was alone, but he waited a bit to answer, just to make sure she wasn't being followed.

"Up here, Holly," he called, stepping from behind the post and waving. Before he could reach the stairs, she bolted toward him.

"Oh, Little Joe," she cried, oblivious to the sway of the steps as she climbed them.

"Easy, Holly, the stairs aren't sturdy like they once were."

Somehow she avoided the damaged steps and met Little Joe at the top. She flung her arms around him, kissing him on the lips. "I've missed you so, Little Joe."

He pushed her face away and backed her into a shaft of light. Her face was bruised. "He hit you, didn't he?"

Holly nodded in shame. "He didn't mean to. It doesn't matter anymore, Little Joe. I'm scared for you."

"Fowler'll never get to me."

"Not him, Little Joe. Thurston Smalley. When I told him I wouldn't give him any more information, he threatened me, said if I didn't believe he could harm me, for me just to watch and see what happened to Adam. I don't know how Adam was hurt, but Smalley could be behind it after what he said. I wanted you to know that because I love you, Little Joe." She hugged him tightly.

Little Joe felt awkward. He still had feelings for her, but no longer that strong. He stroked her hair. "Why did we have to meet like this?"

"I'm scared Smalley might see us together and have us killed. He's a man who'd do it. That's why I went back to Big Jim. He'll protect me."

"The law will protect you, Holly."

She trembled. "No, Smalley's bigger than the law."

Little Joe patted her. "No one's bigger than the law. I'll take you to Sheriff Coffee and get this straightened out."

"If you say so, Little Joe."

Little Joe lifted her chin and kissed her mouth. As he broke from her lips, he glanced down the stairs. His muscles tightened.

Standing in the doorway watching them was Big Jim Fowler.

CHAPTER 23

"It's not what you think," yelled Holly Lucas.

Fowler shook his fist at her. His other hand held a can of coal oil. "I can see what it is." He started for Holly and Little Joe, scooping up a length of two-by-four from the floor, then charging up the stairs which trembled under his footfalls.

Little Joe pulled a pale Holly Lucas away from the landing and shook her. "Now listen to me, Holly. When he gets up here, I'll distract him long enough for you to get down the stairs and escape."

"He'll kill you, Little Joe."

Fowler's pounding footsteps drew closer. Little Joe released Holly. "Do as I say, get away and get help."

Fowler stood at the top of the stairs, panting like a wild animal. "I'll get you now for interfering with Holly and me."

Fowler took a step toward Little Joe.

Little Joe pushed Holly aside. "Do as I said. He's a madman."

Fowler sneered, shaking the can of coal oil. "I'll finish what I didn't get done at the opera house!"

Holly gasped. "You set it on fire?"

"It doesn't matter, does it?"

"You tried to kill us, didn't you?" Holly caught her breath and charged full into Fowler, surprising him. He dropped the can and shoved her aside with his powerful arm. She stumbled toward the edge of the platform, ran full into the rail and staggered as her foot slipped off the ledge.

Little Joe leaped for her. He grabbed her arm and jerked her back to safety. As he did, he caught a glimpse of Fowler charging at him. Flinging Holly to the floor, Little Joe jumped aside and heard overhead the whoosh of the board Fowler had swung at his head. "Run, Holly. Go get help."

Shaking her head, Holly climbed to her hands and knees as Little Joe's words sank in, then stood up and raced for the stairs.

Fowler glanced over his shoulder. Seeing Holly dash by, he lunged for her, turning his back on Little Joe.

Little Joe dove for Fowler. His shoulder cut the big man down at the knees. Fowler cried out from pain and surprise. Little Joe rolled away in time to catch a final glimpse of Holly as she disappeared down the stairs.

Jumping to his feet, Little Joe charged for the stairs, but Fowler stuck the two-by-four between his legs and tripped him. Little Joe tumbled to the edge of the platform, realized the danger and scrambled away just as Fowler climbed to his knees and brought the two-by-four down with a crash where he had just been.

Both men pounced to their feet. Little Joe tried to circle around behind Fowler and make a dash for the stairs, but the big man always stayed between him and his escape route.

His eyes focused on Fowler, Little Joe backed across the platform. He was trying to draw Fowler closer so he would have more room to maneuver. He moved back another step and Fowler advanced. It was working. Another step or two and Little Joe knew he could make a dash around Fowler for the stairs. Retreating a last step, Little Joe stumbled over an ore cart rail. He kept his balance until his foot caught on the parallel rail. He fell hard, his head banging into the plank flooring. His eyes blurred for a moment, then cleared long enough to see Fowler's hulking form above him, his arms drawn back over his head, clutching the two-by-four. He saw the club start down for his eyes. It seemed an eternity before his reflexes took hold. He moved his head just as the board reached him. His head exploded with lights and a buzzing, and suddenly he was in a nether world between consciousness and unconsciousness. He did not move because he knew he was helpless. Now his wits were all he had, and they were dulled and slowed by the pain.

Fowler laughed. He threw the board down on Little Joe's chest and retreated to the stairs. Little Joe tried to open his eyes, but even in the dimness of the room the light was blinding.

Little Joe heard a sloshing, as if someone were

pouring water onto the floor. The sound made him think how thirsty he was, how much he'd like to have a drink of cold water. He wished Fowler would throw some of the water on his face. Then the odor hit him. It was the worst-smelling water he had ever encountered. It wasn't water. It was coal oil. He lifted his head as best he could, and saw Fowler bent over by the stairs. If only he could get up, Little Joe thought, he could shove Fowler to his death; but his strength failed him.

Then the chance passed. Fowler towered over him, sneering. "So long, Little Joe Cartwright. Nobody can save you now."

Little Joe moved a bit, his hands and legs seeming to answer his brain's call. But what now? He opened his eyes, squinting against the brightness. He could make out Fowler standing over him. Fowler held his hands together and then broke them apart real quick. A fire blazed between his fingers. "No," Little Joe managed.

Fowler laughed, backing away toward the stairs. Then he tossed the match at Little Joe. Little Joe's hands flew instinctively to protect his face, but the match fell short. The room seemed to explode and a wall of flame flew up with a roar between him and Fowler. Hell could be no more frightening than the wall of fire dancing between him and the stairs. Heat rolled over Little Joe. He knew he must get up or die. He wasn't ready to die. He looked at Fowler, who shimmered through the yellow and orange flames like a demon in Hell's mirror. Fowler's eyes and mouth were wide with pleasure. Then he laughed and turned around, starting down the steps with his heavy footfalls. His laugh lasted but two strides before a step gave way. Fowler stumbled forward and his leg snapped with a pop.

Little Joe pushed himself up to his knees. The smoke was growing heavy and he was having trouble catching his breath. He saw Fowler struggling on the stairs, screaming wildly, lunging in agony. He was trapped in a Hell of his own making. Then a cloud of black smoke enveloped the stairs and Big Jim Fowler disappeared, though his horrible screams grew as crackling flames shot up.

The blistering heat battered Little Joe's face, and he retreated on his hands and knees even farther from the stairs. The smoke was thick and he had almost given up, except for a rectangle of light ahead of him. It was so bright that he shut his eyes. The pain of the fire behind him was greater than the hurt of the light ahead of him. He crawled in that direction, not understanding the light source until he remembered the ore chute. That was his chance, his only chance, if he could just make it. But his equilibrium was bad and his energy depleted. His hands brushed against hot metal and he screamed. Then the rectangle disappeared in a cloud of smoke. It was gone. He would die, burned to death. His hand brushed up against the hot metal again. It was a rail. The rail for the ore carts.

He felt the hot rail and followed it on hands and knees. It seemed forever without a window, and then all of a sudden it loomed before him. He crawled as fast as he could on battered knees and blistered hands, coughing and heaving for breath. His lungs ached as much as his head. He felt a hint of cool air brush against his face and he dove forward. Then his head was outside the opening and the chute was beneath him. Little Joe pulled himself fully into the chute, then pushed himself away from the building. He gathered speed, exhilarated to be escaping with his life. At the end of the chute he seemed to fly for a moment. But in the next instant he crashed into a dirt embankment and everything went black.

Sheriff Roy Coffee jumped up from his desk at the banging on the door. A screaming woman burst into his office. He recognized her as Holly Lucas. "What in tarnation's the matter, ma'am?"

"Jim Fowler's attacking Little Joe in Montgomery Mine!"

Coffee grabbed his hat and darted past her out the door. He jumped on his bay gelding and turned the animal toward Mount Davidson. The mine building was spewing black smoke. Others must have noticed too, because fire bells began to ring. "Giddy-up," he yelled, slapping the reins against the horse's neck and galloping to Mount Davidson. Behind him he could hear the clang of several fire wagons.

Up ahead, smoke was billowing from second-story windows and flames licked at the wall and roof. Coffee struck his horse again, getting everything he could out of the gelding. As he watched the fire take hold, he knew the building could not be saved, but he had to get there in time to save Little Joe and Fowler. He thought of Ben Cartwright, with one son stoved up in the hospital and possibly dying, and a second son in danger of burning to death.

Drawing as close to the fire as his panicked gelding would allow, Coffee jumped from his horse, which spun around and galloped through the approaching throng of firemen and spectators. Coffee ran as near the building as he could, but the flames were blistering hot. "Little Joe, Fowler, anybody, you in there?" he yelled.

Only the crackle of the flames answered him. Above him the whole second level was ablaze. Fire was crawling down the stairway, which suddenly collapsed, showering the rest of the room with sparks and burning cinders. A blast of hot air followed the collapse, washing over Coffee like the breath of Hell. He retreated.

There was nothing he could do now but watch and keep others from getting too close. Fortunately, the building was isolated and wind was low. The fire should not spread. The throng gathered in a crescent behind the sheriff on the slopes of Mount Davidson. Lacking adequate water, the volunteers, like the spectators, could only gape at the flames climbing the building.

Coffee did not know how long he had watched

before Holly Lucas was by his side, winded and breathless.

"What about Little Joe?" she pleaded. "Where is he?"

The sheriff shrugged. "Ma'am, I haven't seen him. I guess he's still in there."

"No!" she screamed. "He can't be! Why does everyone I love burn to death?"

Coffee couldn't answer her. It was more a statement than a question anyway, but it jogged his memory. Wasn't she the young lady who a few years ago had seen her entire family consumed in a fire? Why hadn't he remembered that about Holly Lucas before now? Damn shame the way her folks died. He looked from her to the fire and then back again. But now she was gone!

All at once the crowd gasped. Coffee saw Holly Lucas running toward the door. Coffee darted after her. She had a good start, but he knew he could catch her, until he tripped over a rock and felt flat on his chest. It knocked the breath out of him and he gasped for air, then tried to scramble onto his feet. He stood up in time to see her disappear into the building. It would be suicide to follow. Coffee knew she must come back quickly or she would die. Suddenly, a sheet of flame fell from the second floor and the entire wall was on fire. There would be no escape for Holly Lucas.

A group of firemen rushed up to Coffee, grabbing his arms to help him back down the mountain. Vigorously, he shook them off, mad that he hadn't caught Holly Lucas. He shook his head in failure, despite the reassurances of several people who had seen his attempt to stop her.

As the fire reached its peak, the crowd backed down the hill, retreating from the heat. Coffee sighed. How could he tell Ben Cartwright about Little Joe? Damn if he didn't wish he'd retired before now. He was getting too old to be sheriff, especially when a young woman could outrun him.

"Look," shouted someone from the crowd. Others picked up the cry and took to pointing around the side of the building, by the railroad spur. Some people started applauding and others ran in that direction.

Coffee glanced over his shoulder and saw a man staggering down the mountain. He couldn't believe his eyes. It was Little Joe Cartwright. Thank God!

"He'll be okay," Dr. Paul Martin said to Ben Cartwright, nodding toward Little Joe in the hospital bed beside Adam's. "Dislocated shoulder's been reset, and the blisters on his hands will heal without any scarring. The burns on the neck are comparable to a sun blister, so he'll do okay. He's lucky."

"Wish Adam were as lucky," Ben said. He looked from Little Joe to his oldest son.

Behind Ben, Roy Coffee let out a deep breath. "I feared he was a goner, Ben, and feared having to break the news to you."

"The Bristlecone's getting about as unlucky as the Montgomery, Roy. I figure it's time we Cartwrights gave up on mining and concentrated on ranching and timber."

From the chair at Adam's bedside, Lucia Sinclair arose. "It'll hurt Adam, you giving up."

"We've been hurt plenty as it is. I laid off all our men this afternoon. The Bristlecone is shut down until we get a buyer." Ben saw tears in Lucia's eyes. Adam was lucky, Ben thought, to have a woman like her interested in him.

"I just wish you could wait until he comes to," Lucia managed.

"Me too, Lucia," Ben replied, "but . . ." He let the sentence hang unfinished.

Anger flared in her eyes and in the curl of her lip. "He'll get better, you mark my words." She rubbed her hand gently across Adam's face and a single tear ran down her cheek. "I'm not giving up on him." She turned her head away and dashed down the aisle as she broke into tears. "I'll be back later."

"Tough situation, Ben," said Sheriff Coffee.

Ben just nodded.

"Little Joe," said Coffee, "I'll be back in the morning to ask you a few questions. Nothing that can't wait."

"Thanks, Roy," Little Joe replied, settling gingerly into the bed's white pillow.

Ben accompanied Coffee outside, passing Lucia seated on the front steps. She wiped hurriedly at her cheek, then smiled weakly. "I didn't mean to be rude, Mr. Cartwright, but Adam's got a lot invested in that mine. I know you've got a lot invested in Adam, but so do I."

"I'm glad about that, for you and for Adam." Lucia seemed pleased by his words.

The sheriff and Ben walked from the hospital toward the center of town before splitting up and going their separate ways, Coffee to his office and Ben to the Washoe Club. He reached the entrance the same time as Monville Pyburn and Clarence Eppler.

"Little Joe's okay, isn't he?" asked Eppler.

Ben nodded. "He'll do fine."

Both men grinned, then laughed, but Ben didn't understand what was funny about another son in the hospital.

"I should've known," Pyburn said, "you'd never give in to selling your stock without a fight." Both men laughed.

"Nothing's changed," Ben replied.

"Don't be coy with us, Ben," said Pyburn. "We've heard the rumor going around."

"What rumor?"

"The one that says your latest assay reports are better than three hundred dollars a ton." Eppler laughed. "You're a sly one, Ben."

Ben shrugged ignorance, but the two men wouldn't believe him. Ben could only scratch his head. Nothing made sense anymore.

CHAPTER 24

The night had been long, Little Joe restless. Periodically coughing up the residue of the smoke in his lungs, he grimaced as his burned and sensitive hands moved across the stiff sheets. In the next bed Adam rested peacefully. Beyond him, Lucia Sinclair was slumped forward in her chair, her face drawn. Little Joe wished Holly Lucas could have been there. Though no one had said anything, he knew that Holly had perished in the fire. She deserved better.

As dawn softly illuminated the drawn shades on the tall ward windows, Lucia shifted in her chair and shook her head, her eyes straining open. Slowly she stood and stretched, then bent over Adam and kissed him gently on his bandaged forehead. Weakly, she smiled at Little Joe. "Morning, you feeling better?" she whispered.

"A little," he answered. "My hands hurt the worst." He studied Lucia a moment. "Why don't you go home, get some bed rest. You shouldn't push yourself too hard."

"Thanks, Little Joe. I just owe Adam an apology."

Little Joe nodded. "There'll be time for that."

"I hope so." She began to cry. "Maybe I should

go for now." Turning away and running her fingers through her mussed hair, Lucia walked out of the ward.

Little Joe watched Lucia leave, hunger gnawing at his stomach. He craved breakfast, but it would likely be an hour or more. He rolled over in bed and stared at Adam. At first when Adam moved, Little Joe dismissed its significance. Then Adam turned on his side. His eyelids quivered. With his sore hands Little Joe pushed himself up from the bed. "Adam, Adam."

Batting his eyelids, Adam shook his head. Then his eyelids popped open and he was staring blankly at Little Joe. "Where am I?"

Little Joe laughed. "The hospital."

Adam scratched the bandage at his head. "What happened to you?"

"It's a long story, Adam, a long story."

"What about the Bristlecone?"

Little Joe swallowed hard. "Pa's shutting it down, Adam, even if he has to sell it to Thurston Smalley."

Adam bit his lip. "I failed."

Little Joe slid gently back onto the bed. "Maybe you lost the mine, but you got Lucia Sinclair back. She's been at your side around the clock, save for times she went home to change, like now."

Adam closed his eyes. "The Bristlecone," he said bitterly.

"At least you're talking," Little Joe said. "Things'll be better without the Bristlecone."

After a breakfast of oatmeal and toast, Adam

and Little Joe sat up in their beds, waiting for Ben and the sheriff. Lucia arrived first, her head lowered like her spirits.

"Lucia," called Little Joe across the ward, "someone wants to speak to you!"

She lifted her chin and saw Adam upright in bed, a smile upon his face. She dashed to his bedside, with tears streaming down her cheeks. "You're okay!" She stood over him a moment as he nodded. "Now it's my turn to apologize," she said softly. "I was a fool."

Adam shook his head. "It's behind us, Lucia, if we just forget it."

"We can, Adam, we can." She bent over and kissed him on the cheek. Then, with a smile gracing her face, she pulled her chair against his bed and sat down, holding his hand.

Little Joe slid gingerly under the sheets and rolled over, allowing Adam and Lucia a bit more privacy.

"Now, boys," Sheriff Roy Coffee said to Ben and Hoss as they pumped Adam's hands, "don't wear him out. I've still got a few questions for Adam and Little Joe. You let me get that done and I'll go about my business."

Ben turned around and slapped Coffee on the back. "Roy, you're sure throwing a wet blanket on the best news we've had in weeks!" Ben laughed. "Adam's all yours."

"Tell me what happened, son, before your accident."

Adam's brow furrowed in pain. "I remember gathering samples when Jesse McMatt clubbed me. That's all I recall."

"Do you remember anything about the explosion?"

Adam shrugged. "No, sir, but was McMatt killed?"

The sheriff scratched his chin. "Killed a miner named Vorley Deaton, but McMatt wasn't injured. This doesn't make sense."

"Roy," said Little Joe, sitting up quickly in his bed.

Turning to Little Joe, Coffee said, "Go ahead."

"Holly Lucas wanted to warn me that Thurston Smalley had threatened Adam to her, saying he would be in an accident soon. He had extorted information from her that I had . . ." Little Joe paused and looked at his father. ". . . That I had unwisely given her."

Ben shook his head. "So that's how information was getting out. Roy, you think Smalley hired McMatt to kill Adam?"

"Don't know for sure, Ben, but I'm gonna find out. Now, Little Joe, what happened in the fire?"

"Holly sent a note, said it was a life and death matter and for me to meet her at the Montgomery Mine. She warned me about the threat to Adam. It would've been nothing more than that, but Big Jim Fowler followed her there. He attacked me, then set the place afire like he said he had done the opera house. As he tried to escape, the stairs collapsed, trapping him. I fell out the ore chute. Holly ran for help, but I don't guess she made it."

Roy shook his head. "She made it, son, and got me. When she thought you were still inside, she went crazy and ran in to find you. It was suicide to go in there, Little Joe, but she did it for you. She must've thought a great deal of you."

Little Joe bit his lip. "More than I thought."

Coffee looked from Little Joe to Ben. "I wouldn't put any of this past Thurston Smalley, Ben, but you know it's all hearsay. I still can't figure how Vorley Deaton figures into this, unless he dropped Adam in the ore cart. The cart must've shielded Adam from the explosion."

"That would explain why the doctor saw the explosion bruises and cuts on the miner," Ben interjected, "but not on Adam."

Coffee nodded again. "I think we're on to something, boys, but nothing that would hold up in court. Maybe it's time to try a little bluff. Hoss, as I recall, you're still my deputy. Why don't you get your gun and come along with me?"

"Deputy?" Ben looked at Hoss.

"Yeah, Pa, when Adam and Little Joe got in a fight! Oops!"

Ben looked from Hoss to his bedridden sons. "Somebody's got a lot of explaining to do about what happened while I was in San Francisco."

Little Joe slid under the covers. "I'm feeling a mite poorly right now," he said.

Adam put his hand to his head. "My head's

spinning, Pa. Maybe we can let this wait until —"

"Until next year," interjected Little Joe.

Jesse McMatt sat at a back table playing checkers with another out-of-work Bristlecone miner. The union hall was filled with displaced miners, some reading, a few napping on the long, hard benches, some just staring across the room, and others idly conversing with one another. With a thousand dollars in his pocket for killing Vorley Deaton, McMatt was waiting for Adam Cartwright to die so he could collect the remainder of his bounty. Then he would leave Virginia City. It was a good feeling, almost as good as the two sticks of dynamite pressed against his leg in his pants pocket.

Every time one of the mines closed, the rumors always started that the Comstock Lode had peaked and it was time for miners to move to the next boomtown. But McMatt wasn't one to participate in such mindless speculation, so he just played checkers out of boredom to pass the time away. For pleasure it would never match the thrill of killing a man, even a dumb miner like Vorley Deaton. After losing his third consecutive game, McMatt started setting up the board again, until he saw over his opponent's shoulder a miner pointing at him. McMatt froze. Beside the miner stood Sheriff Roy Coffee. What did he want? McMatt patted the dynamite in his britches pocket as the sheriff approached.

"Jesse McMatt," Coffee said, reaching the checker players.

McMatt nodded. Had Thurston Smalley squealed? He would take care of Smalley if he had. "Sheriff," he acknowledged as he dropped a handful of checkers.

"I need a word with you, McMatt." Coffee's hand was resting on his gun belt, near his revolver.

"I'm always ready to help the law," McMatt said. "Go ahead."

"In private, McMatt."

McMatt shrugged. "My luck's been running bad all morning, Sheriff. I've lost three games straight, but I feel my luck's changing. I figure I'll stay put."

"Don't try my patience, McMatt. Come along or I'll arrest you."

McMatt scratched his chin. "Arrest me? For what?"

Coffee's eyes narrowed and his hand slipped over the butt of his revolver. "Murder, if I have to."

The room went quiet and McMatt's checker-playing opponent pushed himself away from the table.

That son of a bitch Smalley, thought McMatt as he rose from the table, his hands wide of his waist. "That's serious talk, Sheriff. You see I'm an unarmed man."

Coffee nodded. "Serious talk's all that'll get your attention. Now, let's move outside."

McMatt knew the sheriff was in his fifties, two decades older than himself. He figured he could take Coffee if he had to, though the flint in Coffee's eyes told him it wasn't a sure bet. McMatt started for the door, watching the sheriff over his shoulder. He felt the suspicious stares of every miner in the room as he emerged onto the street. Maybe it was time to clear out of Virginia City. He might do that, but not without a final message to Thurston Smalley.

On the plank walk Coffee stopped. "This'll do."

"Okay, Sheriff, what's this all about?"

Coffee's hand still rested on the butt of his pistol. "Thurston Smalley's telling folks you tried to kill Adam Cartwright."

"Thurston Smalley is a liar, Sheriff."

Shrugging, Coffee continued. "He says you came to him, knowing he was interested in buying the Bristlecone. He says you offered to help matters by killing Adam Cartwright, if the price was right."

McMatt felt the two sticks of dynamite in his britches. "And what did Smalley say was my going fee?" He studied Coffee to see if this was a bluff. If Coffee answered $5000, he would know for sure Smalley had squealed. If the sheriff gave the wrong amount or avoided an answer, it might well be a bluff. "What was my asking fee?"

Coffee's eyes narrowed. "I'm asking the questions."

Was the sheriff bluffing or just cagey? "You seem to have all the answers, Sheriff."

Coffee lifted his hand from his revolver and pointed his finger straight at McMatt's nose. "I've got the answers. Right now I just can't make them stand up in court, but I will. My advice to you is not to leave town for a few days."

"Can't afford to go anyplace since the Bristlecone shut down, Sheriff. I don't have a job."

"And I don't think you have a conscience, McMatt." The sheriff turned and walked away.

McMatt stood and watched him cross the street. Damn him! Damn Thurston Smalley! When the sheriff had disappeared, McMatt turned toward the union hall, but he saw too many scowling faces staring at him through the dingy windows. Cursing, he turned around and strode down the street. When no one was looking, he turned between two buildings. Hidden in the shadows there, he pulled the two sticks of dynamite from one pocket. From the other he jerked blasting caps and short fuses. Carefully, he inserted the blasting caps and fuses into the dynamite. Then he stuck a stick in each pants pocket and headed toward Thurston Smalley's office. He had an unscheduled appointment with the Vulture of Virginia City.

Thurston Smalley smiled to himself. The Bristlecone was crumbling just as he had planned. He leaned back in his chair and propped his feet on his desk. The shades were drawn and the room was dark, except for a lit coal-oil lamp at the end of his desk.

340

Adam Cartwright had yet to die, but as long as the Cartwrights sold the mine, Adam's survival didn't matter. In fact, if Adam lived for a while in a coma, it would distract Ben from the sale, make him weaker to deal with. Of course, Ben Cartwright wasn't down yet. He had closed the mine, yes, but he was giving it a good go, trying to prop up the sale price by floating information that assay reports had worked out to almost $400 a ton. Smalley enjoyed bringing down a man of Ben Cartwright's stature. By the end of the week he would own the Bristlecone. Then the real fun would begin, when he sold stock he could manipulate.

He heard someone knocking at his door, then banging on it. Whoever it was could wait. With a crash the door flew open and Smalley jumped to his feet, slipping his hand into his coat pocket and cradling his derringer.

A big man entered and Smalley shrank back toward the wall. He recognized Hoss Cartwright, but he played dumb. "Whoever you are, the saloons and eateries are down the street."

Hoss stomped across the room to Smalley's desk and bent his hulking figure over, as if he could swallow it. "You're Thurston Smalley, aren't you?"

Smalley began to pull his hand from out of his coat pocket, but Hoss reached over the desk and grabbed it in his viselike grip. Smalley gasped and released the derringer.

"Keep your hands where I can see them," Hoss commanded.

"I don't keep valuables in this office," Smalley said, "so you're wasting your time."

Slowly, Hoss shook his head. "You're the only thing I'm after. There's an explosives man around here who's saying you paid him to kill my brother."

Smalley bit his lip. Damn McMatt! "No truth in that," Smalley lied. "You know mining towns and the stories that get started."

Hoss's eyes widened and he shoved at the desk. It crowded Smalley against the wall. "When I find this coward, I'll beat him to a pulp. And if he mentions your name, I'll come back and do the same to you."

Smalley's lip trembled. "You're mistaken, whoever you are."

"Hoss Cartwright's my name and you made a mistake messing with the Cartwrights." He backed away from the desk. "I'll be back."

As suddenly as he had entered, Hoss Cartwright disappeared. Smalley tried to push the desk back in place. It barely budged. He squeezed past it and scurried to the door, closing it but unable to latch the smashed lock.

For once Smalley felt vulnerable. He must get a warning and an offer to McMatt. He would give McMatt $5000 to kill Hoss Cartwright quick. Suddenly, controlling the Bristlecone didn't seem as important as eliminating Hoss Cartwright.

Roy Coffee and Hoss Cartwright met at the corner opposite Thurston Smalley's office.

Hoss grinned. "Smalley's scared."

Coffee nodded. "McMatt's leery, but I think we've raised enough doubts in their minds. It's just a matter of waiting."

"Smalley may have a small gun in his coat pocket," Hoss warned.

"McMatt's as treacherous as a snake, so keep an eye on him," Coffee countered, then pointed down the street. "Here comes McMatt. He didn't waste a minute." The sheriff grabbed Hoss's arm and pulled him around the corner.

Hoss patted his revolver. "I ought to kill him now."

"Couldn't let you do that, Hoss, no matter how much he deserves it." Coffee squinted at McMatt. "Best I can tell, he's unarmed. That ought to make it easier."

McMatt was jittery, looking over his shoulder, staring at each approaching pedestrian. When he reached Smalley's office, McMatt noticed the busted door, then looked both ways down the plank walk before barging inside.

"Come on, Hoss, let's go." Coffee dashed across the street with Hoss behind him. They crossed the plank walk and eased over to the door, drawing their pistols. Several spectators stopped and Coffee waved them away.

From inside, McMatt's and Smalley's voices carried out the door.

"You fool," Smalley yelled, "coming here now, like this. And you've been doing a bunch of talking."

"Damn you, Smalley," McMatt shot back, "you're the one that's been talking to the sheriff, telling him I came to you to kill Adam Cartwright."

"I haven't talked to the sheriff, you fool," Smalley snarled. "You've let him trick you, McMatt. You stupid fool."

McMatt cursed. "He was bluffing."

"He may have been, but Hoss Cartwright was here asking about you. He doesn't know your name, but he knows you tried to kill Adam."

"I'm clearing out, Smalley. You can weasel out of this one on your own. I just want my five thousand, and I want it now."

"Adam Cartwright isn't dead," Smalley replied.

"But you will be if you don't give me my money."

Smalley stood silent for a moment. "As long as you get out of state and don't come back, ever, I'll pay you."

Sheriff Coffee nodded to Hoss. "I've heard enough." Gently, he pushed the door open and walked in, Hoss behind him. Both were inside before Smalley or McMatt realized it.

"I want the money now and —" McMatt seemed to understand something was amiss. He glanced around and stiffened.

Then Smalley understood his predicament. "Oh, my God," he said.

"As loud as you talk," Coffee said softly, "you boys are in some pretty deep trouble."

Smalley stepped cautiously from around his

desk. "Don't tie us into anything bad, Sheriff, and there's money for you, more money for you than you've made in a lifetime behind a badge."

"Don't tempt me to shoot you, Smalley," Coffee growled.

Turning to Hoss, Smalley tinged his words with desperation. "I'll back out of the Bristlecone and leave you Cartwrights alone."

"I may look dumb," Hoss answered, "but I'm not dumb enough to trust a snake."

McMatt slowly slid his hand into his pants pocket.

Smalley ranted, "Sheriff, you know I can buy any judge, any jury in the state, and get off free. You might as well take my offer."

"Your bribe, you mean?" Coffee replied.

Quickly, as attention was focused on Smalley, McMatt lifted the globe off the lit coal-oil lamp on Smalley's desk. Then in one swift movement, he jerked a stick of dynamite from out of his pants, grabbed Smalley for a shield and stuck the slow-burning fuse into the lamp flame.

Before Coffee or Hoss could react, McMatt was standing before them with a lit stick of dynamite.

McMatt sneered. "Now, gents, you best get out of my way before I blow up Virginia City."

CHAPTER 25

Thurston Smalley whitened at the hiss of the dynamite. "No, McMatt! I can buy our way out of this."

McMatt shoved the stick of dynamite at Smalley's face. The manipulator grimaced and twisted away, then staggered as his knees turned mushy for a moment.

"Now back out, Sheriff, both of you," McMatt commanded. "You don't have much time."

Coffee and Hoss scrambled outside, the sheriff yelling to passersby, "Clear the streets! Clear the streets! Dynamite!"

Women and children screamed, then stampeded in panic. Some men unhitched horses and galloped down the street while others trotted for a safe vantage point.

"Somebody sound the fire bells," Coffee shouted.

Within seconds the street was empty within fifty yards of Smalley's office, except for Hoss and Coffee. "Spread apart, Hoss," Coffee said. "When the fuse is low, he'll throw it at one of us. Let's stay far enough apart he won't get us both."

Hoss eased away from Coffee. Both men aimed

their guns at the doorway as McMatt emerged, holding Smalley as a shield.

"It won't work, McMatt," Coffee yelled. "You're a dead man no matter what happens."

McMatt sneered at them, waving the dynamite over Smalley's head.

Hoss watched Smalley carefully. The little man had apparently regained his resolve and was slipping his hand into his coat pocket. Slowly, steadily, Smalley lifted his hand, holding it flat against his waist. Hoss saw a glint of metal that had to be a derringer.

"Get out of my way," McMatt yelled at Coffee.

Smalley let his hand fall to his side, then crooked it behind his back.

Hoss heard a pop. McMatt staggered forward, grasping at Smalley with both hands to keep his balance. The stick of dynamite fell at their feet.

Smalley screamed and kicked at the hissing explosive, but with each attempt McMatt's weight pulled him off balance. Both men tumbled forward and the dynamite disappeared beneath them. Smalley flailed, kicked and screamed at McMatt.

"Run, Hoss, run!" yelled Coffee, and both men darted away.

Then the street erupted in a cloud of dust and smoke, the first booming concussion followed instantly by a second, both breaking windows and rattling doors all along the street. Hoss dove behind a water trough, feeling the sting of dirt against his neck. He peeked over the trough and watched the cloud of dust settle, all the time thinking of Adam and how close a call he must have had with McMatt. Finally standing up, Hoss brushed his clothes off. Through the haze of dust and smoke, he saw the twisted forms of Jesse McMatt and Thurston Smalley in the street.

The Vulture of Virginia City was little more than carrion.

Ben Cartwright looked out the hospital window toward the Bristlecone. Its stamp mills were silent, its hoist works still, its walks empty. It had been a gamble, a bad gamble, as it turned out. He shook his head. He had failed at so few things in life that this was hard, especially because of its toll on his family. Taking a deep breath, Ben turned around to face his three sons, Adam and Little Joe propped up with pillows in their hospital beds, Hoss sitting backward on a chair between them. Lucia Sinclair stood beside Adam, holding his hand.

"With Thurston Smalley gone, we can expect a fair price on the sale of the Bristlecone," Ben said. "Somebody's already trying to do us a favor. A rumor's going around that our ore's assayed out at $389 a ton."

Ben shook assay reports at Adam. "The Nina and the Pinta are both below twenty dollars a ton, like they've been for weeks."

"What about the Santa Maria?" Adam asked.

Ben shrugged. "These are all the reports I have."

Little Joe sat up in his bed. "Were those the

ones Adam got before the explosion? The ones I had assayed?"

"That's right," Ben said. "What did they assay out to?"

Smiling sheepishly, Little Joe admitted, "I didn't ask and I didn't look."

"What!" exclaimed Ben.

Little Joe shrugged. "I'd told some things earlier I shouldn't have, and I just didn't want to ruin things again. I had the assayer seal the envelope. I took it with me when I went to meet Holly at Montgomery Mine. Where are my clothes?"

"Under the bed," Lucia said.

Hoss leaned over from his chair and pulled a basket from beneath Little Joe's hospital bed. The clothes Little Joe had been wearing in the fire had been cleaned and folded. Hoss lifted his brother's shirt, britches, and socks from the basket, finding beneath them Little Joe's pocketknife, a few coins, the crumpled note from Holly Lucas, and a sealed envelope. Hoss handed the envelope to his father.

Ben ripped the end off and pulled out the report. He shook his head and reread it, then seemed to pale. He looked over to Adam, and his face cracked into a broad grin. "The samples assay out at $389 a ton."

Adam shouted with glee, and Lucia bent over and kissed him.

"That's good, isn't it, Pa?" asked Hoss.

"Yes, sir, that's good, Hoss. It's the mother

lode. We can pay off the Bank of California on time. Best of all, it means the Ponderosa, all of it, will stay in the Cartwright name."

Hoss smiled widely. "That is good, then, isn't it?"

"It means," said Adam, "I was right about the Bristlecone."

"I knew you were all along, Adam," shouted Little Joe.

Everyone laughed.

"We'll reopen the Bristlecone and put the miners back to work," Adam said. "After that, I want to see Billy Makovy of the *Enterprise*. I promised him a story, and boy do I have one for him!"

Calder, Stephen   MAY   1996
Bonanza 5: The money hole